justifying JAMIE

ANNA BROOKS

REASON TO RUIN

#READYTOBERUINED

The first time I heard his cheesy pick-up line, he made me laugh. The next night, I fell madly in love. Then he shattered my world without speaking a word, leaving me with an empty heart and a hollow soul.

Still, I tried to fix what was broken, only to be humiliated beyond repair. I couldn't believe the same man who promised me heaven so ruthlessly put me through hell with lips that once worshipped me.

I thought that was the end of us, but then a life-altering discovery threatened more than just me, and the least likely man to stand at my side was the one who refused to leave it.

To Jenny, my friend and editor who has been with me since day one. I appreciate you and I love you.

justifying JAMIE

ONE

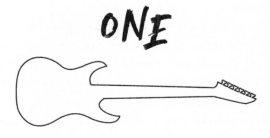

Jamie
three years earlier.

"RUIN. RUIN. RUIN." THE SOUND OF THE BAND'S name being chanted gets louder as the seconds pass, and I can tell it's gonna be a kick-ass performance. The crowd is already pumping us up, and their energy is what sets the tone for tonight's show.

The four of us stand in a circle—one arm around each other's backs and the other straight out in front of us, hands stacked on top of one another's—rocking back and forth.

The smoky air gets thicker, and everyone around us senses what's about to happen because they all shut up. Stagehands, roadies, sound techs... everyone gives us a moment. "Unleash the fury, boys." Mike initiates the pre-show ritual we started when we were eighteen with stars in our eyes, and even though it's the lamest thing ever, we won't start a show without doing it. It's tradition, and nobody fucks with tradition. "Give 'em hell, give 'em fire."

The rest of the crew reaches between us so we're all meeting in the middle of our huddle. A lot of tattooed hands and fingers, rings and leather bracelets all wait for it. Everyone raises their hands at the same time. "Let's goooooooo!"

Mike catches my eye, and his lips quirk like they always do. He hates our chant but got outvoted all those years ago when it came time to make a decision. True to almost everything with Mike, we should have listened to him. He's the levelheaded one and always has been.

I'm the crazy one who dyes my hair and is always the life of the party. My brother, Liam, is the opposite; he's quiet, and although he liked to have fun, being in a relationship with Meara while on the road made it so he spent a lot of time alone.

Gabe hardly spends any time alone. He's short-tempered and rarely holds back with anything... ever.

The four of us spent a decade together, and when Liam decided to leave the band to be with Meara, we all supported him. Now we have Kolby as a replacement, and he's good shit. But he's also a dick. If he wasn't almost as good as Lee on the drums, we'd have found someone else by now, but he keeps his personal shit away from the band, so it works for us.

After Liam left, we kept everything status quo even though it wasn't the same without him. Nothing is really, but we had decisions to make when he decided to quit. He chose his family, and we chose the band. We love it. We love the life, the experiences, the women, the road. All of it.

We love nights like tonight. And as the crowd grows impatient and gets louder, it reminds me why we chose to go on without Liam. As we head toward the stage, Kolby lifts his chin at me, and I do the same. Show-fuckin'-time.

Jimmy, our roadie, stands at the curtain, and as we walk out, he hits each of us on the back with an open palm three times before we rush onto the stage. Another tradition. We won't start without him here and without getting a good luck slap from him.

The stage is dark, but the glow up stickers mark our spots so we can take our places. I hook my strap over my shoulder and adjust my earpiece one more time even though it'll likely be out by the end of the show since I dig being enveloped by the sound of my amp on stage. There's a quiet hum, and a vibration thrums through my entire body a split second before the lights blind and the noise deafens.

Fans scream. Bass vibrates. Screeches and cheers replace the jolt of electricity, and we do what we were born to do.

We rock the fuck out.

Mike doesn't waste any time before he's working the crowd. Women reach for him, and guys split their fingers, flashing the universal sign every red-blooded male does at a rock concert. I get bras thrown at my feet and laugh when a thong lands on my shoulder. *Yeah, I love my job.* It's ninety minutes of sweat and soul, and by the time we head off the stage, the shots I took before the show have worn off, but the natural high I get from performing replaces the buzz.

Kolby heads off the opposite direction as we head to the small room where we'll hang out with our fans. "Gotta take a piss, bro. I'll be right there."

The decision to do the meet and greet post-show was made unanimously. There were too many times when we were late getting on stage because we didn't want to rush the fans who paid good money to meet us. It was just too much of a pain, and it ruined the pre-show vibes we wanted, so now we do it after.

Sometimes, we'll chat and take photos with fans for hours, and sometimes, it only takes twenty minutes. "You guys ready?" our manager, Ian, asks as soon as Kolby sits down behind the long table.

We've all slammed a couple of bottles of water and wiped the sweat off our faces. "Yeah, we're good. Send 'em in."

The door is pushed open, and the line trickles in and the noise level increases. We sign shirts and a few pairs of tits, then stand and take pictures and shoot the shit with our fans. Ian brings us some beers and a scantily clad woman walks around with a tray of shots. "Thanks." I grab one off the tray and wait for Gabe to give one of his infamous toasts.

He clears his throat, stands on the table, and holds his shot glass in the air. "Here's to the girls who say they will; here's to the girls who say they won't." He winks at the redhead hanging on his leg. "Here's to the girls best of all, and guys you know I'm right." We give a collective laugh of affirmation. "Here's to the girls who say they don't, but you know they will tonight."

The men grunt in approval, and the women pretend to be offended as we toss back our shots, but after a few minutes, they forget Gabe's misogynistic bullshit and are practically panting to go back to the bus. I grab a bottle of water from the table and take a long swallow, glancing around the crowded room. I remember when we'd perform and nobody would even be in the audience; now we sell out stadiums and tickets in a matter of hours. We have fans with tattoos of our lyrics and signatures. It's surreal sometimes.

"You straight, dude?" Mike stops in front of me and crosses his arms. I've had a headache all day, and it's getting worse, so I lift my chin at him. "I'm actually gonna head out. Still feel like shit from last night." Instead of sleeping like Ian told us to, we went to a strip club down the street and didn't crawl into bed until about three hours before sound check this afternoon.

"Same, man, we'll be right behind you."

"Want company?" a high-pitched voice comes from my right. I stare down at her… blond hair—fake, of course— big tits that at first glance seem natural, barely there black tank, and a pair of jeans so tight I question if it's worth the effort trying to take them off.

She licks her lips, and I shrug. Why the fuck not, might make me feel better to get sucked off. "Sure."

I meander out of the room and hear her heels following, then nod at Wesley, one of our bodyguards. He pushes open the door to outside and peers around before motioning for me to follow. By the time we're through the dark parking lot and on the bus, she's stumbling into me. When I sit down, her ass lands in my lap, and her mouth attaches to my neck.

"Chill for a second." Damn. I pry her off and grab another bottle of water from the mini fridge, then settle back down. I don't have time to even get this chick's name before the rest of the guys get on; along with some eager pussy.

"Chelsea!" A screech makes me groan, and I see the redhead rushing toward the girl on my lap… Chelsea, I presume. It doesn't take long for their conversation to fade, and the redhead to go back to Gabe.

My phone vibrates in my back pocket, and I'm actually grateful for the distraction. "Sit up a second, babe." I nudge the girl leaning on my chest, and she drunkenly lifts her upper body. I grab my phone out of my jeans and sit my ass back down. Not a second later, her face is in my lap, just not the way I originally wanted it to be. She went from drunk to passed out in a matter of seconds. Fuckin' fantastic. Gabe snorts, and I flip him off before I unlock the screen on my phone to read the incoming text from my brother.

Liam: Meara's in labor. I'll keep you posted.

"Holy shit."

"What's wrong?" Mike narrows his eyes at me, the uneasiness in my voice evident to him and the other guys as I get their attention as well. Part of spending so much damn time together is you get to know absolutely fuckin' everything about each other.

"Meara's having the baby."

A collective whoop and a few cheers sound in the common place on our bus. "Lee's gonna be a dad," Gabe mutters. "Damn."

"I know, man. I can't believe it. We need to start driving up there. Hey," I call for the chick who's straddling Gabe. She turns around and raises a brow. "Get your friend. We've gotta take off."

"So soon? We haven't even played yet."

Her whiney voice sends a sliver of irritation down my spine. I'm going to be an uncle, and the woman who I love like a sister is having a baby. I need to be home. Like now. I ain't got time for this chick's attitude.

Gabe must sense my frustration because he pats her on her ass that's bared since her skirt rode up to her waist.

"Another time. Go rustle up your girl. We'll get you a cab."

The way she jumps up and stomps her feet as she pulls her skirt down is an indicator of what's about to happen. "Whatever. Fuck you."

"Not tonight."

"Come on, Chelsea." She shakes her friend who moans but sits up. "We need to go. These assholes are kicking us out."

I tune them out and push to my feet, striding to the front of the bus to find Ian. Our manager is hanging around outside with some of the crew and roadies. I get his attention. "We need to take off as soon as we can. Meara's having the baby."

Ian's face splits into a huge grin. He's been with us since the beginning and has been through everything the same as us. He fought hard for Lee, but in the end, he knew he couldn't do anything to keep the original four of us together. "No shit?"

"Yeah. I just got a text from him."

His eyes go over my shoulder, and he sighs. The man has warned us time and time again about these groupies and has had to intervene in the aftermath more times than I can count. But hey, it's part of the life. The two girls stumble off the bus, and with one holding the other up, they sway as they head toward the parking lot. I lift my chin at Wesley. "Make sure she's not driving."

He nods and follows them. This isn't the first time he's had to do something like this, and even though it's technically not part of his job, he doesn't complain. He's the shit. We don't normally have any problems, but all it took was once when some psycho grabbed a knife and tried to stab the girl who was sucking Gabe's dick in an insane bout of jealousy.

Ian decided that we'd always have at least one body-guard with us on tour, and since then, we've hired some-one from Royal Ace Security because they're the best.

"I'll get everyone rounded up, and we'll hit the road in a few hours." Ian claps his hands together.

"Thanks."

"It's what I'm here for."

As soon as we knew Meara's due date, Ian rear-ranged our schedule to be as close to home as we could so we'd be around in the hopes that the baby would be on time. Luckily, it worked. We're in Kentucky right now with a show scheduled in a few days in Milwaukee, then Chicago. So not only will I get to meet the baby right away, but I'll get to hang out for a couple of days after.

There's a nervous energy in my gut, and I don't like it. It doesn't happen often, but the last time it did was when I had to tell Meara about Lee's fuckup last year. I try to push it aside and pray for a safe delivery and a healthy baby.

I shoot a text to Liam to let him know our schedule.

Me: We're on our way soon. Be there early morning.

Not surprisingly, he doesn't reply immediately. I pace up and down the bus while the guys all keep to them-selves. Mike reads a book, Gabe's got earbuds in, and Kolby plays a video game. True to his word, Ian has us on the road almost exactly three hours later. And about four hours after that, on a bus in the middle of Illinois, I get a phone call.

"Tell me good news, brother," I answer.

The other guys all tense up and wait.

"She's the most beautiful thing I've ever seen in my life." My brother's voice is filled with pride.

I sigh and fall back into the seat, giving a thumbs-up for everyone else. "Shit, man." I wish I was there now. Not later, but right now. "Happy for you. No idea how much." If anyone deserves good things after what they've been through, it's him and Meara.

"You need to hurry. I want you to meet her. Fuck, Jamie... just hurry."

I can't imagine the fear he's feeling right now. Being responsible for a baby girl and keeping her healthy and safe in this crazy world we live in. "We'll be there soon. It's all good, Lee. Everything's gonna be awesome."

About three hours after I hang up the phone with my brother, I'm back home and staring at the most beautiful baby I've ever seen sleeping in her father's arms. She even smells good; her fresh, clean scent purifies the antiseptic odor of the hospital. "She's amazing. You did good, man."

Liam lifts his head, his nervous eyes going from his daughter to his sleeping wife who looks so small curled up in a ball, then to me. His leg bounces nervously. "I can't fuck this up."

"You won't."

"I can't, Jamie." His voice wavers, and he shakes his head. "I can't fuck this up."

The guilt runs deep with him for the mistakes he's made with both his wife and the band. His demons were what made him such a good songwriter, but now that they're gone, he takes everything on and worries too damn much. It pisses me off that he still does this to himself. "You won't, Liam." He starts to protest, but I cut him off. "This is where you're meant to be. This is what you fought for and what you worked so fucking hard for. You won't mess it up, you hear me?"

He swallows and stares over my shoulder at nothing.

"Liam, come on." The undiluted pain in his eyes guts me. "Dude. You're an awesome husband. You're gonna be a great dad. You need to stop living in the past and focus on living the future you fought for. And you won that shit. Look at where you are. Look at what you made, man. This is where you're supposed to be, and this is what's right. I know it. You know it. Trust that."

He sucks in a breath and nods as he exhales, coming to a decision. "Stop swearing in front of my daughter."

I chuckle. "She doesn't understand me yet. When she starts talking, I'll tone it down."

"All right, but remember that when you have kids. Turnabout is fair play."

When the baby fusses, Liam doesn't hesitate to rock her. I take a step back and watch him console his daughter and talk in a high-pitched voice I've never heard before. And a really fuckin' small pang of jealousy hits me at what he has that I don't.

TWO

Mercy

COFFEE.

That's the only thing on my mind. Even though I'm already running late, I have to stop at the small café right inside the hospital. Not only is it part of my daily routine, but without caffeine, I'll surely fall asleep standing up today.

Accustomed to long hours, I know all the tricks to doing whatever I have to in order to pull off double shifts, and coffee is essential... like a vitamin. I mastered sleep deprivation in nursing school, but the insomnia I've been experiencing decided to come to the party late. And it's been almost debilitating the past few months, making my usual tired exhausted.

As I stand in line for caffeine, I cover a yawn. I've worked two doubles in a row this week and am covering a ten-hour shift for my friend Nikkie while she's on vacation. I had the day off and could always use the overtime, so I signed up for her hours.

Right now, though, I'm regretting it because I can barely keep my eyes open as I shuffle forward to get my coffee. The wait is unusually long, and as I contemplate if I should skip the line and go to the vending machine that's next to the elevator for a soda instead, the squeaky giggle of a woman in front of me draws my attention.

"I know, right?" She twirls her long blond hair and bites her red lip, so blatantly trying to flirt with the guy ahead of me in a Valley Girl accent that is so not indicative of the Midwest.

I don't hear what the guy said that made her laugh like a hyena, but I roll my eyes at how obvious and embarrassing her behavior is. It's one thing to be into a guy and have a conversation, but to blatantly throw yourself at him while you're acting like a literal idiot is something all women should be ashamed of. No man is worth your dignity.

We shuffle forward, and I get a whiff of the spicy-sweet cologne he's wearing. Damn, he smells good. So does his leather jacket.

She clutches his arm and pushes up on her pointed black shoe and whispers something in his ear that has a small gauge in it. I study his profile as he listens. He's tall and lean, but not skinny. Toned. His tattoos peeking out of the collar of his black shirt give him the mark of a bad boy. I bet he has at least one sleeve of tattoos; something I've always found attractive.

What catches my attention the most, though, is his hair. It's short on the sides and spiked in the middle, but when the light hits it, I swear there's blue in it. Something about him is intriguing. I suppose it's his look. I see guys with tattoos all the time, but not with the whole rocker vibe this guy has. It's somehow really sexy, and I hate to admit that I get why this girl is all over him. But if he were to give me that attention, I'd probably just say something stupid and embarrass myself. I tend to do that because I'm a total dork sometimes.

He leans down and replies to the woman who then reaches into her black leather purse and pulls out an envelope. She hands it to him, where he presumably writes his number and hands it back. Why wouldn't she just put his digits in her phone? She clutches his hand with both of hers and squeals like a damn pig. I wonder what animal is next.

My God... who does that in line for coffee at six fifty in the morning?

I take another step when they do and finally get close enough to hear his voice loud and clear. "Black for me and whatever the pretty lady wants. Something sweet, I'm sure, just like her."

The laughter that bubbles up my throat is uncontrollable, and when his head starts turning, I drop mine to hide my face. My shoulders shake, and I stare at my shoes, unable to stop the giggling at that cheesy line. I'm a bit slap happy and can't help the little snort that escaped me when I try to inhale.

I think about something sad to control myself; like *Bambi* or the ending of *Titanic*. But instead of it having the effect I want, it makes me mad because there was totally room for Jack on that damn door. Rose was a selfish bitch. Then I remember the scene in *Steel Magnolias* when Shelby (spoiler alert) dies. That does it; there's no way I can laugh thinking about that. I clear my throat and somber up, all traces of humor gone.

Finally, I feel rather than see the space in front of me clear, and when I risk looking up, I'm happy to find the lovebirds are gone, and I'm next in line. The barista Cole waves with one hand and holds a tumbler of ice water in the other. "Hi, Merc. Usual?"

"Hey, Cole," I reply with a smile as I step closer to the counter. "No, not today. Can I get an Americano?"

"Sure thing. Tired?"

"That's an understatement." I hand him some cash and scurry away before he can give me any change. He's here almost every morning, and when he isn't busy, I usually chat with him for a few minutes. He's a really nice guy, around my age at twenty-six and also at my height of five feet seven with a mop of curly brown hair.

A quick look around tells me my entertainment for the morning has left, and I bite back another laugh as I think about that guy's lameness again while I wait for my coffee.

"Something funny?"

His baritone voice behind me scares the crap out of me. Where did he come from? I twirl around so fast that my elbow hits the cup in his hand. In slow motion, the Styrofoam lands on the floor with a force so hard the lid blows off and piping hot black coffee magnetizes to my blue scrub pants.

"Oh shit," he mutters.

I freeze in place, which is ironic since my legs are on fire, and take a deep breath. My exhaustion catches up to me, and I keep my eyes closed as I squeeze my hands into fists, trying not to cry or scream, I'm not sure which. I finally raise my eyes, and the moment they catch his bright green ones, he smirks. "Now *that* is funny."

"You're an ass."

"And you're beautiful."

I guess it's anger I'm going with. "Listen, dude." I push up on my toes to make myself feel better about the height difference. "Those phony lines and your…" I wave my arm between us. "Bad boy charm won't work on me, so take all that crap and shove it up your ass."

He smiles then, full-on with his white teeth practically sparkling, and if I'm not mistaken a glint of silver on his tongue from a bar in the middle of it. He shifts toward me an inch, so close I can feel the warmth coming off his tall, lean body as his sexy as sin smell invades my senses. "Not big on things being shoved up my ass, but if you're game, I'd be more than happy to play."

I glare, my eyes spitting fire as I fall back to my heels. If he wasn't so damn hot and so sure of himself, I'd be insulted. But clearly, he finds the entire situation hilarious, which it really is. I usually always find humor in everything that I can. Life's too short to willingly be unhappy.

"Damn. Are you okay? You're not burned, are you?" Cole comes around the counter, and before I answer him, I notice the man's brows furrow as if he just realized his coffee could have legitimately done damage.

"I'm fine, Cole, thanks. My scrubs soaked it up before it hit my skin. But now I'm going to be even later because I have to go home and change after already waking up late and running out of milk for my oatmeal. Have you ever eaten oatmeal with water?" I don't wait for a response and continue. "Well, I had to this morning, and it's gross. And then on top of that, my blow-dryer died on me." I take a breath. "Rest in peace." I'm totally sad to see her go; she's been with me since high school, and her death came as a complete shock.

Cole nods while trying to fight laughter as he wipes

15

the mess up with a mop. "I'll keep yours warm until you get back."

"Thanks." I start to back away but call Cole's name. "Can you get Donny over here a new cup?"

His green eyes light up bright with amusement. "My name's not Donny, babe."

"No?" I giggle dramatically in mock disbelief as I start my exit and tap my index finger to my chin. "Really? With all that charm? I could have sworn it was Donny. Do you prefer Don? Or do you only go by *Don Juan?*"

His lips tilt up, and the most beautiful, deep laughter I've ever heard sings to my soul. Rushing away, I'm thankful not for the first time that I don't live far away. I could wear my extra scrubs, but I keep forgetting to bring them back to keep in my locker. On the way home, I call my boss and tell her of my conundrum. I might live close, but the walk is about fifteen minutes. And in that time, I can't stop smiling as I think about that guy, despite my shitty morning.

By the time I get back to the hospital, grab my Americano, and am making my way to the elevator, I'm over a half an hour late.

"Sorry, sorry," I yell as I run past my co-workers, my black Nikes squeaking on the linoleum floor. Once I reach my destination, I throw my stuff in my locker in the break room and go to the nurses' station to look at patient charts and start my rounds.

"We're fine, girl. Take a breath."

I sigh loudly at Beth and wrap my stethoscope around the back of my neck as I try to slam some caffeine. "Thanks for covering for me."

"No problem. I'm just about to go to three-oh-seven."

"I'll go."

I wave at the lactation consultant as we pass each other and then knock on the door to three-oh-seven quietly before opening it. "Morning," I whisper, not sure if anybody is asleep.

The first-time parents look up at me with tired smiles. "Hi," Mom replies.

"Morning," Dad mouths.

As I'm washing my hands, I hear the little peep of a baby and can't help but hurry to see the tiny pink bundle wrapped in her mom's arms. "She's gorgeous," I whisper in awe as she yawns, her itty-bitty fists squeezing. Her cheeks are rosy, and her nose nothing but a little button. I think all babies are beautiful, though, but this one is just a little extra. Probably because Mom is stunning. Her face is flawless without makeup, and she just had a baby less than twenty-four hours ago. Not all women can get away with the badass look she has going on, but it suits her perfectly. I briefly think about the guy from the coffee shop and how they both have the same vibe.

"I'm Mercy. I'll be your nurse this morning."

"I'm Liam, this is my wife Meara, and the little princess is Melody."

Swooning, I put my hands to my heart. "What a beautiful name."

"For a beautiful girl, just like her momma," Dad adds. Running his tattooed knuckle down Meara's cheek, he gazes at her with such love it makes my eyes burn. That right there. That isn't a line; that is genuine emotion.

I push aside the heartache that I'll never find a man who will look at me like this guy is looking at his wife. Or that the good ones are already taken. Or that I'll never have a baby of my own. I love my job immensely, but I hate the sorrow and self-pity I feel at this moment, so I take a breath and grab the cuff from the IV cart. "I'm just gonna get your blood pressure really quick."

And then I go to work.

By the time my shift is over, I'm dead on my feet, which barely get me home. It doesn't take long for me to take a shower and collapse on my bed, not waking until almost noon the next day.

THREE

Jamie

"I THINK IT'S OKAY TO WALK AWAY," I WHISPER TO MY
brother.

He doesn't look up from his beautiful
daughter when he answers. "I know." It's as if he's still in
shock.

A few minutes after he doesn't move, I try again. "The
couch is four feet away. I'm pretty sure you'll hear her if
she needs something."

"But what if she stops breathing? I won't be able to
see if I'm not watching her."

"That's not going to happen, but I'm right here. I'll
watch her if it'll make you feel better."

Sighing, he turns around from the bassinet and then
sits across from me on the black leather couch in his living
room, resting the back of his head on the cushion. "That
wasn't so hard, was it?"

"Shut up."

"How's Meara doing?"

They just got home this morning, which shocked me.
I thought when someone had a baby, they stayed in the

hospital for like a week, but apparently, a day and a half is enough. He already looks ragged, and it makes me feel for him, knowing it's just going to get worse. I've heard stories about how infants don't sleep and how hard it is for some parents at first. It's not like they're strangers to not getting decent shut-eye—my brother used to be a rock star, and Meara owns a bar—so I know they'll pull through just fine.

"She just pushed an almost eight-pound human out of her tiny body. What do you think?" I raise a brow at how damn defensive he is. He always was, though, when it came to Meara. From the first time he saw her when we were just kids, a part of him always belonged to her. In all my life, in all the places I've been and people I've met, I have never seen a love like theirs.

He closes his eyes and then pinches the bridge of his nose. I'd give him shit about being in the same clothes he wore yesterday, but he looks straight-up beat. "I'm exhausted, so there's no way she's not feeling it a thousand times more than me. God, I don't know how she did it. She's so small, but she was so strong."

Liam and I are the same age, but from the time our parents got married when we were four years old, I always took on the role of the older, wiser brother even though, truth be told, he's the smarter one despite what he thinks. He always knew what he wanted, and even though the road to good intentions was rough, he set himself up for a pretty sweet gig. He's a business owner and the one who's married and has a kid now, but I still feel the need to look out for him. "I'm right here, Lee. Go up to bed and get a nap in with your wife while you can."

"I don't want to go up there and wake her. She barely

slept, and she's not going to have a choice but to wake up to nurse, so if she's snoozing, I'm leaving her. Plus, you've never been alone with a baby in your life. No way in fuck are you using my daughter as a guinea pig."

"I've been alone with babies before."

He huffs. "When?"

I actually have to think on it but can't remember a time that I did. Normally, the thought of babies or, more specifically, me having babies makes me queasy… I shiver at the thought of being tied down. "Okay, so maybe I haven't, but it can't be too hard. You just pick 'em up by their ankles—"

"Fuck off."

I laugh at how easily he's provoked. "I'm proud of you, bro. And you're doing great."

"It's only been a day, not too much to fuck up in a day."

"Give yourself credit and get some damn sleep."

His knees bounce. "I don't know if I can. I feel all speedy. I'm agitated, but at the same time, I'm focused. It's weird."

"I bet you are, but if you tried, you could probably knock off for at least a few minutes." My phone vibrates, so I pull it out of my pocket to find a group text from Ian.

Ian: Fire at Stage 20, show cancelled tonight. I'll keep you posted but looks like we won't reschedule. Enjoy the next two days off. Departure still set for Saturday at 7.

I shoot back a reply of acknowledgment. "Damn. There was a fire at Stage 20, so the show's cancelled, which means I don't have to leave for sound check, so you can definitely go take a…" I trail off when a light snore from Lee filters through the room. "…nap."

Laughing to myself, I stand and take a picture of him so I can post it on social media, and then go to the kitchen to grab a bottle of water. I think for a second about what caption I want to use beneath the picture and laugh as I type it in on Ruin's profile. We all have access, and each of us tries to post once a day to keep our visibility really high and our names on people's minds, which sells tickets when they see we're in their town.

Baby Melody and Mama are doing perfect, but Daddy, on the other hand... #andtothinkheusedtobearockstar

He'll pretend to be pissed at me, but even though he isn't technically a part of the band anymore, the fans still want to know what's going on with him. And his family. Meara was around a lot, so everyone who follows us knows who she is. She was actually in a couple of music videos in the beginning. God, that was so long ago, before we had the money to hire actresses and models. Damn... sometimes I forget just how far we've come and how much more we can accomplish.

I don't say it to Liam, but it's hard to digest still, looking behind me and seeing someone who isn't him behind the kit. He isn't just my bandmate; he's my brother. As much as the other guys are like family, Liam actually is and that naturally gave us a tight bond on the road. It might make me a punk ass, but I miss him on tour and was even resentful at times that he left us, but more specifically that he left me.

We dreamed up this band when we were kids. We'd spend hours and hours thinking of names. He'd go through pads of paper writing lyrics while I broke the skin on my fingertips messing around with hooks for something we never thought would be possible. I never thought we'd be selling out arenas and winning awards and having our music on movie soundtracks. Truth be told, I didn't understand how he could leave that, even for Meara.

I understand it now.

Seeing him tired but *so fuckin' happy*, I know he made the right decision. It's what's best for him and for Meara, who I love like she's blood. And damn, for the first time ever, I really, truly understand him.

Because if I had what he does, I'd give anything and everything to keep it and stop at nothing to protect it. It's sometimes hard to remember that the kid I met when I was four who went from stepbrother to friend, to best friend, to *brother* is a fucking husband and now a father.

I meant every word I said to him in the hospital, and I know he's going to rock this dad gig. Lord knows I couldn't do it. On stealthy feet, I head over to Melody's bassinet and stare down at her, and damn… I never knew it was possible to love something so tiny so much. She is perfect. She almost looks like a porcelain doll, and if I didn't see her chest rising and falling, I'd think she was fake. Smooth skin and pink cheeks and puffy little lips. Her nose scrunches, and her arm flails as she fusses. Out of instinct, I lift her out carefully and cradle her in my arms before she wails and wakes Lee.

I might not have ever been alone with a baby before, but I'd die before I ever did something that could hurt her. I treat her like glass and hold her snug against me, and a part of my heart cracks, the jagged piece held tight in her itty-bitty fist.

Lee's still sleeping, and Meara must be, too, so I take Melody to the kitchen so I can hopefully keep her quiet so they can get a few more minutes of rest. "Hey, doll face." I rock her in my arms and am thankful when she opens her eyes but doesn't cry. She's just precious. So small but the impact she's gonna have will be huge. I can see it in her eyes; she's going to be amazing. "Hi, beautiful."

"Hi to you, too, handsome."

I don't lift my head but reply to Meara with a chuckle. I didn't hear her come into the kitchen. "Your mom thinks she's funny."

"I know I am. Gimme my baby." I reluctantly take my eyes off the most precious baby I've ever seen and hand her over to her anxious mother, who looks amazing after just giving birth yesterday.

"I was trying to keep her quiet so you guys could sleep."

She shrugs. "Must be motherly instinct or something." Meara heads to the kitchen table, a small wince hitting her face when she settles into the seat, then grabs a u-shaped pillow from the table. Carefully, she rests it beneath Melody. "Or… it could be because my boobs hurt like a—"

I look away when she reaches into her shirt. "I don't want to hear that shit or see your tits."

She laughs but starts whispering when Melody fusses again. "There you go, baby. There you go. Okay you can look now, Jamie. It's not a big deal. It's not like you haven't seen a boob before… or signed them."

"Well, if they're gonna show them to me, I'm gonna look. But my sister-in-law's tits are something I never want to see, no offense. I'm sure they're nice."

I turn and catch her smiling down at Melody before she looks back up to me, her hair a toned-down blond I haven't seen before. That, along with the baby in her arms, makes her look so grown up. Which she is since we all are past our mid-twenties now. "They're usually small but having them this big makes me want to get a boob job. Liam really lik—"

"Seriously, Meara. Stop talking about your boobs."

She giggles, and I lean on the kitchen counter, able to see her from the neck up and not see the actual deed, which is what I'm going for. Meara has always been gorgeous, and her spunky personality makes her that much more beautiful. She's got a glow about her that I've never noticed before, and as she nurses my niece, it's almost breathtaking.

"Do you want one of these?"

"A boob?"

Her manicured brow shoots up to her forehead. "No. A baby, you dork."

"Sure." I shrug.

"Really?"

"Yeah, I mean, not now." I shudder. "Maybe in a while, but why not?"

She stutters. "Uh, because I'm talking about a baby, not a bass."

"So?"

"So. You have to find a woman first, and not someone who you knock up and send a check to once a month."

"I know that, Meara."

She widens her eyes. "So that means you need to find a woman, Jamie."

"Well, yeah. I will... eventually. I'm still having fun, still lovin' the life and livin' the dream."

She swallows, and a flash of pain crosses her face.

Shit. "This is Lee's dream, Meara. He doesn't want to be anywhere else but here. With you. With both of you."

Her shoulders square back as much as they can, and she plasters a fake smile on her face. "I know."

"Do you?"

A sigh leaves her, and she shakes her head, putting a clear end to that topic. "You need to get on that baby making thing, like now. I'll even break the no-hookup-at-Kelly's rule if you go find her tonight."

She must be sleep deprived. "Sure, Meara. I'll go to Kelly's and meet the girl of my dreams. We'll fall in love and have babies and live happily ever after. That's exactly what'll happen tonight."

I hear Liam padding into the kitchen. "Why didn't you wake me?" He comes into the room and crouches down in front of Meara, not even giving me a second glance. "I told you to wake me when you did."

"I've been up like three minutes. Not much you can do to help me, honey. I'm the one with the boobies."

"Yeah, you are." The sultry tone makes me gag.

I push up from the counter as he grabs a chair so he can be close to his girls. "On that note, I'm out."

"Bye, Jamie," Meara says. Liam doesn't even acknowledge me as the two females in his arms are the only things he cares about right now.

FOUR

Mercy

MY SISTER, CHARITY, LIES LENGTHWISE ON MY COUCH in the clothes she wore to yoga. Facing the TV, she's watching some stupid reality show. I pace in circles around the glass coffee table, dropping my hair from the knot I had it in on the top of my head as my mom cackles into my ear. I shouldn't have answered when she called.

When will I ever learn?

"Yes, Mother. I know he's my age and already made partner."

Charity laughs, and I glare at her, give her the *Friends* fuck you with my hands, then head to the kitchen to get a soda.

"I don't know why you have to be so difficult. It's just dinner." My mom chastises me as she did when I was eight and refused to eat peas. And then again at ten when I snuck a stray cat into the house. And of course, when I was thirteen and dyed my hair with lemon juice. Hell, I heard it last month when I didn't apply for a promotion at work because, God forbid, I'm actually happy in my measly little nursing job.

"Oh, I don't know, Mom. Maybe because I've never met the guy, and I already know from the way you're describing him that I won't like him."

"You're never going to get married if you don't date."

I rest my head against the freezer. "I'm not going to marry some guy just because he's rich and having his family name attached to mine will be good for Dad's firm."

She huffs on the other end of the line. "That is not why, Mercy, and I'm insulted you'd think such a thing of me." I wait for more from her but don't get words, just a sniffle.

Great. She's crying. I put my soda away and grab a beer. "Fine, Mother. I'll go out with him."

"No. Don't do me any favors."

I grit my teeth together to stop myself from saying what I really want to. "Where and when?"

"Tonight. Rustic View at five o'clock. Don't be late."

"Fine. Bye." I drop my cell on the counter and go plop myself in the corner of the couch. "What is her problem?" I snap at my sister.

She holds up her hand and ticks off the points on her French-tipped manicure. "Popularity, vanity, money. Is that enough, or do you want more?"

I purse my lips. "I suppose that's enough for now."

"Who's she setting you up with this time?"

This time. Yeah, this definitely isn't a singular occasion. I've been out on at least a dozen dates set up by my mother, and each one was worse than the last. She refuses to believe that I'm happy with my life and doing just fine without a man. Sure, I plan to eventually marry and have kids, if I find the right person, but I'm not going to force it. I love my life. I love my friends and my job. I'm happy.

As much as I want the white picket fence and golden retriever, I don't need a man to make me whole.

I'd rather be in the position I'm in right now than the one so many of my friends who married young are. Some of whom have kids and are either unhappy or in the process of a divorce because they rushed into things too fast.

I shrug at Charity. "Some lawyer. She didn't say his name, but apparently, Dad's trying to steal him from the firm where he just made partner."

"Probably Chad Worthington. He's a nice enough guy but doesn't seem to be your type."

"I don't have a type."

"Well, from what I remember of him, he's not it."

My neck tilts. "How is he not my type if I don't have a type?"

"I picture you with... someone who isn't so clean cut. Someone who wants to go out and have fun. Not that I'm saying he's a loser, just that I feel like you need someone more adventurous."

"Maybe he is."

"Why are you sticking up for him?"

I release a sigh and shake my head. "I'm not. I'm just frustrated. I really don't want to have dinner with him, and I feel like if I go into it already bitter, it's just going to make it worse." It's not only that. I don't want her worrying about me, but part of the reason is because I'm sick of being disappointed. I let myself get excited at the prospect of a good guy, and then I'm continually let down. I'd rather be alone than deal with dating and weeding out the losers. Or the ones who have more hair product than me. Or the guys who talk about themselves the entire night, or even worse... the ones who talk about their mothers. No thank you. I already have a toxic mother, no way would I want to be with someone whose mother still wipes their ass.

"Why are you going if you don't want to? But better yet, why have you gone in the past? I don't get that. You're normally not one to let anyone tell you what to do."

I wish I had an answer for why I am the way I am, but I don't. I'm just me. I know my worth, and I'm proud of what I've accomplished, even if my mother isn't. I donate a dollar every time I'm asked at the grocery store, and I fill up those plastic bags the mailman leaves once or twice a year for a hunger campaign. And I fill them up with the good stuff, not just the stray can of baked beans or the almost expired canned pumpkin that I buy every Thanksgiving when I say I'm going to make a pie and never use.

I hold the door open for the person behind me, and if I get to a four-way stop at the same time as another driver, I always wave them through even if I have the right-of-way.

I'm not perfect, but I'm a good person, and I appreciate everything I have. Including my mother. I try to tell myself at least she cares. At least I have a mom who's still alive, and even if her execution sucks, her intentions are usually always good.

"You wouldn't understand," I grumble at my sister. "You married your high school sweetheart, who happens to be a neonatologist. You're going to make partner at Dad's firm probably by the time you're thirty. I *settled* for nursing and have no potential husband."

She sits up and crosses her legs, then runs her fingers through her dirty blond hair. "That doesn't explain why you go when you don't want to."

"It's just easier, Charity. If I go, then she gets off my back for a month or so before she starts up again." I sigh and pop the top on my beer. "Besides, when I go, I get a free meal. And since she always sets me up with trust fund babies, I always get lobster, and it's always delicious."

"Speaking of…" She glances up and down at my outfit, her brown eyes much like my own narrowing. "You need to change."

I look down at my joggers and sports bra. "Nah, I'll wear this. Turn him off."

"Hate to break it to you, but a sports bra probably will have the opposite effect and turn him all sorts of on."

"You're right." I stand and grab her hand. "Come help me find something that says *I'm only here because my mom forced me.*"

She takes my beer and sits on the end of my bed while I rummage through my closet. In the end, I wind up in a pair of tight light wash jeans, ballet flats, and a black turtleneck I dug out of the back of my closet. Totally plain and boring and hopefully will send him the signal that I'm a prude.

Because I refuse to get stuck needing a ride, I meet him at the rustic yet modern restaurant, and the hostess points me in his direction. He smiles when he sees me approach the table. His teeth are nice and white, and I'm surprised to find he's actually quite tall when he stands.

"Hi." He walks a few feet to me and holds out his hand. "Chad Worthington. It's nice to meet you."

The tilt of his lips seems genuine, and I find myself caught off guard a little. "Mercy. Same."

"Would you like a glass of wine?" He holds my chair

out, and as soon as my butt hits the seat, I grab the specials list off the table.

I shake my head and set the menu back down, already knowing what I want to eat. "Water's fine." What I want is to scarf this food down and get away from him. He seems nice, but I really want to be anywhere but here. This always makes me feel like such a loser.

The waiter comes over, and as Chad orders the special for both of us, I study him. I didn't ask him to order for me or tell him what I wanted, so it should irritate me, but he's actually not bad. His blond hair is parted on the side and touches the top of his ears. His fingers are long, and when he shook my hand when I arrived, I discovered they were softer than mine, which is a turn-off. The blue in his eyes is brought out by his navy blue suit, which is expensive as hell. And his white shirt is crisp.

He thanks the waiter, and once he walks away, Chad gives me his attention. He adjusts his tie and clears his throat. "I'm sorry. I'm very excited to meet you, and I've gotta say I'm a little nervous."

Aww. That's sweet. "Please don't be. I'm just me."

"That's exactly why I'm nervous. I hear about you at work all the time." That surprises me. "Your father tells me you're a nurse."

I lift a curious brow. "My mom said you worked at another firm."

"I do, but since your father and my boss are trying to build a partnership with the law offices, I see him often. And he talks about you almost every time I see him."

Makes sense, I suppose. "He doesn't lie." I smirk at the unintended lawyer joke. "I work in postpartum."

"What's that?"

"It's where mom and baby go after labor and delivery, which is where I used to work."

"Why did you switch departments?"

"I wasn't planning on it. I just saw the posting and thought I might like a change, which I do."

"Nice. How many babies do you usually see a day?"

Wow, I'm surprised he's asking questions about me. Usually, these guys like to talk about nothing other than themselves. "It really depends. Some days one and other days four. The most deliveries I ever saw in one day was nine. But it was like a full moon on Friday the thirteenth in October, so I wasn't surprised."

He takes a sip of his water but doesn't set the glass down. "You're superstitious?"

"Not outside of work. See, if anyone says anything along the lines of it's slow or they're bored, the rest of the shift goes downhill from there. Without fail, a full moon brings twins. Friday the thirteenth always means a doctor is sick. Stuff like that."

"So if you're walking down the sidewalk, do you step on the cracks?"

"Yes." I smile.

"Walk under a ladder?"

I gasp. "I'm not a glutton for punishment, Chad. No sane person walks under a ladder."

"Will me having a black cat deter you from letting me cook you dinner at my place sometime?"

My brain takes a second to catch up with how slick he just asked that. "You have a cat?" I ask in disbelief.

"Does that surprise you?"

"It does, actually."

He leans back in his chair and crosses his arms. "Why?"

"You're just all… suit and tie guy."

"Guys who wear suits and ties can't have cats?"

"Well, I thought not, but apparently, I was wrong."

He smiles. "It was my grandmother's cat, but she passed away two years ago."

"I'm sorry."

"Thank you. She, the cat, not my grandmother, doesn't like me. I can't even get near her to pet her, and when I feed her, she hisses at me until I back away."

"Oh no, that sucks."

"Yeah, but every morning when I wake up, she's lying on my feet, so I figure she can't hate me that badly. I think she's just pissed and confused because she lost her person."

I lift my glass to take a drink when the waiter sets our meals down. We both halt conversation and dig in. After licking the melted butter off my fingers, I swallow the last bite of my savory crab. "This is delicious."

"It is. Thank you for agreeing to meet me tonight. I know these setups are always a gamble."

"Tell me about it."

"I'd like you to tell me more about you, Mercy."

I wipe my mouth and set my napkin back in my lap. "What do you want to know?"

"Whatever you'd like to tell me."

For the next hour, I talk about myself. He listens and laughs when appropriate, then pays the bill and leaves a sizeable tip. He holds the door open for me and holds my hand as he walks me to my car. After I press the button that unlocks the door, he puts his fingers on the handle and tells me I look beautiful. Then he kisses my cheek and softly shuts the door behind me. And when I look in my rearview mirror, I see him watching me drive away.

FIVE

Jamie

KELLY'S PUB IS MEARA'S BAR, HANDED DOWN TO HER RE-cently from her parents. Everyone in our group—family, friends, and even fans—hang out here all the damn time.

We meet to drink and watch sports and play games in the old-school arcade on the second floor. We perform here a lot, too, and it's where Lee does acoustic sets when the nerve strikes him, usually for a charity. A lot of things happen within these four walls, but one thing that never does is hooking up.

It isn't an unwritten rule because it's carved in stone. There are too many complications that could arise from it, so everyone knows if they go to Kelly's they're not get-tin' any that night. The fact Meara even joked about lifting the ban earlier today is hilarious. We don't need some dis-gruntled chick causing problems for Meara and we defi-nitely don't need guys who feel threatened trying to start shit, which happens more often than we'd like.

Gabe usually attracts the problems, though, because of his reputation. He loves women, and women love him.

They flock to him more than anyone, and he's up for anything. He parties hard and fucks harder, but fights with such tenacity it's a wonder he hasn't been arrested more than twice. He doesn't take shit from anyone and is the first to stand up for someone he cares about.

Mike and I get our fair share of pussy, and it's actually a good thing Gabe is such a magnet for chicks because he weeds out a lot of the crazy ones for us. Fun as some of those girls can be, the majority are psycho, so we stay far away.

It was definitely different when we were in our early twenties. We all used to be like Gabe—except for Liam, of course—but as we've gotten older, we've settled down a bit. I find myself liking the quiet every once in a while, which is unusual for me.

I don't have anything on my mind tonight except getting a beer and maybe playing a game of pool, though. The unexpected night off is both a welcome relief and an annoyance. After I left Lee's house earlier, I went to my parents' and had a home-cooked meal.

But now I'm ready for a beer.

I walk up to the large wooden door at Kelly's and bump fists with Pierce, Meara's brother, who works as a bouncer on the weekends. "What's up, man?" he greets me.

"Nothin'. Just wanted to grab a beer."

"I heard about the fire at Stage 20. That sucks."

I sigh because it's such a bummer. The owners are really nice people, so I hope they get everything fixed soon. "Yeah."

"How long are you guys in town for?"

"We leave tomorrow morning. Show in Chicago

tomorrow night. Ian scheduled us as local as he could around Meara's due date."

"Cool. Congrats on being an uncle."

"Hey, you too, man. Melody's gorgeous."

"Yeah, she is."

A group of giggling girls come up, and I lift my chin at Pierce as I start my way inside. "Later."

He gives me a two-finger salute as he takes the ID from the first in line.

As soon as I pull the door open, the smell of old leather and pine hits me, and I can't help but smile to myself. There's something about home and the familiarity of everything. And there is nothing better than walking into Kelly's Pub. No matter when I show up, I'll know someone who won't want anything from me but conversation.

I sidle up to a stool, greeting the bartender Nik the same way I did Pierce with a fist bump. "Beer?" he asks.

"Yeah, thanks."

They never charge the band or family for drinks, but we always shove cash into the jar they have beneath the counter for tips. As he pops the top off, I walk behind the bar and locate the jar, dropping a large bill in. Nik shakes his head and hands me my beer as I sit in a stool on the end.

"How've you been?" I ask him.

Nik is a close friend of the Kelly family. Specifically, he's best friends with the oldest brother Declan. "Good, bro. You?"

"Things have been good."

"Haven't seen you in a while, not since Lee left, I don't think. How's the band with Kolby?"

"It was rough at first, but we're all good now."

"Glad to hear it. I listened to the acoustic set you guys did on satellite last week. Shit was sick."

I take a swallow and set my beer on a coaster. "You liked it?"

"Yeah, man. Why? You don't?"

Recording that track was one of the strangest experiences we've had as a band. Even more so than when we were in the studio for the first time and didn't really know what we were doing. "I do. It's just the first single without Lee."

"If you're worried it sounds different or something, I didn't think it did. But I'm not musically inclined except to know when I like a jam, so take it for what it's worth."

"That's good. We didn't want there to be a difference. Even though Gabe, Mike, and I hear those subtle nuances, we were hoping the fans wouldn't be able to tell, ya know?"

He shrugs. "Like I said, I thought it was sick. I'm sure you'll always hear a difference without your brother, but the show must go on, right?"

"Yeah. For sure." We talk for a few minutes before he's interrupted and heads to the other end of the bar.

I sit back and glance around, then do a double take when I see her. The hot chick who spilled my coffee yesterday sits in a U-shaped booth with a man perched on the end of her table.

The desire I have to go to her is so strong it makes my palms sweat. I've thought about her more times than I can count since yesterday. And for some reason, her face popped up when Meara said I needed to find a girl to make babies with.

Seeing her again in the flesh makes me realize

38

thoughts of her were damn near constant. I wanted to hang around the hospital yesterday to find the sexy nurse again, but Meara and Liam needed some time alone after so many visitors, and I'd just look like a lunatic pacing the halls in search of a woman I talked to for a whole minute.

A woman whose name I didn't know, yet I wanted to discover everything about her.

The thoughts of coffee girl were never far from my mind, though. Not yesterday and not today.

I'm surprised as shit to see her here. I'd almost convinced myself she was a figment of my imagination. Unsure if she's with the guy or not, I casually ask Nik, "What's up with her?" I'm hoping he says she's not with the dude, but I have no clue how Nik would actually know. That's like high school shit if I ask that.

He wipes down the mahogany bar top but glances to where I'm looking. "Not sure. She came in over an hour ago and ordered a rum and Coke but hasn't even touched it."

I want to go to her, but I shouldn't. If I do, I'll end up breaking the rules because I can't let her walk away again. Not many women make me laugh or get in my face. Or make me think about them all day. But she did, and I liked it. Too much. So much that I know without a doubt she's the game changer, but it doesn't matter.

We're going on the road again, and things are jiving so well with Kolby. I don't have the energy to put into anything other than whatever it takes to get me and whoever I'm fuckin' off for the night.

Besides, I need to follow the rules. Regardless of how much I want to talk to her again, I behave myself. No matter how badly I want to get lost in those earthy eyes,

I admire her from a distance. As hard as it is to stay put, I do just that.

For about a minute.

Because then the guy slides into the booth next to her. He crowds her and puts his arm around her shoulders, and she stiffens. It's just instinctual; I don't think before I push through a bunch of tables to get to her, green tinting my vision over a woman I have no claim to.

I don't get jealous. I'm not possessive or territorial, and I barely know this girl, but I want to put my fist through his jaw for even looking at her and getting close enough to smell how sweet she is.

It's funny because not a day went by since Liam was with Meara that he didn't growl at somebody who looked at her. I always gave him shit for being a caveman and laughed at him when he'd get all red in the face.

But I'm not laughing now.

No way. My reaction is so visceral and possessive I feel it all the way to the marrow of my bones.

Her brown hair is down, unlike when I saw her the other morning, and I decide instantly I like it better like this. It's wavy and shiny and long enough I could wrap it around my wrist. I can't remember the last time I saw a woman wearing a turtleneck, but this chick makes me want to bite and lick and suck on her neck so she has to wear those ugly ass sweaters, and only I would know that she's hiding my mark beneath the material.

I don't get a chance to think about how badly I want to see her out of her top because I arrive at the end of her table. "Wanna introduce me to your friend, Daisy?"

Her head snaps up, and her mouth falls open, cherry lips forming an O that I'd like to thrust my cock between.

I slide in the opposite side of the other guy and wrap my arm around her waist, palming the outside of her thigh and ass to pull her away from him and to me as if I have the right to claim her.

"Dude, you're—" I see the recognition on his face, and I cut him off. I don't want to deal with fans right now. I don't even want her to know who I am. Not Jamie, the rock star. I want her to know *me*, who I really am.

"Donny, nice to meet you." I stick my hand out for him, and he shakes it. Luckily, he takes the hint and grabs his drink.

Slowly, he stands. "No. Aren't you from—"

"Spain? Yes."

The little cutie next to me snorts, and I raise a brow at the man who still stands in front of the table. "No. I meant the ban—"

"And I meant it's time you leave." I level him with a challenged stare. "Now."

He mumbles something inaudible under his breath, and does the smart thing when he walks away without incident. I take that time to calm my shit.

The little minx tries to scoot away, but I tsk her and apply pressure to her luscious behind as I take a swallow of my beer, leaving the neck to dangle between my fingertips. She feels too good to let go.

I angle my head at her untouched drink. "It's not gonna drink itself."

"I know."

"Is it nasty?"

"No." She swirls the liquid, clear on top from the melted ice with the darker rum and soda on the bottom, making the entire glass amber colored. "I just didn't feel like it once I got it." She sighs and lifts her head so she's looking up at me. For a second, I'm afraid she's going to pull away, but she doesn't. In fact, she settles into me. God, she's pretty. She raises an annoyed brow. "Daisy? Really?"

"Yeah. Isn't it obvious?"

"This ought to be good." She crosses her arms, pushing her perfect breasts up higher in her black sweater. "Why?"

"Because I picked you."

Her insanely beautiful whiskey eyes shine. "You're such a player."

"Hate the game, baby." I wink, and she rolls her eyes. "So aside from being sexy, what do you do at the hospital?"

She pulls her head back, then her lips split into a huge smile, and somehow, she becomes even more gorgeous. "You're good. Not as good as the guy you chased off, though."

My temperature heats with envy, and that irritates the shit out of me. I shouldn't care. I'm never fucking jealous; the amount of ass I get makes other guys jealous, and I like it that way. It's not supposed to be like this. And definitely not over one woman I don't even know. "How so?"

"Do you have a name?"

"Yeah, Donny." I smirk. Gotta give her credit for thinking on her toes yesterday morning.

"No. That was his line. Do you have name, or can I call you mine?"

I smile behind my beer. "No shit?"

"Yeah. Totally lame. At least you have some…" She waves her hand in my general direction. "Charisma."

I blink. Then do it again slowly. Once more. Her nose scrunches adorably when my lids open and close rapidly. "Are you okay?"

"I dunno." I squint. "There must be something wrong with my eyes because I can't seem to take them off you."

She throws her head back laughing, and her neck elongates, and I finally see a sexy map of smooth skin I'd like to explore every inch of. "Oh my God. Is that what you said to that girl to make her giggle like that yesterday?"

"What girl?"

"The one who you ever so horribly were trying to pick up by telling the barista to get a coffee that was sweet like her?"

If she only knew. That woman was a fan who was driving me nuts. We're usually always really respectful to them and have no problems signing autographs or anything, which is what I wrote on the envelope she handed to me. We get recognized often enough, and even more since social media really blew up the past couple of years, but when we're home, it happens all the time. "No clue who you're talking about."

"Come on." She exasperates.

"The only woman I remember from the other day is a pretty nurse in blue scrubs."

Her lips twitch. "Okay, I don't know if you're drunk or stupid."

"I'm not drunk, but I am intoxicated by you."

Without missing a beat, she replies, "So you're admitting you're stupid, then?"

"Oh, Daisy…"

"My name isn't Daisy," she grinds out.

"That's right. It's Gillette." She drops her forehead to the table, and I chuckle when I land the punchline. "'Cause you're the best a man can get."

She lifts her head. "What's your name? For real, though? I wanna know what to scream tonight."

"Okay, my little firecracker. You wanna play?" I reluctantly remove my arm and turn in the booth. "Is your name Summer? Because you're hot as hell." She rolls her eyes again. "Winter? 'Cause you'll be coming soon."

"Do you know the human body has two hundred and six bones?"

I sit back, waiting for it.

"Wanna give me another one?" Her lips press together while she tries not to laugh.

"That's good." Blatantly, I check her out as best as I can from where we are in the booth. I really fuckin' like what I see, and even though I know it's a matter of time before I break the rules, I'm having fun with our little game. "Tell me, baby. What's a nice girl like you doing in a dirty mind like mine?"

Her mouth is open with a reply, but just then, Nik comes by with another beer for me and a fresh drink for her. "Thanks, man."

"Excuse me?" She sits up.

"Yeah?" Nik answers.

"Do you have a napkin?"

He shakes his head. "No. I'll grab one, though. Be right back."

She's smirking and avoids looking at me, so I know she's up to something. It's been fifteen minutes, but it feels like that many years since I've known her. And all I want to do is have that be longer. I want to take her home and bring her with me on the road. Tuck her away so she's just mine, and I can have her whenever I want to.

When Nik comes back a few seconds later, she takes the napkin from him. "Thank you."

"No problem," he hollers over his shoulder.

I know she's waiting for me to ask since she's just sitting here, staring at me with mischievous eyes and an amused and sexy as fuck smirk. "Why do you need a napkin?"

"'Cause you're making me wet." She can barely contain her laughter and ends up snorting, which makes her laugh even harder.

My shoulders shake, and I stare at the ceiling. I can't remember the last time I laughed this hard with a woman. Don't get me wrong, we make noise, and usually a lot of noise since that's how I like it. If I'm fucking a woman, I want to hear what I do to her, and I have no problem communicating that to get us both there. But as soon as we're done, so am I. I've never had the desire to hang around and banter with one of them either before or after.

But her, *Daisy*, all I want to do is be close to her. I can tell she would keep me on my toes, and the idea doesn't scare the shit outta me. In fact, the thought of not having her around scares me more. Not knowing everything about this woman freaks me out. Righting myself, I find her with a defiant brow raised. "Hey, sweet thing?"

"Yes?"

"I'd tell you a joke about my dick, but it's too long."

I've never seen someone look so bored, and I have a hard time keeping a straight face. "So are you going to sleep with me, or do I have to lie to my diary?"

That's a new one. I rack my brain and dig through my pocket to pull out a quarter, then hold it up between us. "What are the chances when I flip this, I'll get head?"

"I lost my teddy bear. Can I sleep with you tonight?"

"Smile if you wanna have sex with me." She tries not to, but it proves fruitless when her lips tilt up. I like this game, but I've had enough. I want it to be over so she can be under me. I reach up and run my thumb across her lips. "You're so fuckin' pretty. Your smile is beautiful," I whisper, all joking aside.

Her cheeks flush, and I cup her face in my hand. She swallows. "I bet it would look better if it was the only thing I was wearing."

"Nah, that shirt is becoming on you... but then again, if I was on you, I'd be coming, too." I end on a whisper but with only centimeters between us.

"I... um..." She stutters.

"I need you to get up and walk your tight little ass out of here."

Disappointment flashes in her eyes. "Why?"

"Trust me. I just need you to do it."

"Why would I trust you? I don't even know you."

I sink my hand in her hair, and damn, it's smooth like silk. Pulling her to me, she gasps, and I cover her mouth with mine. Soft and gentle, the exact opposite of what I feel. I want to ravage her. I want to tear her apart and put her back together again so I can make her mine.

My dick twitches at just the faintest touch of her sweet tongue. Yeah, I've gotta have her. Pulling back, her hooded eyes are confused and full of lust. "That's why. Now trust me. You need to leave before I do something I'll regret."

SIX

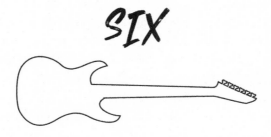

Mercy

MY LEGS ARE SHAKY AS I STUMBLE TO MY CAR. AT first, it was because of how turned on I was, but now it's because I'm pissed. I refuse to take it personally. I won't cry over some stupid, arrogant asshole who was so disgusted by me he essentially kicked me out... shooed me away like I was a dog.

And why did I even listen to him? Why did I leave? It's not like it's his bar. He doesn't own it.

Ugh. I wore my flats as a deterrent, but the bottoms are hard, and they click loudly as I stomp toward my car. This week couldn't get any freaking worse. This night couldn't get any worse.

I wasn't planning on going to a bar after my blind date, but I didn't want to go home to be in my thoughts. Too many of them are swirling around in my head, and I was hoping the noise of a bar would drown them out.

And it was working. I stopped thinking about Chad and how he was nice and sweet and would probably treat me good. But I felt nothing with him. And then that made me think maybe there really is something wrong with me.

What more do I want? He's obviously into me and would treat me like gold. But that's not enough.

I want it all. I want the ridiculous attraction I feel with Don Juan and the sweet, attentive husband material of Chad. But no way does Chad make my panties wet with a look, and there is not a doubt in my mind that Donny is the furthest thing from husband material.

So what do I do?

Give up what seems like a good, decent man to continue searching for something that doesn't exist, or settle for good instead of waiting for great?

"Stop!" I shift on my toes in the parking lot with my fingertips on the door handle of my car, wondering why I respond to this man so easily.

The heat from his body surrounds me, and I feel his chin push my sweater down, then his lips at my neck. He gently kisses me and then sinks his teeth into my oversensitive skin. The shudder that courses through my body makes my legs shake for a completely different reason. His hands span my waist as he toys with the waistband of my jeans. "I want you." His impressive length presses against my lower back, and instinctively, I push against it. "I know the owner and promised I'd never hook up in the pub. I had to make you walk away so I could keep my promise and still have you because Christ, I want you."

I don't even care at this point about anything other than his hands on me and what he'll feel like inside me, and I totally understand why the blond was throwing herself at him yesterday. I'd do just about anything for his attention no matter how much of a badass I want to pretend to be.

The thoughts I was hiding from disappear. I turn and

slide my hands up his neck and into his surprisingly soft hair. My nails dig into his scalp, and his chest vibrates. "So take me."

His green eyes smoldering with unfathomable desire, he slams his mouth to mine. Unlike the gentle kiss he gave me in the booth, it's rough this time and so needy. So perfect. I find myself lifting my leg to wrap around his thigh to get closer. He reaches down and palms my butt, lifting me up and pressing me against my car.

His throbbing erection rubs in just the right place, and I moan when a rush of moisture floods my panties. "You gonna come for me like this?"

"Probably."

I feel his smile against my lips, and he does something with his tongue inside my mouth that makes me gasp. "Just a tongue ring. Wait till you feel it on your pussy later. God, I can't wait to taste you."

"Jesus…" My thighs quiver, and I rip my mouth away, sucking in oxygen as I climax in the middle of a parking lot, in my jeans, with a man I don't even know. And it's the best orgasm I've ever had. I see stars and black at the same time, and I buck so hard the back of my head bangs against the roof of my car.

"Fuck, you're even hotter when you come. Didn't think you could get any better, but I bet when I get you naked and under me, you'll prove me wrong again." My legs fall, and he lets them slide down to the ground but brings my head back toward him. I stare at my shoes feeling *all the things* as I come back down to earth. "Tilt your face up for me."

I manage, just barely, but I do. I lift my chin, and he smiles down at me. "You okay?"

Okay? More like perfect. "Uh… yeah."

"Good. You want more?"

"Uh… yeah."

He chuckles and grabs the keys from the ground that I didn't even realize I dropped. He takes hold of my wrist and drags me around the car, then opens the door and shoves me in the passenger seat, his movements jerky and on edge.

"Where do you live?" I breathe as he climbs into the driver's seat, slams the door to my car, and puts the key in the ignition.

"Not close enough."

I'm not exactly sure what that means, but I'm too turned on to ask questions or even care where he takes me at this point. I just know he won't hurt me. Deep down, way at the bottom of my gut, I know he's feeling what I am, and nowhere in the scenario of us is there such a thing as pain. Not now, and probably not ever.

He drives with little control, his hair still spiked into a fauxhawk not a lot of guys can pull off. His jaw is clenched, making his cheekbones pop, and his nostrils flare as he breathes even harder than me. So lost in the moment, I don't even realize he pulls into a hotel until he puts the car in park, and I jostle in my seat.

"I'm not dragging you through the lobby like a whore. Sit tight for three minutes while I grab a room."

It doesn't occur to me that I'd be embarrassed if people saw me walking into a hotel room with a man and no luggage at two in the morning. But he did. Because he cares. Because he's the most perfect man. He's what I was waiting for. "Okay."

"I want you to stay nice and wet while I'm gone."

Oh God. "What?"

"Put your hand in your pants and play with your pussy. Rub your clit but don't come."

For the love of… I've never been so far gone in my life. I don't even contemplate his demand before I lean back and unbutton my jeans. Then lower my zipper. His eyes are hot and wild on me as I slide my fingers between my slick folds.

My hips shoot up, and I moan, my entire body overly sensitized. "Look at me." His hand wraps around my wrist, and he pulls my arm away, then brings my wet fingers to his lips.

When he sucks them into his mouth, a spasm between my legs makes my hips circle, desperate for more, to be filled by him. "Fuck, you're sweet. Keep touching yourself while I'm in there, but I want your eyes on me the entire time."

"Okay."

He grabs the back of my head and kisses me. I just barely taste myself on him before he pulls back. "Watch me."

Words don't form in my head or come out of my mouth, so I simply nod and rub my clit in small circles. If I speed up, I know I'll come, so I work myself painfully slow. I imagine it's him doing it to me. Shivering when I think about what his tongue would feel like.

He rushes to the desk, and when he takes the keycard across the counter, he turns his head. He's talking to someone else but looking at me with nothing but sex on his face. I've never seen anything hotter in my life. My body shudders as I'm so, so close, but he shakes his head. I don't know if I can hold on or if I even want to.

My fingers are slippery, and they easily slide around in circles and up and down. Back and forth and in jerky movements as the peak gets closer and closer. The door is whipped open, and he starts to drive away before it's closed all the way. "Stop."

"No," I whine, grinding my pelvis into the palm of my hand. "I can't." So close. So damn close.

"I said stop. You don't come without me inside you this time." He pulls my arm away, and I cry out at the loss of sensation. "Gimme."

Before I can understand what he wants, he's licking my hand. All the way from my wrist up to the tips of my fingers. "That's not helping." I pant when he gets to my thumb.

"No shit. But it's mine. I want all of it." He nips at the tip of my finger. "You gonna give me more?"

"Yeah."

"That's good, gorgeous. Really fuckin' good."

My breath hitches as it happens. It hits me fast, but the build was slow. At times, agonizingly so. The first time was fast. As soon as we walked into the room, he threw me on the bed and had us both naked before the clock registered a minute. He fucked me fast and brutal, and I got off on every second of it.

What was happening at this moment was slow and sensual, and he made me feel special. I loved it. I think I love him if it's possible. I want it to last forever. Want to be with him, like this, every moment of every day for the rest of my life.

I continue to smile when his hips still, and he groans into my neck, his deep voice making my belly spasm.

My lips are tilted up as they press an openmouthed kiss right above his collarbone. He tastes good. I'm not surprised because he smells good, too. He is by far the hottest man I have ever seen in my life, so it isn't lost on me that these things were expected with the package of my own personal Don Juan.

The weight of him pushes me deeper into the mattress, and I have to put effort into breathing, but I don't care. As long as I have him, I don't care about anything else. Not my past, not my future, not even tomorrow. The only thing that matters is this moment.

He pulls out of me and kisses my forehead. "Be right back." I cuddle up on my side and wait for him to return. He brings back a warm, wet washcloth and a hand towel. "You need to clean up?"

"Sure." He used a condom, but he got me so wet I soaked the sheets and the inside of my thighs.

I take the towels and roll to my back to clean up as he climbs in beside me. He hands me a bottle of unopened water, and I sip it before handing it back.

"You hungry?"

"Kind of, but not really."

He lifts my hand and turns his so our palms are touching. His fingers are longer than mine and his palm could swallow mine whole. I love him touching me. I want his hands on me every day for the rest of my life. "What does that mean, kind of but not really?"

I feel the soft touch of his calloused fingers through my entire body as if he's staking claim to every part of me. Inside and outside at the same time. "It means I could eat but like… not a steak. Or even a burger. But fries would be good."

"Chips?"

"Those, too."

"Candy bars?"

"I'll never say no to a Snickers." I'll never say no to you because the answer will always be yes.

He links our fingers and tugs me to my knees, then pulls me so I'm straddling him. We're both still naked, and for whatever reason, it doesn't bother me. Usually, I'm self-conscious about my body, but he makes me feel beautiful. Desired. Sexy. His lips are tilted, and his eyes lazy as though he knows exactly what he's doing to me, how every touch and every look undoes me. "Kiss me first, then hop off and we'll go raid the vending machine."

"That sounds awesome."

"Yeah, it does." His eyes point at my lips, and I find myself wetting them. "Kiss me, Daisy."

"Okay, Donny."

For the first time tonight, I take the lead. I press my lips against his and bring my hands up to rest on his strong shoulders. My head tilts to the side, and I slide my tongue along the crease of his mouth. Once he allows me entry, I moan as I twirl the tip of my tongue around the bar in the middle of his, and he brings a hand up to wrap around my throat. I don't fear for a single second that he'd hurt me, but even if he did, I know I'd love it. The very tips of his fingers dig into my jaw, and he takes over, plundering my mouth, devouring it, and owning it.

I feel him hard beneath me, and I'm already so wet that when I grind against him, I slide so easily up and down. He grunts and grabs one of my breasts, his thumb swiping back and forth, teasing my taut nipple. He works one, then the other, making my heavy breasts ache with need.

My hips rock against his, mimicking sex, and my body simply and naturally reacts to his nearness. Every time I go up, my swollen clit rubs against the velvet tip of him. I have to pull my head away to suck in air, and he doesn't waste even a second before he feeds my breast into his mouth.

"Oh God."

The steady rhythm of my hips is interrupted, and I drop my neck to watch as his mouth feasts. My forehead lands on the top of his head, and I watch as he suckles one nipple, then the other. When he pulls back, I get a chance to admire his flat abdomen and the muscles on his chest.

"God, you're so fuckin' sexy. I could stay here forever and fuck you," he confesses.

"Me too."

He thrusts up, and I have to grab the headboard so I don't fall. "I'm not done with you, not nearly, and I only have one more condom. You got any?" He pants.

"No." The fact he even had more than one is something I don't want to think about.

"We'll get creative then 'cause I'm not leaving you tonight for anything." He tilts his head up, grabs my face, and kisses me deep. "Sit up, baby."

I use his chest to push myself up, and he slides his hands down until he's at the juncture of my thighs. Using his thumbs, he parts my folds. "Watch."

Again, my head falls, this time landing on his

forehead, and we both look down. My thighs shake as I ride his cock as pearly white leaks out of the tip. "That's so hot."

"Fuck yeah, it is. Ride me, gorgeous. Watch me come for you. Look what you do to me."

I whimper and try to move faster, but his hands apply pressure and his fingertips dig into my thighs. "Slow."

I don't want to, but for him I'll do anything. "Okay."

He continues to hold me open, both of us watching as I glide up and down his velvet-wrapped steel. Sweat drips from his temples and falls onto his stomach. "You wanna go faster?"

"Yes." I shiver and tears tickle the back of my eyes with how damn much I feel right now. I've never been so intimate with a man before. We're not even having sex, and I feel closer to him than my college boyfriend of three years.

"Then move. Your sweet pussy is so fucking wet, so warm, and it feels so fuckin' good. Fuck, baby. Fuck." He brings his hands to my hips and pushes me down as I press harder.

Our movements become frantic as we both chase it. "I'm gonna come," I whisper, the words barely audible as my breath is stolen.

"Yeah." He grunts, and I watch as he splashes on his tight abs. "Me too. Fuck."

I can't take it anymore and cry out as my entire body locks tight, seconds before I fall apart... or maybe, I'm finally put back together.

SEVEN

Jamie

"YOU WANT THE LAST ONE?" SHE HOLDS UP THE last stick of a Kit Kat. Isn't that a sign of true love or some shit when they offer you the last slice of pizza or whatever? Regardless, I shake my head.

The bed is filled with wrappers, and I yank the sheet up, making the papers fly to the floor. She giggles when I pull the covers over our heads. "Remember doing this in elementary school during gym? It was my favorite."

The dim light casts a shadow over the left side of her face, and I swear every time I look at her, she's more beautiful; in the dark, bright light, or shadowed, she's so expressive and just gorgeous. "Yes, I totally remember that. But my favorite was the scooters. Until they weren't." She licks the chocolate off her fingers and rolls to her side. My T-shirt bunches up by her hip, and I trace the bare skin just below with one finger, watching in fascination as little goose bumps arise.

"Why did it stop being your favorite?"

"Because my hair got caught in the wheels, and it

57

yanked a huge chunk out. I had to go to the emergency room and get a stitch in my scalp."

"No way."

She brings my hand up and presses my middle finger to a spot just behind her ear. "Yup. Right here."

I gently probe the scar and caress the shell of her ear before I slide my hand back down to where it was. "How did that happen?" I can't get enough of her. I just want to keep touching her. And I've touched her a lot. I've touched her everywhere. After she rode my dick until we both came, we took a shower where I fingered her until she came again. After we were done, we got almost a hundred bucks' worth of crap from the vending machines.

We came back to the room, and I was going to give her a break and let her get some sustenance until I heard her moan when she bit into a candy bar.

Immediately, I got hard. I don't even have to try, just her tasting chocolate does it for me. I stopped eating the gummy bears I'd bought and started eating her. And Christ, she's more decadent than anything I've ever tasted. I pulled her over me, and she rode my face while she sucked me off, then swallowed all of me down her throat... every last drop. If I had a ring on me, I'd have proposed to her right then and there. We had to call housekeeping to get new sheets since those had melted chocolate all over them.

That then led to another shower where she fucked herself with her fingers and I jacked off watching her make herself come. It's all been fucking fantastic, the best I ever had. By far. Ever. I don't want it to stop, don't know if I can stop it. I want inside that pussy again. I want to bury myself balls deep and live inside her. And I have one more time to do that tonight. Or this morning. The last time I looked, it was almost two.

"It happened because I'm a moron. See, I used to do gymnastics, but my mom made me stop and—"

"Why did she make you stop?"

"Because my mother likes to try to control every aspect of my life, and when I was a kid, she could. So anyway, I think I was rebelling or something because I knew it was stupid, but I tried to do a headstand on the scooter and well…" She shrugs. "I think the rest is self-explanatory."

"I get it. I ended up in the ER one time because I thought I could fly like Superman. Jumped off the roof and if it wasn't for the bushes, I'd probably be dead." Her eyes widen, and as insane as it sounds, seeing the genuine concern on her face makes me fall harder than I did that day.

I bring her hand to my arm, and she finds the raised skin on her own. Even though I can't feel through the scar tissue, her touch penetrates the barrier somehow… she breaks down all of my barriers. "You broke it?"

"Yeah. And my ankle. I also got a rock to the head, so of course I got a concussion and needed the gash stitched up."

"I bet your mom was terrified."

My body tightens, and she must sense it because her hand glides up my arm and rests on my jaw. She doesn't even ask me, but I tell her anyway. "She left me when I was a baby. Like… the day I came home from the hospital, she laid me down for a nap, packed her shit, and left."

"Where was your dad?"

"Working. He owns a construction company, and up until that day, he worked around the clock. When he came home that night to find a note and a screaming new-born, it woke his ass up that he was wasting his life away at a job. He tried to get her back, but she'd made up her mind."

"I can't imagine that. I'm sorry."

I shrug and take her hand. "It is what it is. He remarried when I was four, and my stepmother is the only mom I know. She's great, and honestly, I don't even think about my birth mom anymore." I hate seeing that look of pity on her face. The last thing I want is for her to feel sorry for me. I want her to see me as a man, her man, one who's strong and capable and will protect her at all costs. "What about your dad, is he still around? You mentioned your mom earlier."

"He is, but I don't want to talk about them." She bites her lip, and I reach up and tug it down with my thumb. Gently pressing in, I let her suck it and can feel the pulses of her mouth all the way down on my dick. I slide it out and bring it to my own mouth, rubbing her moisture on my lips. Wanting nothing that's her to go to waste.

I roll us over so I'm on top of her and stare down into mocha swirls. "What do you want to talk about?"

"You."

I pull my head back. "Oh, yeah?"

"Yeah. I... I'm... I've been wanting to know something, and I... I just want to know."

I hope she doesn't ask me my real name or what I do. I'm liking that she doesn't know that about me yet. Probably part of the reason why I'm feeling so strongly about her is that I know she's here with me, for me, and not because of my money or for a walk on the wild side.

She's not going to post a selfie with a thumb's up and

me sleeping in the background. She won't steal my shirt as proof she went home with me. And I know she'd never try to sneak video while I fucked her.

There have only been a couple of women I've actually dated over the years, and neither of them lasted long because it didn't take long for them to show who they really were; nothing but groupies.

But not her... not Daisy. No. She's real—as real as they come—and I don't want to let her go.

"I'll tell you anything you wanna know, gorgeous." I don't have anything to hide about who I am; I just don't want her to know yet. I want to be with her just a little longer so I can know for sure she's exactly who she says she is... who I think she is. But if she asked, I'd tell her right now because I don't want to lie to her. If she wanted my social security number and the pin to my debit card, I'd give it to her.

Her tongue darts out to moisten her lip, and if it wasn't for the concerned expression on her face, I'd ignore whatever question she had and take her mouth. "Nothing. Never mind."

"No fuckin' way. You can't get all serious, then tell me to forget about it. I want to know what's on your mind. I wanna know you. Everything that I can."

Her teeth sink into her lower lip. "It's gonna ruin the mood and probably the night, so just forget about it... seriously."

"Ask me," I growl and drop my forehead to hers, but she looks away. "Nothing will ruin this night, Daisy-girl. I won't let it. It's been the best night of my life... You're the absolute best I've ever had, and I'm not gonna risk losing that over a question. Ask."

She hesitates for a second, then takes a deep breath. "You just seem to be really comfortable with this whole… one-night stand thing. And I'm not normally… I've never." She takes another breath and finally meets my eyes. "I don't know if it's weird or makes me crazy, but… I don't want to be just a number since it seems like that's what this is. I didn't think one-night stands were supposed to be this… intense, and I don't want to make a fool of myself by being the only one who feels that it's more."

"Oh, baby … no." I frame her face and pull back so she can see me. I want her looking into my eyes so she knows how fucking serious I am. "You're not a number, gorgeous. You're the answer to the equation."

Her lips tilt up, and she giggles. "That was a good one."

"Wasn't trying to be funny," I rumble, and her lips snap closed. "You want the truth? Or do you want me to sugarcoat it?"

"Truth."

She starts to look away, but I turn her head, so she's forced to look at me. "Out of all the one-night stands I've had, nobody has ever, *ever* made me feel what you do. Nobody has made me question my career, nobody's made me want to stay, and I have never imagined my life with a woman, and this will make *me* seem crazy, but I already can't imagine my life without you in it." And that's just the damn truth. Call it irrational or call me crazy, I really don't care. As long as I can call her mine, nothing else matters.

I didn't realize how dark her eyes got until they light up beneath me. "Isn't that what every guy thinks every girl wants to hear? I feel like I'm an idiot if I believe you."

"I get it. It's scary as shit. Hell, what I'm feeling for

you scares me, but I'm trying to only focus on now and not worry about how to make this work with how much I travel and wondering if I'm crazy for even thinking that far ahead."

I wait for her reaction to my confession and tense up as the seconds pass. I actually can hear my watch as the seconds tick by. "You are crazy but not for that reason." She runs her fingers through my hair, and if I wasn't looking for doubt in her eyes, I'd close mine.

"Why am I crazy?"

"Because you don't break off the pieces of the Kit Kat before you eat them. I mean seriously, who bites into it like that? Crazy people, that's who. You probably don't peel your string cheese, either."

The sigh of relief I expel almost hurts my chest. I am crazy, but if I have her, I don't give a shit about anything else. I bite my lip and lunge at her. She screeches but doesn't fight; instead, she wraps her legs around my waist. "You're fuckin' adorable."

"Thanks."

I run my nose along hers, and she swallows when my lips brush her cheek. "I want you again."

"Okay." Her thighs shift beneath me, and I groan.

"Never wanted someone as much as I want you."

"Same." She pants as I roll my hips, rubbing my hardening dick against her.

"I want you to know that."

She nods. "I do."

Fuck if those two words don't make my dick twitch. I'm driving myself crazy with how much I want this girl. How I feel like I need to be inside her. Not just to fuck her, but to make love to her. To claim her.

I toss the sheet off the bed and sit up, ripping my boxers off so I can straddle her. "As much as I like seeing you in this, I want it off." I tug on my T-shirt she's wearing, and she sits up to yank it off. I hate that I have to wrap up but there is no way I'd risk her safety or health, so until I can prove I'm clean, I'll have to use a condom.

My fingers squeeze hers, and I bring them up over her head. Her legs part in invitation, and I slide inside to where I fit perfectly. It's like the first time every time with her. Every time I come, I don't think it can get better, but somehow, it does. Foreheads together, noses brushing, mouths sharing the same air, I make love to her. Slowly. Every time I pull out, I slide back in an inch at a time. Then I leave my cock inside, letting her muscles torture me as they spasm. "You're so deep," she whispers.

Yeah, I am. I pull all the way out of her and bring her wrists together with one of my hands. I grab my dick with the other. "Unwrap your legs for a second."

Her thighs fall apart, and I scoot forward, resting my cock on her flat stomach. She looks down and moans. "See how far inside you I go?" I slide back inside in one smooth thrust. She gasps, pushing against the headboard. "You feel me all the way up here?" I touch above her belly button, to where the tip of my cock reached. "You feel me, gorgeous?"

"Yes."

"You gonna feel me tomorrow?" She mumbles something incoherent as I glide my fingers from her ankles to her knees, then hold her open. "Answer me. You gonna feel me tomorrow?"

"Yes."

I grunt, my balls drawing up and making my spine tingle. "What about the next day?"

"I'll feel you." Her back arches. "God. I won't ever not feel you."

"That's right. You'll feel me forever. I promise you that. Fuckin' forever."

EIGHT

Mercy

I SNUGGLE INTO THE COMFY MATTRESS AND PULL THE SHEET up to my chin and can't believe this is my life. That I found *him*. Or more like he found me. Ever since I saw him at the hospital, I haven't stopped thinking about him. At first, I just thought he was an arrogant pig, but the more time went on and the more I couldn't get him off my mind, the more I realized it wasn't his attitude I kept thinking about, it was his eyes. If I'm being honest, it was what was behind his eyes that I couldn't stop thinking about.

And after the way those emerald irises saw through me tonight and showed me what I didn't even know I was missing, I'll never be the same. I didn't ever believe in that love at first sight crap, and with him, it really wasn't instant, but it's been intense, and I know it'll be everlasting, no matter what happens.

There are things I want to ask him, secrets I feel like he's keeping, but I want to wait until the morning for the bubble to burst. I want just this night with him to be perfect so I'll remember it forever.

The light to the bathroom shuts off, and the bed dips behind me. He pulls me against him and laces our fingers together. I love that. *Love it.* He doesn't just hold me but he entwines himself with me. His breath at my neck tickles, but his lips replace the itch, and I get a full body shiver at his loving touch. "Get some sleep, Daisy."

"Okay."

"We'll get breakfast in the morning, but I gotta go outta town after that."

Sleep is gaining on me, but I still manage to ask, "Where do you have to go?" I don't know if I want to know the answer, but I had to ask. Curiosity got the best of me.

"Not far but any distance away from you is too much." If it was up to me, I'd never leave his side. And even though he said he feels the same way, I still worry that it's too fast. Too much, too soon. Hell, I don't even know his name... but maybe that's part of why it's so good. The mystery. The allure.

He buries his face in the back of my head, and I soak up the feeling of him holding me. I'm normally not a big cuddler, but with him, it's like his body was made to hold mine. Like it was made to fit inside me perfectly.

"This is crazy," I confess into the dark.

"I know," he agrees, and his arms spasm around me. "But it's crazy good."

Putting my weight into him, I squeeze his hands interlaced with mine. "I know."

"We'll talk in the morning, gorgeous."

"Okay."

"This isn't over. You know that, right?"

Sighing, I melt into him even further. "Yeah."

"Promise me, this isn't over."

He likes me. God, he likes me so much he doesn't want to let me go. "Promise."

It doesn't take long before his arm around me gets heavier. My eyelids get weighted down as well, and before I know it, my phone vibrating on the nightstand wakes me up. I quickly untangle myself from his embrace enough to grab my cell, then unlock the screen and read the text from my sister.

Charity: Where are you? Why aren't you answering?

Shit. I slide out from between his arms and go to the bathroom to call her back. I close the door, then sit on the top of the toilet and get a sinking pit in the bottom of my stomach when I see seven missed calls. I don't know how I didn't hear them vibrating.

"Where are you?" she answers after only half a ring.

"What's wrong?" I whisper-yell.

"Mom's in the hospital."

My throat dries, and I can only choke out a cry.

"She was attacked by a patient. We're still in the ER, but they're going to move her soon."

"I'm on my way."

"Okay. Hurry, but drive safe."

I yank the door open and let the light from the bathroom help me find my jeans. I slide those on and grab my shoes and purse, then rush to the door. "Crap."

When I turn around, I find Donny still sleeping. He looks so young like this, all restful and relaxed. I don't want to wake him because I don't want to waste the time explaining that I have to leave, plus I don't have it in me for some type of emotional goodbye. And I know that's exactly what it would be, too. And then the thought hits me that he might not want to see me again.

What if he was just saying all that stuff to get laid? How do I know he wasn't lying, and after we parted ways tomorrow, he'd never call me?

The thought of not seeing him again makes my throat spasm, but I can't focus on that right now. I have to believe in him. Trust that he feels what I do, that his word is true. I grab the first thing I can find, which is a piece of paper with the hotel's logo on it, and leave him a note with my number on it.

I press a kiss to my fingers, then his scruffy jaw, and memorize everything that I can in case he turns out to be someone I think he's not. I want to remember him just like this. He stirs slightly but falls back to sleep. I grab my shit and haul ass outta here with so much fear in my stomach that it cramps up on the drive.

I'm fearful about my mother, but mostly, I'm afraid of my future, or lack thereof, with Donny.

Somehow, I arrive at the hospital, and out of habit, I park in the employee parking lot. As I'm jogging through the brightly lit blacktop toward the ER entrance, I roll my eyes at how dumb I am for making myself walk this far.

By the time I make it inside, my brother-in-law Mark is heading out. He offers me a sympathetic smile. "Hey, Merc." His strong arms wrap around me, and he squeezes. "She's okay. I'm going to get Charity some clothes because she ran out in her nightgown."

I pull away from him and rush toward the electric sliding door. "What room is she in?"

"Seventeen."

"Okay, thanks."

"You need me to grab you anything while I'm at the house?"

If I did, I wouldn't even know what it is right now. I have so much whirling around in my head that I actually have to look down to remember if I put my shoes on. I grab the ends of Donny's T-shirt I'm still wearing. "No, I'm good."

The bright light from the ER shines like a beacon as I rush inside. I don't have my badge on me but have no problem getting to her room quickly. Her face is toward the window, but she turns her head as soon as I walk in. I have to fight to keep my jaw hinged. She looks terrible. Aside from the cast on her right hand, her usually impeccable light brown hair is tousled. The right side of her face is purple and swollen, and beneath her left cheek is a butterfly bandage.

An attempt has been made to wipe away whatever makeup she had on because she still has black smudges under both eyes, and her lips are a pale pink, not the coral they usually are. She's probably more miserable about that than what happened. Appearances mean everything to her.

"Mom," I whisper.

"They didn't need to call you." She turns her head and winces but still manages to glare at my sister. "I told you not to call her."

"She'd want to know, Mom."

I step all the way inside and touch her good arm just above her IV. "You hangin' in there?"

"Yeah, I guess. I told them I was fine, and this is all unnecessary."

After giving a gentle squeeze, I skirt around her bed and hug my dad. "What happened?" I ask so only he can hear.

He shakes his head and takes hold of my arm. "I'm gonna take Merc to get some coffee, okay."

"You can talk in front of me," my mom snaps without even opening her eyes. "I was there, so I know what happened."

"True. But that doesn't mean you need to relive it." He puts his hand on my shoulder and steers me out of the room despite her protests. We walk down the hall and stop at the vending machines in the waiting room. I smile, remembering laughing with Donny as we raided the vending machine in the hotel.

My dad grumbles something about bad coffee as he waits for his to brew, and I wait for an explanation. "She was called in for an emergency surgery, a broken leg from a car accident. I don't know the details. The guy was former military and currently a police officer, and I guess when he was waking up from anesthesia, he displayed some concerning signs. The anesthesiologist and your mother both sustained wounds, but more so your mom because she was apparently in a headlock getting her face punched while the anesthesiologist sedated him again."

I hold my hand to my throat. "My God."

"She says it's the first time it's ever happened in all the years she's been a surgeon. Totally unpredictable and so rare she forgot it was even something that could happen."

"Wow. I don't even know what to say... I want to go back by her. She looks terrible."

"She's trying to hold it together, Merc. She fought hard when they said they wanted to keep her overnight for observation, but I think she didn't want to appear too combative, either. Once we move rooms, I think I'm gonna take off. Go home so I can get a couple of hours of sleep and bring back some of her things in the morning before I take her home."

I lean into him as we go back to her room. My mom and I have always had a rocky relationship, but since I was a baby, I've been a daddy's girl. All of the pictures of me as a child are either with my sister or my dad. But still… she's my mother. It doesn't matter how badly she treats me, how much her favors come with strings, or how she constantly makes me think I'm a failure, I'll push it all back as good as I can and try to be the kind of daughter she'll eventually be proud of some day. "Okay. I'll stay until the doc comes in the morning."

"Your sister insists on staying, too. Mark went to grab her some clothes."

"I saw him on my way out."

"Is he bringing you back anything?"

I shake my head. "No. I'm okay."

"Yeah, that big T-shirt looks really comfortable."

My face heats up at my father's joke, and I bite back a laugh at his not-so-subtle dig.

Mom's still awake when I get back, and Charity is already sleeping. Mark comes back, and he sets her bag on the floor. I toss a blanket over her and grab one for myself, then settle in for the night, my dreams filled with green eyes and whispered promises.

My mother gets discharged in the morning, and for the next week, I sleep at her house every night, taking some personal time from work to be with her while she recovers. But unfortunately, as each day passes, she gets worse. She doesn't even apply lipstick or comb her hair. Her physical wounds are healing, but her will is fading. And fast. I wasn't expecting her to spiral.

I've been so busy dealing with her, but I haven't forgotten him. The liar, the asshole. The player.

He never called. He never fucking called, and I'm mad. I'm sad, and I'm hurt. I feel stupid. No matter how I try to hide it, I know I'm acting unusually quiet, but I can't help it. If I'm not dealing with my mom, I'm replaying that night in my head and wondering what I did wrong and how I fell for his lies.

He was so convincing. He made me believe. But more so, I felt it. I swear I felt him in my soul, and as irrational and unconventional as it is, I know he ruined me for anyone else.

It's day seven post-Donny, and as I sit on the edge of my mother's bed, I find myself staring into space. "What's the matter with you?" she snaps. "You'd better not be like this because of me." She's always been kind of short with me, not sugarcoating anything and getting right to the point, but this thing where she snaps for no reason at all is new. And deep down, I feel like it's just the beginning of the end.

"Like what?"

"Miserable."

I didn't realize I was acting a certain way. I knew I was off—there was no way to hide it—but I didn't know I was putting off a vibe that I was miserable. She's been so depressed since the attack, I decide that telling her about my pathetic mistake would make her feel better and give her something else to focus on. And maybe, just maybe she'll give me some advice. Some real, solid, motherly relationship advice. "I met a guy a week ago. The night you were hurt, and incidentally, the same night you set me up with Chad." Who's called and even stopped by every day since my mom's been back home. She refuses to let him see her, but he brings magazines and candy… anything to try to cheer her up.

She doesn't respond as I tell her my problem, just watches and listens.

"I thought he was the one. It was… it was a perfect night, and I thought it meant so much more, but he never called. It's only been a week, but I already know he never will, and it feels like my heart is cracking."

I wipe the tears before they fall, and she shakes her head. "No man is worth that. Stop it right now." I'm not surprised by her response, but I don't want to listen to it. I prepare to leave because it's impossible for me not to feel emotional about this. About him. "You may think I set you up for selfish reasons, but rest assured, it's for you."

"Mom, no offense, but the guys you set me up with are kind of lame."

She purses her lips together. "They might be lame, but they're not cheaters. They're not going to not call. They'll treat you like a princess and worship the ground you walk on. Marriage with a man like Chad wouldn't be perfect, but it'd be safe. It'd save you from that." She motions to my tear-stained face.

"But I didn't feel that… that spark with Chad."

"So what? The spark fades away after time anyway, so what difference does it make if you don't start with one to begin with? You'd live your life with a husband who cared and loved you, and a man who would make a great father. Those things are more important than a stupid spark, Mercy."

She rolls to her side, and I close my eyes, wondering

if that's really how she's felt her whole life with my dad. "Okay, Mom." I pat her shoulder to placate her and take the opportunity to leave the room. Closing the door behind me, I sniffle and go downstairs to find my dad sitting behind his desk in his office.

I'm not surprised; it's where he spends most of his time, which is why it's fit for a king. Large mahogany desk, oversized leather chair, bay windows that look out into the garden, and floor-to-ceiling law books that take up the walls on either side of the room. He even has a chandelier. It's pretentious, but he's not.

My father is the most down-to-earth man I know. He works hard but always has time for his kids. As I step inside and sit on one of the two cushioned chairs, I wonder if my mom feels the same way. That he'd do anything for her, that he'd drop everything to be wherever she needed, that she was loved. "Hi, Daddy."

"Hey, pumpkin." He sets his reading glasses down and leans back, the chair groaning with his weight. "What's with the long face? She not doing any better?"

I shake my head and cross my arms, more upset about what she implied about love than anything, but I can't tell him that. "No. Not really. Have you heard any more from the specialist?"

His blue-gray eyes slide down as he nods. "Unfortunately." He angles his head at the door. "She wasn't coming down, was she?"

"No." I sit up, eager to hear the news on her prognosis.

"It's not good." The regret in his voice is almost palpable. "He doesn't think the nerve damage can be repaired. Not in the way your mom would need in order to operate again. I'm afraid she'll never step foot in an OR again, but more so, I'm afraid of what that's going to do to her psyche."

A stress headache forms between my temples. "Dammit." The patient who attacked her crushed her hand, breaking a couple of bones and causing extensive nerve damage. She had surgery already to fix it as best as they could, but the surgeon wasn't hopeful. And since my mom is stubborn and in denial, we got a second opinion.

"She wants yet another opinion, but we flew this last one in from California. He's the best in the country, and even he agrees with the initial diagnosis. I don't see good things for the future, Mercy. Best prepare yourself for this wave to pass because if we let it, it'll take us all under."

Three months later

My arm is shaky as I pull the heavy wooden door open, my legs even wobblier as I take a seat on a stool. I really need to get back to the gym. I haven't gone since my mom's accident. God... it feels like forever but like yesterday at the same time. I can't think about her accident without remembering that night. It's such a gift and a curse that each minute is etched in my brain.

"Hey. I know you."

I lift my head and force a smile at the woman behind the bar, and even though it's been a few months since I last saw her, I recognize her immediately. The wife of the man who looks at her like she's the world. "Hi. How are you?"

"Oh, ya know. Sleep deprived and happy. How about you?"

"Same." But my reason isn't because I have a newborn at home. Mine is entirely different. I wish it was because I had a baby at home.

She laughs and leans a hip on the bar. "I don't remember ever seeing you here. Have you been in before?"

"Um, yeah. Just once a few months ago." The best and worst night of my life.

"Well, you came back, so that's good."

Not intentionally, I don't tell her. I'm only here because I'm meeting Chad for a midday drink since I'm off of work and he's going to have a long night at the office. This place is by his building, but I didn't realize it was the same place I met *him* that night when Chad text me the address earlier today. If I knew, I'd never have agreed to meet him here. I'd leave, but he just texted that he's on his way, so I'll wait a minute. Once he gets here, I'm going to try to convince him to go somewhere else.

Being here brings back all the memories, so many that I feel like the air is thicker and it's getting almost harder to breathe. I can't freak out. After inhaling through my nose, I smile at her. "It's a really nice bar." I glance around at the arcade on the second story loft. "I love the little game room up there; it's really neat."

"Thanks, we try. What's your name again? I totally forgot. To be honest, I'm so damn exhausted I'm surprised I even remember you. I should have listened to Lee and not come back to work yet." Of course her perfect husband wanted her to stay home longer. Why wouldn't he?

"It's Mercy. And I wish I had a newborn as an excuse, but I forgot yours, too."

"I think your job is a good enough reason. You see a gazillion people, and I'm sure the hours are long, so I'd forget everyone's names, too. I'm Meara Kelly hyphen Anders."

I raise a brow, not to be judgmental, just curious as to why she hyphenated her name. I always wondered why women did that. If I ever married someone, I'd jump at the chance to get rid of my surname and belong to him.

"I know, I know. It screams *feminist movement*, but well… I own Kelly's and—"

Duh. "Oh my God. I didn't even put two and two together with the name." I laugh embarrassingly, and it's probably the first time I've cracked a genuine smile in months.

She waves me off. "You're fine. But since I own the pub, I just didn't want to get rid of it when I married Lee. But I also wanted his name since I'd scribbled it in my notebook since I was like ten, so hyphenated is the way to go."

I tilt my head and run my fingers through my hair. "You married who you had a crush on when you were a kid?"

"Yeah, it's annoyingly cute."

I try to hide a smile, but she shakes her head. "No way, what is that look?"

"Nothing. I just totally thought you and your husband were ridiculously cute and totally in love in the hospital." And you make me insanely jealous, and I wish I was that in love with a guy who was equally in love with me instead of the feeling being one-sided.

Her bright white teeth shine against her pink lips. "Aww. That's awesome you thought that. We are, and it's pathetic, actually. But I love him, and he hasn't gotten rid of me yet, so…" She has a look in her eye, the same one

I'd seen on her before. The one that made me instantly jealous, and I still hated that I felt that way. It wasn't that I begrudged people on their happiness; it's that I want it too.

And I thought I had it. I thought I had the night to end all nights. But in reality, I had the night that ended me.

I sip my Coke while she refills a pitcher of beer and then hands it to a guy at the end of the bar. "Here." She pulls her phone out of her pocket. "What's your number? I'll text you so we can maybe meet up for coffee or something sometime."

"Um. Okay." I wasn't expecting that, but she's really nice, so I spit off my number, and she smiles. I doubt she'll ever call; she's probably just saying that to be nice. As soon as I'm finished, I feel a presence next to me.

"Hey."

I look up to see Chad and smile at him. "Hi."

"I'm sorry I'm late. You still want to grab a quick drink?"

Want to? No. Need to? Yes. The past few months have been insane. Since he now officially works with my dad, Chad decided to take it upon himself to step up to be there for my family… and for me.

I have to admit, he's been helpful. He's bridging the gap between work and home for my father, and he's actually been a strong shoulder for me because things with my mother have gone from bad to worse. He's been completely appropriate and one hundred percent a gentleman. He's been the best friend a girl could ask for.

As the days have gone on, it's been easier and easier to be around him. I start looking forward to him calling because I know that if I need something, he'll be there for me, and aside from my sister, I've never had that before. And I like it. I knew... I knew that he was husband material. He's husband material without any type of connection, but according to my mom, that should be good enough.

"Can we go out to eat instead? I'm starving," I lie. I just need to get out of here, away from the memories that still are so vivid it's like I'm living them. I look over at the booth where I met *him* in and can feel his arm around me, can hear his husky laughter, can taste his lips. My throat tingles with threatening tears, and I start to stand, not giving Chad a choice if we stay or we go.

"Anything you want." I knew he'd say that either way. God, he's such a nice guy. Why can't I feel anything for him?

Meara is on her phone leaning on the bar. I wave to her, and she smiles bright and mouths that she'll call me. Chad takes my hand and leads me out of the bar. "Do you know her?"

"Just from work. She had a baby a few months ago." The day I first saw him.

"Oh, neat. What do you feel like eating? Italian? They remodeled that place on the corner after they got a new owner, and I've heard it's really good now."

"Sure." I'm not in the mood to eat at all, but I'll never say no to some alfredo. Just like I'll never say no to a Snickers. Or Donny.

After a quick lunch where I choke down some pasta, Chad walks me to my car, placing a kiss on my cheek before I get in. As soon as I pull away, it happens, but I hold it in. I wait until I'm around the corner and yank my steering wheel, running my tires into the curb and jamming the shifter into park. My breath tangles in my throat, and I let out a loud cry, so fucking hurt by and in love with a man who doesn't exist for me anymore.

Every time my phone rings, my heart races, praying it's him. But it never is, and I know deep in my gut that it never will be. It kills me to know how wrong I was. How I was so foolish and insecure with myself to allow his lies to hurt me.

I dry my eyes and head to my parents' house where I can wallow in misery with my mom. After I'm inside, I toss my purse on the table and walk quietly up the carpeted stairs. I pass the room I grew up in, a bathroom, and my brother's room before I reach my mom's bedroom.

Knocking is pointless since she won't get out of bed for anything other than to go to the bathroom. I open the door slowly and peer inside, finding her in the same position she was in when I checked on her this morning. Curled on her side, she stares out the window with a blanket up to her waist and bare feet.

"Hey, Mom." I walk around and sit on the floor, leaning my back on the window so she's forced to look at me. She blinks but doesn't say anything back.

We've had three different psychologists come to the house, but she refused to speak to any of them.

When the nerve damage in her hand was officially confirmed as irreparable, she sank into a deep depression that seems to only be getting worse by the day. My father is at his breaking point, feeling helpless after enduring her verbal abuse for months.

The specialists all say to just give her time. Talk to her like normal, treat her as if she's an active participant in the conversation, so that's what I do. "I just had lunch with Chad."

For the first time in months, she smiles. "He makes you happy, and that makes me happy."

My eyes widen in shock at her statement because that's the most she's spoken at once in weeks. "Yeah, Mom. He makes me happy." I lie, but if it'll help her get better, I'll say whatever I have to. I'll do whatever is necessary to help her get better.

NINE

Jamie
nine months later

"**H**EY, BIRTHDAY GIRL." MY VOICE IMMEDIATELY raises a few octaves when my niece's face pops up on the screen. I miss her. I haven't seen her for about three months, and it breaks my heart that I'm not there.

"Hi, Uncle Jamie." Meara holds Melody's wrist and makes her wave when she talks in a high-pitched baby voice. "Say, I wish you could be here." Spit bubbles come out of Melody's mouth when she giggles the sweetest, most innocent baby giggle known to man.

That pull in my gut from not being there makes me sick, but I've gotta work. And right now, we just finished up a European tour and are doing some dates on the East coast so we won't be home for another couple of weeks. I understand why they had her party now, but I still wished they would have waited until we could all be there, or at least me. Chances are Kolby will go back to California since we'll have a short break, so it'd be me, Gabe, and Mike. "I wish I could be there too, chunker." Melody babbles something baby, little spit bubbles coming out of her mouth. "Did you get my present?"

Meara rolls her eyes. "Stop calling her chunker; she's gonna get a complex. And she's one, Jamie. She doesn't need Power Wheels yet."

"You're small enough to fit in that Jeep, Meara. You can take the little chunker for a spin."

"Whatever. I have this thing called a real car I chauffeur her little butt in all the time as it is." She shakes her head. "It is adorable, and she'll love it... in about three years."

I chuckle and see my brother in the background talking to a guy I don't recognize. "Hey, who's Lee talking to?"

She turns her head. "Oh, that's Chad. My friend's fiancé."

"You have a friend?"

"Yes. Why? It surprises you that I have a friend?"

"Yes," I answer immediately.

She narrows her eyes at me and presses her lips together. "If I wasn't holding my daughter right now, I'd swear at you."

I wink. "I know. Hey, have I met your new friend?"

"No, I don't think so. Next time you're home, maybe."

"Is she hot?"

"Dude. She's here with her fiancé."

I smirk and nod. "Yeah. That means she's hot." Nobody's as hot as my Daisy, though. And no matter how many women I see in a crowd, her face is the only one I ever see. Her melted caramel eyes shining up at me, and her dimpled smile sweet and sexy at the same time.

God, it's been a fuckin' year, and I can't get the bitch

outta my head. I haven't told anyone about her because the damn truth of this fucked-up situation is that I fell in love with a woman who played me like a damn fiddle. She wound my strings up so tight they snapped with just a blink of her eyes.

My pride won't let me admit she deceived me, my heart won't let me forget it, yet my dreams force me to remember each second of that night. I relive it minute-by-minute almost every fucking time I close my eyes to sleep.

It's gotten to the point I have to take NyQuil to get decent shut-eye.

Mike sticks his head outside where I'm talking to Meara to warn me we're about to go on. We're in Florida right now, I think at least. I can't even keep track anymore.

"On in ten, Jamie."

I nod, letting him know I heard him. Time to get in the zone.

"Is that Lee you're talkin' to?" Mike asks.

I shake my head. "Meara and Melody."

He smirks. "Ask her if she got my present."

I press the button on the screen to flip the camera so she can see him as he stands in the doorway, and Mike lifts his chin. "Yes, she got it." Meara sighs. "I thank you, Melody thanks you. And Liam most definitely thanks you."

Mike's shoulders shake as he tries to hold in his laughter. "Yeah. I bet he does."

"What was it?" I ask, the question meant for either one of them.

Mike answers. "You tell him, Meara. I've gotta go warm up... these pipes don't make the ladies drown without some lube first." Meara makes a gagging sound, and I shake my head. "Happy Birthday, Melody," he sings before he takes off, and I stand, ready to end the conversation so we can do our pre-show ritual.

I flip the camera again so she sees me. "What did Mike get her?"

"I swear, you guys are so clueless when it comes to babies. He got her a freaking karaoke machine."

"Ha. That's awesome."

"No, it's not. He should have gotten her one of those fake kid ones, not a professional quality machine with speakers loud enough to fill an arena. Besides, she can't even use the damn thing for years. What the hell am I going to do with that huge box for that long!"

Her irritation makes me laugh. "She'll be using it sooner than you think, I bet. But hey, I've gotta go, though. Tell Lee I said hi and to answer his fucking phone. Kiss Melody for me. And make sure I meet your hot friend next time I'm home."

"Yeah, okay. I'll let you meet my friend, and with one look, she's going to leave her fiancé to be with you. Go break a leg. Literally."

I throw up a peace sign and then tuck my phone in my pocket and head inside. The other guys are all in the dressing room, Mike warming up for vocals and Gabe tuning his guitar. I throw back some Fireball and shake out my hands, then tune up as well before handing it off to a stagehand who will go set it up.

We silently gather close to the stage and put our hands in. "Unleash the fury, boys." I play along like always, and I don't know if the guys can tell, but I'm not the same. Not since her.

I have so much love and hate for her that the feelings clash and form something eviscerating. The fire I used to have has burned out. I hate that I let one woman get to me, but it's beyond my control. The attraction was out of my control, and the fucking pain is out of my control. If I had my way, I'd forget about her and fuck her out of my system, but it doesn't matter how many groupie skanks I screw, she's still the only damn thing I think about.

My performances on stage have been the best ever, though. I see now why my brother was the way he was. How he wrote haunting melodies and poured his soul onto paper. How that confusion and anger played out in his music on stage. It's the only thing I have left anymore.

Tonight's show is over before I know it, and after I find some pussy for the night, I bring her back to the bus. I still get excited whenever I see a brunette. Even if her hair is shorter or longer than my Daisy's, I know she could have cut it, and in a year, it could have grown out, too. But every time one of these chicks turns around, it's not who I want to see.

Their eyes aren't the color of whiskey, and they don't have that little dimple on their chin. Their voice isn't soft and sweet, and their laughter doesn't make my guts twist.

Which is why the redhead currently riding my dick doesn't have any of my attention. The only reason I even got it up tonight was because I was imagining Daisy. Her voice, her smile, her laughter... her mouth and how hollow her cheeks would get when she was sucking me. How fucking tight her pussy was and how damn wet she got for me.

It's pathetic, really, how fucking tore up I am over her. How wrecked I'll always be over the one that got away.

How thoughts of her are the only thing that makes me come anymore, if I can come at all.

I ignore the squeals and mewls, yanking the groupie off me to stand. My jeans are at my ankles, and I yank them up, frustrated as hell at the bitch for playing me like she did and making me fucked up over her lies. And straight up fucking me up. "Time for you to go."

"What?"

"Leave."

"But…"

I yank open the door that leads outside and ignore her protests. What did she think? That we'd magically fall in love and I'd want her to be the mom to my kids? My feet pound down the steps, and I run into the rest of the band sitting around an electric fire pit relaxing with a beer.

Groupie chick stumbles off the bus and our bodyguard Lincoln walks to her to steady her. He shakes his head at me and I shrug, grabbing a Lite out of the cooler. "Where is everyone?" I ask as I plop down on a fold out chair.

"Dunno, they all took off. Since we're only an hour from his house, Ian of course went home to boink his wife." Gabe laughs.

"You seen the tits on her?" Kolby whistles. "I'd leave you pussies to boink that cunt, too."

"You ever fucked a married chick?" Gabe asks.

Kolby laughs with his mouth closed and reaches behind him. "Gentlemen." He clears his throat. "I think Gabe has just begun a round of shot or not."

"Dammit," Mike groans but takes the plastic cup of Fireball Kolby poured. I do the same, as does Gabe. Kolby just keeps the bottle in his hand.

We have this thing, where if someone asks a stupid question, we have to play a round of this dumb-ass game. But in reality, it always turns out to be a blast. And honestly, I could use as much distraction as I can.

"I have knowingly fucked a married woman." Gabe asks.

Not surprisingly, Mike shakes his head, and the three of us take our shot. Kolby fills all of our cups again.

"I purposely sent a dick pic." Gabe laughs, and the question from him isn't a surprise. What is a surprise is when he doesn't drink.

Kolby shrugs and takes a swig.

"Dude. You know that shit's on the internet somewhere," Mike chastises him.

"I sent it to Kim; she spreads that shit, and I'll blast her pussy all over social media." He rests his elbows on his knees, and the way he talks about his ex-wife pisses me off. Everyone knows that she was an awesome woman, but Kolby treated her like shit. He cheated on her left and right, and his personal life dragged his old band down, causing them to kick him out for being such a fuckup. Kim divorced him, and he contacted us after Liam left.

The rest is history.

"I got snowballed," Kolby says with a straight face, and we all burst out laughing. Nobody takes a shot, and everyone looks to me.

I've had a few tonight, probably more than I should, so my tongue is loose. I've kept all the shit about Daisy shoved deep down for a year now and even though I've been distracted at the most inopportune times, nobody's said anything. "I've woken up in the morning to an empty bed and broken promises."

I toss back the Fireball, and when I straighten up, they're all staring at me. "What the fuck?" Gabe asks. "We didn't start this shit to turn into a bunch of baby back bitches."

He's right. We didn't. We started this dumb ass game to pass the time. To let one night roll into the next and to the next and the next. Because that's what our lives have become... mine has at least. And it doesn't make any sense. I shouldn't be this messed up over her. Not ever but definitely not still.

"Nah, I know you're right, man."

"Are you all fucked up over some chick?" Kolby leans back in his chair and crosses his arms. "Because I'll tell you from experience, ain't no female worth that shit." He and his wife divorced because he stopped putting in any effort to be a halfway decent dude. I don't blame her for leaving his ass.

I shrug. "Never thought I'd be."

"And I never will be." Gabe raises his glass, and we all do the same, then throw back some more alcohol.

I drop my cup to the ground and cross my feet at the ankles. Gabe goes on about how he'll never live with a chain and some other shit about being a bachelor for the rest of his life. And I think about how, at the rate I'm going, I will be too.

TEN

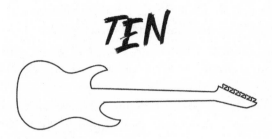

Mercy
two years later

YET ANOTHER DAY HAS PASSED... ANOTHER WEEK, ANother month gone... and then two years. Just like that. A snap of my fingers and a blink of my eye, my life is passing me.

I'm exactly where I should be, too. Engaged to be married to a very kind man and plans for a future that includes kids and a house with a white picket fence. My mom is healthy again and has been for the past year and a half. Mostly because she's been busy planning Chad's and my wedding. The wedding of the century. Hundreds and hundreds of people have RSVP'd, and everything is going according to her plan.

Things have been great on paper, and I only think about *him* every now and then. Usually... no, always, I think about *him* when Chad and I are having sex. I can't call it making love because I don't love Chad, not in the least... not that way. It's not fucking because he's too gentle for that. He never pulls my hair or wraps his fingers around my throat. Every time, without a doubt, it's *him,* it's Donny I'm imagining inside me, and the only reason I can climax is because I remember how he made me feel.

I'm not proud of it, and I'd never admit it out loud, but that's just the truth, and I've accepted it. I need to be happy for what I have and not dwell on the past. I've taken my mother's advice and moved on without the spark.

I pick up the pace a little bit as I walk home, excited to see Chad and tell him about my day. We've become close, and despite not being in love with him, he's one of the best friends I've ever had. The best, actually. Almost on the same level as my sister.

And that's sad.

The man in your life should be your man first. He should claim you with an arm around your waist and make you feel like you're coming out of your skin when he's inside you.

Chad doesn't do that.

What he does do is listen. Whenever I talk, he gives me his undivided attention. He shows me he cares. Always. Showers me with gifts and is there for me no matter what or when. When I'm bitchy or moody or frustrated, for whatever reason, he lets me vent to him. I got so lucky because I know I'll never find someone who loves me as much as he does, and that's what I need to focus on.

There's always time to fall in love, right? I can learn to love him… can try to make our relationship into one I've always dreamed about, can't I?

He moved into my apartment about a year ago since it was close to both of our jobs. Unfortunately, his cat passed away the week before he moved in, and it tore me up to see how upset he was over an animal that hated him.

It was an adjustment at first, having to share my space with somebody, but I got used to it rather quickly because every morning he woke me up with a cup of coffee and breakfast in bed, and on the weekends, he made dinner. It's actually nice having someone to help shoulder the responsibility of bills and car maintenance. And I know when we have kids, he'll be a great dad. Involved. Active.

What more can I ask for?

I give myself an internal pep talk about how lucky I am on my way home. When I get to the door and see Will, the neighbor below me, I wave and smile. "Hey."

"Hey, Merc. How are you?"

"Good," I answer automatically. "You?"

"Same. Wedding's getting close, isn't it?"

Unconsciously, I shiver. He narrows his eyes at me, but I smile and try to cover up the slight repulsion I feel about marrying a man I don't really love. "It is, so exciting!" I fake my enthusiasm.

He must buy it because he smiles back, and I sigh in relief. "It sure is. Have a nice night." He nods and holds the door open for me. "Thanks. You, too."

I rush up the steps and insert my key, pushing the door as I unlock the deadbolt. But my movement freezes as soon as I'm inside the apartment. It looks the same. Soft gray curtains on the windows, light brown couch, dark wooden coffee table. The TV is new since Chad wanted a big screen, and it covers the entire wall, sitting above a shelf with the cable box and DVD player on it.

My kitchen is on the smaller side, only large enough

to fit a round table with two chairs, which sits between the living room and kitchen and acts as a divider.

But next to the table is a suitcase. "What's going on?" I toss my keys in the dish at my entryway and hang my purse on the hook.

Chad stands and drags the suitcase behind him. "I'm leaving."

Those two words make my heart skip a beat and not in a good way. Leaving? "What? Where? Do you have a business trip or something?"

He shakes his head, disappointment dripping off him, and takes a step closer. Reaching out, he caresses my left hand, fingering the ring there. "You don't want this."

It takes me a moment to process what he just said. "I… what?"

His soft blue eyes roam over my face. "You don't love me, Mercy. At least not the way I do you. I know you tried, and the fact you're willing to go through with this tells me how much you really don't care." I try to say something, but he gives my arm a little tug. "You don't care if I get hurt, if I live our marriage knowing that I'm not who you really want. If I have a child with a woman who's only with his or her father for convenience."

"Chad, I do care. I don't want to hurt you at all. Ever. You're such a good man, and I—"

He cuts me off and abruptly takes a step back, almost tripping over his suitcase. Anger laces his features, something I rarely see on him. "Cut the shit, Mercy. You're with me out of obligation. It took me a while, over two years, but I finally see it."

"What are you talking about?"

A bitter laugh escapes him. "If you think I don't know

your mother pressured you into being with me, you're completely wrong. I gave it time, gave you the opportunity to be honest with me for once, but you never did. You might be able to live a lie, but I can't. Not anymore. I deserve better than that."

The backs of my eyes start to burn, and the same feeling makes its way down my throat and into my stomach. I can't deny it. I tried, I've been trying, but the entire time I've been with Chad, all I could do was wait for it to get better. I had more chemistry with him on our first date than I do right now. I don't know how it happened. So fast but at the same time, it's been unbelievably slow, living with and pretending to love someone who isn't right for me.

"I love you enough to let you go. I want you to be happy."

"You do make me happy."

"Not the way I should. Not the way you want to spend the rest of your life."

What can I say? How do I deny the truth? I don't, I guess.

He nods at my finger. "I'd like you to keep that as a memory of me."

"I can't." I start to take the engagement ring off, and he laughs. And not the kind of laugh that I'm used to with him every time I tell a joke. But a kind of laugh I've never heard from him. Disbelief, almost.

"You don't even try to tell me I'm wrong. Don't try to fight for me, for us. For a marriage that's supposed to happen in three weeks."

Dropping my head, I squeeze my eyes together. He's right. I'm a horrible person because I don't give him back what he gives me, but I thought it was enough. It is enough. "I'm sorry. Chad, I—"

"Just stop. Stop trying to justify it and figure out what it is you really want because it's not me."

I can't form a sentence but open my mouth to say something. And not surprisingly, nothing comes out.

He laughs again. "I got a job offer in Minneapolis. I'm moving there tomorrow. Your father knows; I told him about a half hour ago. I'm sorry it didn't work because I really thought we had something, but at the end of the day, I want to be with a woman who can't imagine her life without me in it, not one who is excited at the thought of me being out of it."

He reaches out and grabs the back of my head, then lifts me up to my toes. His mouth finds mine, and he kisses me. Hard. Fast. Then he walks out the door and out of my life... and I don't try to stop him.

I don't do anything for three weeks. I barely sleep, can hardly eat, and at work, I'm surprised I haven't gotten fired. Every night, I tried to call Chad to explain, but he never answered. Not that I thought I deserved it, but it would make me feel better that he knew I did love him in a way. But after two weeks, he disconnected his number.

It's a surreal feeling because I miss him, but I don't. I feel bad that I hurt him, but I'm relieved. I'm irritated that I have to listen to my mother lecture me about how stupid I am, but at the same time, I've never felt more free even though I'm locked in my thoughts.

Which is why I came to a dive bar tonight. To get my mind off all the things I can't stop thinking about. To drown my sorrows in a glass and not be around anyone who knows how pathetic I am. But as soon as I sat down, so did this guy. And he distracted me enough to forget why I was here. He bought me enough shots to make a linebacker pass out.

"What's your name?"

I sip my fourth... no, I think it's my fifth rum and Coke and debate answering him. I'm not sure if there's a protocol about this sort of thing. The last time I went home with a guy, or to a hotel, rather, he called me Daisy and I called him Donny.

But now I'm here on the day I was supposed to be getting married, wallowing in my sorrows and trying to forget that it's my fault my mother fell apart again. But that's not why I'm here. No, I came to forget.

Truth be told, I don't know what the hell I'm thinking. If I was smart, I'd have gone to Kelly's and spilled my guts to Meara, who, in the past couple of years, I've grown pretty close with, and I value her friendship tremendously. Especially since she was one of the only people who didn't make me feel even worse about the fact that Chad left me.

I give my head a shake. I didn't come here to think about anything. God, I just want to forget.

Instead of contemplating names, I should be thinking about if I really want to do what I know is going to happen whether I give this guy a name or not. He isn't playing around. I know that, too. But I also know it doesn't matter what I tell him my name is because he'll forget it by the next morning anyway.

And fuck it, if it's going to happen, I want it that way. I want to have a night when I don't have to do any of the thinking. I just want to feel something other than guilt and shame. I want to feel passion again. I want something to make me think I'm not broken anymore.

Donny ruined me. He gave me everything in one night and then took it away and tarnished something that was once shiny and beautiful. Chad leaving me three weeks ago did nothing but cement the fact that I never got over *him*. I never forgot the way he made me feel and how I fell so hard so fast because I swore he was it. Donny was mine.

But nope.

I'm so messed up. I feel horrible that Chad felt the way he did, but he was spot-on, and I truly want the best for him. Because he's right; he deserves better than me.

I strung him along and made him be the one to call it off even though I should have. I should have been woman enough to admit to him how I really felt, but somewhere along the way, I lost myself.

I lost the me I was before him.

And I want her back.

The guy I met about three hours ago runs his finger across the top of my hand. My bare left hand. I refused to keep the ring. It cost a crap-ton of money, and I don't deserve something so beautiful. I found out where Chad worked and sent it in the mail along with a note apologizing. He signed for it, but I haven't heard from him, not that I blame him.

I don't have to wait long before I make either the best or the worst decision of my life because this guy says, "You do wanna know whose name you'll be screaming tonight, right?" He's clearly put enough time into getting me wasted enough to lower my inhibitions so I'll go home with him, so he wants an answer.

His lips are tilted up in an overly confident but not quite cocky smirk. And that's my undoing. The stupid pickup line.

"Yo, babe. You still with me?"

If I continue to think about it, I won't do it. So I stop thinking. Stop giving a shit. "Daisy."

He holds his hand out, and I put mine in his. "It's nice to meet you, Daisy." Something about the way he says my name with a smoky-smooth voice that I'm sure makes women drop their panties for is ridiculously sexy. Everything about him is, though. He reminds me of Donny. There's a swagger about him that tells me if I don't go home with him, he'll just walk to the end of the bar and find someone else, and I don't want that. I want him to want me.

I want to feel desired. I want to feel something other than the hurt that weighs me down and pulls so heavy on my heart that I find it hard to breathe sometimes.

I'm done feeling sorry for myself. Done holding out for a man who doesn't even exist anymore. Who never really existed in the first place. From this moment on, he's gone.

He looks at my drink, then back at me. "Wanna get outta here?"

I don't hesitate. "Yes."

"I was hoping you'd say that." He throws cash on the bar and holds his hand out for me. I put my fingers in his palm, and he takes us to the curb where some cabs are waiting. "My place or yours?"

No way in hell am I going to tell him where I live. For some naïve reason, I'm not worried about him hurting me. Hell, even if he did, I guess I deserve it for being so stupid. But I do believe he's clearly a man-whore, and nothing more. The fact that I'm about to get in the cab with a complete stranger doesn't scare me, but the hesitance I'm already starting to feel makes my stomach churn.

He winds his hands through my hair, his fingers tightening on my scalp. He does something with his lips on my neck that sends a shiver down my spine, then brings his mouth to my ear. "I'll take you to mine."

I crawl eagerly when he pushes me in the back seat. I push against him when his hands go between my legs. I do have enough sense to look at the sidewalk so I don't trip as he drags me up to an old Victorian house. As I kick off my shoes on the way through the dark hallway, I briefly entertain that this is a bad idea.

No… not bad, necessarily, just regrettable.

When he gets me to his room, he shuts the door and is on me before I have any more time to think. So I take advantage and do nothing but feel.

I let him use my body as much as I use his. I take out the pain and the rejection and the fear that I'm going to be alone for the rest of my life out on this guy and his dick. I don't let anything into my head but the moment, and I promise myself to enjoy it because I'm never doing something like this again. Ever.

My head is pounding, and I gasp as I sit up. The movement makes my stomach lurch, and I grab a half-drank bottle of water from the floor and slam it, not even caring.

A hand reaches for me, and I jump out of the bed, pulling the sheet with me. I end up running into the dresser and wince at the pain in my hip. Oh my God. The guy from last night is naked, propped up on an elbow. "You leavin'?"

Oh my God. I need to get out of here. What was I thinking? This isn't me. I never should have been here in the first place. I shouldn't have let him buy me those shots. I know what I was thinking, but in the light of day and with a sober head, I realize just how much of a mistake this was. How stupid I am. "Yeah, I'm getting out of here." I slide my jeans back on beneath the sheet and turn my back to him as I pull my shirt over my head. "I need to get to work." I put my cross-body strap where it's supposed to go and look around the floor. "Where are my shoes?"

"You took 'em off when you walked in. They should be by the front door."

"Okay. Thanks, I guess." Then like a lame idiot, I wave and hurry to his door as vomit bubbles in my stomach for multiple reasons. I'm such a moron.

He chuckles. "Had fun, babe."

I catch myself lying through my teeth. It wasn't that it wasn't fun, it's that I don't remember most of it. And I'm not sure if that's a good or a bad thing. Right now, I'm going with good because I have a feeling I made an ass out of myself last night. "I did, too."

ELEVEN

Jamie

THE DOOR TO KOLBY'S ROOM OPENS, AND I DON'T EVEN bother turning around to see what skank comes out this morning. I hate it when he brings chicks back here, especially groupies because they almost always show up again randomly.

It's like Rule 101; don't let her know where you live. But he doesn't technically live here. We're only home for a couple of nights, and since my house is so big, he crashes with me instead of flying all the way to California. Which, if I'm being honest, I don't know why the hell he goes back there when the only tie he has there is his ex-wife. His family is all in Kentucky, so it surprises me that he chooses to either be here, or back in California in an apartment by himself.

We've been home one night, and he already hooked up, which isn't a surprise really, just annoying I have to deal with these chicks in the morning.

"Shit." I hear a curse in a familiar voice, and whip my head up from the toast I'm buttering at the sound. Sweet, smooth, and sexy as all fuck. Unforgettable. The knife clatters to the island when I recognize her hair, too. The longest, softest, shiniest brown hair I've ever seen in my entire life.

I remember running my fingers through it, pulling it, falling asleep with it all over my face and loving the fact that her scent was with me in my dreams.

Her short legs that appear long from her skintight jeans and an ass so round I can feel the weight of her globes in my hands. I can practically taste her skin, the salty sweat from me working her over almost as delicious as the honey I sucked from her pussy.

God, her pussy.

The tightest. The wettest. The best.

Up until her, I thought they were all the same. Some of 'em a little different, but none of them so slippery snug and sinfully savory they kept me up at night. Like a junkie searching for their next fix, I tried to get high and settled for tainted drugs, because the most potent dose was given to me three years ago, and no matter how much rehab I partook in, I never forgot how the buzz of her felt. How faded her eyes made me feel. How drunk on her taste I got. How just the thought of her sobered me up.

Her.

Jesus Christ, it's *her*.

She bounces on one shoe as she slides the other Chuck on, and at the sound of the knife colliding with the marble island, she looks up. Her eyes widen with shock, her face pales more than it already was, and she falls back into the wall, knocking down a frame that shatters on the ground. Yeah, that's just how my goddamned soul destructed when she disappeared.

My heart pounds so damn loudly that I can fucking

hear it in my ears, blood thickening and making my veins stretch painfully. "What the fuck?" I growl.

"Oh my God." Her voice is now pained and scratchy, her stomach surely in her throat if she's feeling even a quarter of what I am.

I dreamed of seeing her again in so many different ways and at so many different times. In my mind, sometimes I'd be happy to see her and other times I'd be pissed she left me with a bogus number. Depending on my mood, I'd envision just grabbing her and pulling her to me, smelling her again and feeling her soft curves, reminding me that she really was real. Sometimes I'd jog her memory by being gentle; other times, I'd be rough, and it'd be savage as shit, but she'd love it.

A few times, I thought about screaming at her. I even thought I'd just bend her over and fuck the liar right out of her. The fucked-up bastard I am, I vividly pictured shoving my cock down her throat until she gagged so she couldn't tell any more goddamned lies. And it did things to me I shouldn't be proud of, but at this moment, right now, I want nothing more than to thrust my cock in her pretty little lying mouth until her lips turn as blue as my fuckin' balls.

I never thought I'd see her like this... not here. Not now. Not coming out of another man's bedroom. Not this unexpected and this soul-shattering.

Hell no.

Her voice was the same goddamned voice I heard muffled through my plaster wall last night. I was woken up by it, but in my sleep-deprived unconscious-consciousness, I didn't register that it was her. Probably because I heard it so often in my sleep that I thought I was dreaming again. The promises she made and the lies she told mash together, and the throbbing in my head makes me grab my hair to release some of the pressure. "What the fuck!"

"Oh my God." Her trembling hand flies to her mouth, and she puts effort into swallowing.

Kolby's door slams, and he drags his feet as he pulls a shirt over his head, wearing nothing else but a pair of boxers. "Jesus. What's with all the noise?"

"Did you fuck him?" I know she did, but I'm not thinking clearly. I'm not thinking at all. I'm doing nothing but feeling. My skin is stretching, and my throat is itching. My hands shake as I pound them on the island. She jumps, and I turn my head to glare at Kolby who has a confused look on his face. I don't think my question can get any clearer, but I ask him. "You fucked her?"

He pulls his head back and looks at me like I'm wearing lipstick or some shit. "You two know each other or something?"

Son of a motherfucking bitch.

The lack of hilarity in his question is unprecedented. "Do we know each other? Yeah, I fuckin' know her, Kolby." I stupidly gave her parts nobody else ever had, and she crushed them.

I've thought so much about why I couldn't stop thinking about her over the years, and I think when it comes down to it, it's simply because I didn't know why. Why did she lie? Why did she leave? Why did she give a fake number?

Kolby's eyes bounce back and forth between the two of us, and he mouths the word *Daisy*. His head drops, and he rubs the back of his neck before slowly focusing on me again, and he almost looks embarrassed, something I've never seen from him before.

"Kolby?" she asks. And it takes me a second to realize why she asked. Jesus, she didn't even know his name. I guess that's the norm for her. God, she's a good liar. Such a pretty one, too.

I wonder if she laid awake with him, whispering about her past and the future they thought they would venture into together. I refuse to let my mind wander to how many other guys she's done this with and how easily she lied to me and played the innocent little girl when she was really nothing but a whore to begin with.

While she questions him, I take the time to really look at her. And fuck me if she isn't prettier than I remember, no matter how much I don't want to admit it. She's clearly lost weight, which I don't like, but her hair is longer, her tits seem even bigger somehow, and her lips would bring me to my knees if my hands weren't clenched on the countertop. But none of that makes up for the fact that the bitch fuckin' lied about her goddamned phone number. She made a fuckin' fool of me.

Despite myself, I hate hearing the nerves come from her and take a breath to calm myself before I give her my attention again. "You didn't even know his name?"

"No, he never..."

Kolby cuts her off. "If a bitch doesn't ask, I don—"

Again, not thinking, just feeling pure, straight-up rage, I get in his face before he can spit another syllable. "Don't call her a bitch." I can think she's one, I can even call her one because of what she did to me, but he can't. Nobody else can. In all the years we've been on the road, there have been very few altercations between members, but right now, I want to rip his fucking throat out. No, I want to rip his fuckin' dick off and shove it up his ass.

I have to squeeze my eyes shut to force the vision of murdering him with my bare hands away.

He stands his ground like the smug bastard he is. "Didn't know who she was to you," he says loud enough for only me to hear.

Like that would ever stop him. I shove him away, and it takes every single ounce of restraint I have not to break his jaw. It's not about him. It's her. Everything is about her. "I thought she was something. But not anymore." I turn to her and spit with disgust, "She's nothing to me." Then I swipe my keys off the island and lumber out, avoiding her beautiful fuckin' eyes.

TWELVE

Mercy

I STAND IN THE HALLWAY, JUST BARELY, STILL WITH ONLY ONE shoe on as uncontrollable tears spill down my cheeks. I can't catch my breath, I can't see straight, I can barely keep my heart pumping.

"He'll, uh… come around or some shit." Kolby says, unconvincing.

I lift my head and try to do something. Say something… anything, but it's impossible. All I can feel is nothing and everything.

Everything that I can feel, though, it's all empty. My heart, my stomach, my soul.

Confusion. God, so much confusion.

How can he be mad at me? I left him my number. I wrote him a note. He didn't contact me, so I wasn't the one who ruined whatever the hell happened between us that night. It was all him. He's the liar, the one who promised things and then disappeared.

Even still, he's the only thing that's been on my mind, or at least in the back of it. Through everything I've been through the last couple of years, he's never been far enough away to completely forget. I tried so hard to figure out what went wrong… what I did wrong.

How could I be so wrong about what we shared?

But now the question of why he's pissed at me lingers and makes it all even that much worse.

"Well, this was fun, but if you don't mind, I got shit to do." Kolby nods toward the door, and I fight back the bite of humiliation I feel at being dismissed like a whore. I've always had too much pride to allow a man to treat me that way. Laughing to myself as I slide my other shoe on, I realize that's exactly what I am.

I slam the door behind me, and when I get outside, I look around and figure out his house is close enough to my apartment to walk, so instead of trying to get an Uber, I start the trek. I need the fresh air to try to come to terms with what I did. Who I hurt over the past few weeks. Between Chad and now the obvious repulsion Donny feels toward me, and being dismissed as if I was a paid hooker by Kolby, I don't know how it gets any worse.

There is no way I can go into work, so I call in on the way and lie about being sick with the flu. Even more guilt for letting down my friends and co-workers. God, what is wrong with me?

I can't get in the shower fast enough or scrub hard enough. The water burns, but it feels so damn good to wash the night off me. I stay in until the water runs cold, and then I get out and put on a pair of my brother's sweats and an old college hoodie of his, then curl up on the couch.

The banging on my door doesn't let up, and I drag myself off my makeshift bed and yank it open to find him, tattooed arm raised, hand in a fist ready to pound again. Angry, palpable energy radiates off him, so I respond with anger of my own because fuck him. "What are you doing here? How do you know where I live?"

He doesn't answer either of my questions and just stares at me, his mesmerizing green eyes full of question. His chest heaves, and he finally drops his arm. It's raining, so the ends of his hair sparkles with little droplets of water. He looks like he's put on some muscle since I last saw him. Damn… why is he so sexy? He suddenly pushes his way into my apartment, and in an instant, my small space is filled with his animosity.

I'm not doing this. I already feel like shit. I'm so ashamed and embarrassed at my behavior. I'm mad at myself, and my heart hurts so badly I can't take his anger right now. Not on top of the anger I already feel at myself for being so stupid. It takes all I have to stay standing right now and to pretend I'm not dying inside. I'm not a good actress. I'm so bad that I didn't even make my high school's production of *Peter Pan* as a tree.

I'm so terrible at faking things that Chad knew I wasn't in love with him and left me.

Yeah, he needs to leave before he sees that he's the only one who I've ever wanted, and even after all these years, it hasn't changed. No matter how irrational and how much I want to hate him. I yank the door back open. "If you're just going to come here and yell at me, you can leave. How did you know where I live anyway?"

He slams it shut and pushes my back against it, caging me in. My heart thunders, and my pulse echoes in my ears. I love him being close. I hate him for smelling so good. I missed him or at least missed the thoughts of what could have been. And at the end of the day, I think that's why I never got over him, because I was convinced that one night was going to turn into the rest of my life, and when that didn't happen, I was left with unanswered questions.

"I followed you this morning, and I've been sitting in my car staring up at your window wondering what the fuck I'm supposed to do. How I'm supposed to feel. But better yet, why the hell I feel anything for you when you obviously don't and never felt shit for me."

What a liar. "That's not true, Donny."

"My name is Jamie. It's not Don. It's not Donny. It's not Juan." The admission makes my breath catch. I'd sit up at night in the arms of Chad and wonder what his real name was. I honestly thought he'd have one of those romance novel names like Pierce or Royce or Declan. I never imagined his name would be so simple… the opposite of the confusing man himself. "And you're not Daisy."

I shake my head. No, I'm nothing. Not anymore. Apparently, I never was either, and he proved it when he never contacted me. I even went back to the hotel a couple weeks after that night and discovered the room was paid for in cash by a Mr. Juan Donaldson.

"We did make promises, and maybe they didn't mean anything to you, but they meant something to me."

Fuck him. How can he lie straight to my face? "Yeah, okay, Jamie." And fuck him again for being such a liar. It meant so much he never called. I meant so much I didn't even deserve a phone call. Whatever. I was an idiot for thinking I mattered that night. I was and I am an even bigger idiot for thinking I knew this man. The man I met was gentle, he was sweet. He's not this asshole I'm in front of right now. He's making it real easy to get the closure I desperately needed years ago. But just being in his presence makes me realize that I'd be a doormat if he asked me, because I want him to walk all over me if it meant that he'd be touching me again.

I knew he was keeping stuff from me that night, I knew, and still, I wanted more. I should have given him an ultimatum. Shouldn't have let him inside me in all the ways he was with a crook of his finger.

He settles his hands on either side of my face and tilts my head up. His fingers shake as they slide around and cup the back of my head, the tips digging into my scalp. The heat from his body pressing against mine gets hotter as the seconds tick by, and I fight my legs from giving out. "Say it again."

"What?" I say the word, but no sound comes out. He has me speechless with the need dripping from his voice. It's not natural what he makes my body feel, no matter how hard my brain fights it.

"My name. Say my fucking name."

My tongue moistens my lips, and I take a shuddering breath as I watch his heated eyes trail fire across my mouth. I hate him right now, but I love the way he's looking at me. Again. With the same intense desire as I remember, except now there's an aggression in him that wasn't there before. "Jamie," I whisper.

His forehead falls to mine, and the sight of the vulnerability on his face is too much to witness, so I close my eyes and lose the fight to stay upright. My hands come up to wrap around his wrists, and I dig my nails into his skin to keep from sliding to the floor. He slants an arm down my back and wraps his long fingers around my waist to hold me up. And it feels so good, so right. Like it's where I was meant to be. "Again."

Everything in my chest flutters and flips. "Jamie."

He demands, "Again."

"Jamie."

"You."

"What?"

"What's your name?"

I open my mouth to tell him, but his hand on my scalp tightens. "Look at me." No. It's too much. I can't. I shake my head, but he isn't having it. He growls, his body tightening and displaying power without him actually doing anything. "Fuckin' look at me. Goddammit, look at me, baby."

His commanding tone and fierce demand make my eyes snap open, and I gasp at the feral possession on his face, remembering how that look made me melt.

"Tell me your name."

"Mercy," I whisper, nervous for his reaction.

He licks his lips and repeats it in that deep, husky voice of his. A voice that I swear I'd hear randomly on the radio or in a crowd of people. "Fuckin' beautiful. Mercy." My name has never sounded sexier or hotter than right now, rolling down his tongue and out of his mouth. "You're a fuckin' beautiful liar." The moment of erotic harmony vanishes, and his possessive eyes turn hard. Dark. Demanding.

I try to pull away, but there's nowhere to go. "Let me go."

"Why are you a liar, Mercy?"

"Let me go."

"Not until you answer me."

I want him to let me go, and at the same time, I want to stay here forever. I want him to stay forever and never let go, never leave me. But he doesn't deserve answers. Not when he was the one who never called. "I don't owe you shit." How dare he act like he deserves answers.

"You do."

"I absolutely do not. But ya know what I'll tell you? I think about it all the time. That night. You. And…" I shake my head. "You made me believe in us and then…" I blink to push the tears away. "I told myself that it was too good to be true. That I meant nothing to you, and everything you said was a lie, and I was right. You never c—"

He clamps his hand over my mouth. "Shut up," he practically hisses, and for the first time, I'm actually scared of him. He senses it because he cups my jaw, and the anger leaves his face. "You know I'd never hurt you."

"Okay." I'll say whatever the hell I need to in order to get him to leave me alone. Because he already hurt me more than I've ever been hurt, and he didn't have to take a fist to me to do so.

"You know I wouldn't, so stop acting scared. And stop lying to yourself. You know every word out of my mouth was the truth. I didn't even have to *say* a word because you felt it, so don't try to convince yourself that I'd believe your bullshit for a second. You know damn well what we shared was more than just a one-time thing. *You know.*"

I twist my head away, and he drops his arm and steps back. The pressure of his body against mine vanishes, giving me a chill inside and out.

He glares at me, and somehow, every time I look at

him, the intensity of his eyes darkens, the lines on his face sharpen. He stares down, trailing his gaze up my body slowly as if he's memorizing me. I feel him everywhere. His hands might as well be caressing me because it makes me powerless to do anything but stand here and be a victim of his scrutiny.

But as he reaches my face and then hesitates, I know what he's thinking. I see the disgust written all over him and rightfully so. I don't even try to hide the tears that spill over my cheeks, knowing I somehow ruined whatever it was we had and prevented anything from ever forming deeper and not understanding why.

I thought if I ever saw him, I'd simply ask him why he never called. But not anymore. I don't care why because it's obvious he's the liar. He's just too stubborn to admit it. I just know that despite his anger, I'd do anything he asked. And I hate myself for that. I hate him for making me feel like this.

"Oh no. You don't get to fuckin' cry about this. That's not how this is gonna work."

There's nothing I can say, so I don't. There's nothing that can work anymore, either. I can't help the emotion taking over, and I can tell he's fighting not to touch me. To comfort me. Because I know that deep down, what we shared was more than a one-time thing. If he felt even a little of what I did that night, there's no doubt it was more.

But then his face twists in disgust. "Kolby is a piece of shit." He continues with his explanation. "He fucked around on his wife. Repeatedly. She finally divorced him when he gave her a fuckin' STD."

I gasp at the knowledge, my own health something

I didn't even think about. All I could get in my head was how destroyed I felt emotionally. Shit.

"Yeah. You might wanna go see a doctor."

God, he's an asshole.

He drops his head and rubs the back of his neck. The tips of his hair aren't blue anymore, but it's a little longer than before. When he heaves in a breath and looks at me again, I brace.

"I heard you."

"What? When?"

"Last night. I heard you with him." His voice is sinister, and I can practically see the rage he's trying to control about to break free.

THIRTEEN

Jamie

"H E KNOWS WHAT YOU FEEL LIKE."

"Stop it."

I clamp my jaw shut, but only for a second, the territorial possession I feel over her making me irrational. And an asshole. Or a bigger one than I already am. "I heard you when he made you come."

She wipes the tears that silently fall from her eyes, and I love seeing them there. I love seeing her just as fucked up as I feel. "Why do you even care?"

I hate knowing I'm hurting her, but this is fucked up. We would never work, not anymore. I always thought if I saw her again that things would be different. That I'd give her a chance to explain why she left a fake number or even a number at all. Why would she leave a dumb-ass note telling me she'll miss me until I call her. If she had no intention of continuing what we started, why didn't she just leave? It's obvious now that she's just like all the rest. Just a whore who spreads for anyone.

It burns my gut to think that, the acid tearing a hole in my esophagus, but it's the truth. I spent too many nights thinking about her, that the dream is straight up better than the fucked reality. "Does he know what you taste like, too?" It's an evil dick move, but I can't even describe the level of resentment I feel right now. The envy. Jealousy.

It's as if she's a part of me that someone took right out from under my nose, and I'm staring at her, close enough to touch, but if I reach for her, I'll get burned. The burn might be good, though. Maybe that would take away from the absolute crushing in the center of my chest where she holds a permanent place.

She tries to take a breath but finally loses it, and she sinks to the floor, her legs giving out without me holding her up. The dam breaks, making her quake as tears pour out of her eyes, and I squeeze my hands into fists to stop myself from going to her and holding her. Christ, I want to hold her. I want to tell her everything is okay, that I'll make it okay, that I'll fix us. But I can't.

It's not okay and it'll never be.

I'll never get over this. Never get over the girl of my dreams fucking one of my bandmates. She was so sweet and so clean, but now she's just a number, only a notch... a line in a song. She'll never be only mine again, and I can't stand it.

I could even get over her leaving me the wrong number. I would have let her explain, and no matter her explanation, I'd forgive her and move on. I'd pick up where we left off and love only her until I die. Because truth be told, the moment I saw her, I was over the stupid number. It's not that. It's her fucking Kolby that has me in a near black-out rage.

The weight of the boulder blocking my path is heavy on my shoulders. Despair slithers up my spine and chokes me, and I can't take it anymore. I don't even know why I'm here. No clue what I was hoping to accomplish by seeing her again. I thought maybe if I saw her again, the obsession I've felt for her would go away.

It didn't. Right now, it's hollow. It's heavy and fucking hollow at the same time. It's so much of everything that it doesn't have a name. It's jealousy and possession and loss and anger. It's fear. It's all the things and then some, and I can't. Fucking. *Take it.*

"Fuck!" I punch a hole through the wall and pace in a circle. "Fucking shit, Mercy."

"I'm sorry."

"You can't apologize when you fucking liked it." She can't even deny it, so she doesn't say anything. She stares at me with so much pain that I physically ache. "I can't do this."

She panics for some stupid reason, like she cares. "It was just sex, Jamie. It didn't mean anything."

But she means something. She always meant something, and what I thought she meant is no longer. It's not bittersweet thinking about the one who got away; it's a fucking nightmare that will haunt me even when I'm awake. Every time I look at him, I'll be reminded. "His dick was inside you. I heard you moaning, heard you coming because of him. And you're not some sort of groupie, Mercy. Those bitches don't matter. You matter. You knew you mattered."

"No, I didn't!"

I slash my hand through the air with jerky movements. "Bull-fucking-shit."

"Whatever. I can't do this anymore. Just go." She nods at the door. "Leave!"

She's right. I should leave, and I will but not yet. I crouch down, getting eye level with her. My hand itches to feel her soft skin, so I cup her jaw and tilt her head up, my thumb rubbing lovingly across the apple of her cheek. Allowing myself this one last touch. "We spent hours laughing and then hours fucking, then hours talking. You think I spend that much time with some bitch I wanna just use to get off?"

She looks so fragile, so small sitting on the floor, knees to her chest and tears streaming down her face and rolling over her lips. Lips that have probably been wrapped around Kolby's cock. Lips that moans from one of my fucking bandmates fucking her came from. "It doesn't matter. I'm sorry. Christ, I'm so fucking sorry, but I can't look at you and not think about it." I don't even know what I'm apologizing for.

She must have given up because she drops her head, resting it on her bent knees. I stand. "See this?" Her head rises and being this close is almost my undoing. A fresh swell of tears fills her eyes when she looks at the tattoo on my neck, her lips quiver, and her breath hitches. The daisy. The permanent reminder of her that I look at every fucking day, and I'll continue to look at every day for the rest of my life. The daisy I had tatted two years ago as a reminder of the one who got away. The one who lied. The one who taught me never to let my guard down again.

"You know what it means. And you know what we could have had. So when you sit here and cry about what you lost, just know that it's all your fault."

I slam the door to her apartment and stomp my feet all the way to my car. The engine revs, and I peel out, taking my anger out on the road. With no destination in mind, I go to the one place I shouldn't.

Kelly's.

I've been in here so many times, both before and after her. But the difference is, after, I can't even look over at the booth. And tonight is no different.

I walk straight in, and when I see Meara behind the bar, I grunt. Shit. Anyone else but her. She'll take one look at me and know something is up, and I do not want her grilling me.

"What's wrong?" she asks before I even sit down.

"Nothing."

"Uh-oh."

I plop my ass on the stool and point at a bottle of Jack. "Give me the whole damn thing."

She hesitates. "Oh, shit. It's a woman."

"Give it here, or I'll go somewhere that will."

"Fine, but only if you give me your keys."

I take them out of my pocket and throw them at her, where she expertly catches them. Without a word, she hands me the glass bottle and pops the top for me. I take a swing, and the burn that usually accompanies alcohol is void, probably because I've been burning up inside for three fucking years.

It still doesn't make sense. She doesn't make sense, except she's the only thing that's right. God, this is so jacked.

I don't know how long it's been, minutes or hours, but somehow, everyone ends up at Kelly's. Then I remember that it's for a goodbye drink since we're back on the road tomorrow. They all give me a wide berth, and Meara hugged me before she went over to sit by Liam.

I can't stand to be by Kolby, sitting across from him at a table all night, so I hang at the bar and talk to Nik the whole time.

I shouldn't have come, and I definitely shouldn't have stayed after the others arrived. I'm in no state to be around people, and I'm barely holding on by a thread. I'm coiled tight but preparing to strike any minute. I managed to keep my shit together in order to drive here after I left her apartment. But that's all I've got in me.

It's not until Liam finally comes over and asks what's up my ass that I lose it.

Instead of giving him an explanation, I stumble over to the table where Kolby, Gabe, Mike, and a few other people from Meara's family sit. I didn't even wait for him to look up from his phone before I slam my fist on the table. "She was mine."

Kolby's head flies back so fast it bounces off the wall, and his mouth falls open. "What?" He knows exactly who I'm talking about, so the fact that he's acting shocked pisses me off even more.

"I'm in love with her, I've been forever, and I can't have her now because you did, too." My words are slurred, even to me. "You fucked her, but you fucked me over, too because now I can't have her anymore."

He holds up his hands in a placating gesture. "Dude. Take her. I don't want her."

"Why wouldn't you want her? She's perfect." My head wobbles when I look over at the booth next to us where I first kissed her. Where I fell in love with the perfect woman in the blink of an eye, the single beat of a heart. It wasn't planned, but it happened. And I never got over her. "I did what you said, Meara."

She smiles lazily at me, probably a little confused and a lot curious. "What did you do?"

"I went out that night and found her. Rember?" I sway as I lift my hand and point at the booth. "You told me I could break the rules, but I didn't. No." I shake my head. "I didn't rake the bules, but I found her. You told me to go out, and I did. I found her, then I lost her, but now I know she's gone forever."

"Jamie." Mike's always the logical one. I might be drunk, but I can see he's about to try to calm me down, so I turn back to Kolby.

"She feels good, huh? I know she does. Tastes 'licious, too," I hiss at Kolby.

My brother throws my arm over his shoulder. "Think you've had enough, man. Let's get you to bed, but on the way, you can tell me all about it."

"No." I try to fight him off lamely, but he successfully pulls me through the crowded bar and out the back door. "He ruined it. You ruined it," I yell at Kolby even though he's not here.

"Chill, bro."

"Don't chill me, bro. If you heard Meara getting banged by someone else, you'd never be able to get that out of your head."

His jaw clenches, and even in my drunken stupor, I know I crossed a line. "Don't. Do not bring her up. Brother or not, drunk or not, I'll kick your fuckin' ass if you bring her into your shit."

"Jamie, I barely even remember it. It was just sex." Kolby's voice comes from behind me, and I spin around, but Liam holds me up as I lose my footing. "I didn't know she was yours."

"She isn't mine. Not anymore. I fucking loved her, and you ruined that."

"How did I ruin it? You're the one who won't get over it."

How can I get over it? A woman like her... you don't get over her. Ever. I never will. It's been three years since we spent one explosive night together, and it will haunt me until the day I die. I crash into the wall, and Liam holds me steady since the alley is turned on its side. "She's a memory. A good one... sweet, beautiful. But it's gone now. You ruined it."

"I'm not the one standing here drunk off my ass when there's a girl who you claim to love somewhere around here, and you won't go to her." I don't claim shit. I do love her. I never fucking stopped.

"Wasn't my dick in her last night." I sneer.

"Okay, you're done." Liam clasps my shoulder and steers me toward his car. "Can you go grab Meara and tell her I'm taking him to our place?" I don't fight him, and once he pushes me into the back seat, I pass out.

FOURTEEN

Mercy

"LET'S SLOW IT DOWN A LITTLE SO WE CAN RUIN YOU some more." The lead singer, who's name is Mike if I remember right, drawls the sensual words into the microphone. The crowd screams around me, and the lights do a cool thing where they fade and change colors before shining bright again.

"I think I just had a mini orgasm." Charity sighs. "And I'm happily married, but yeesh."

I laugh, finishing off my beer and setting the empty cup into the other three I have stacked at my feet. As I watch the band work the crowd like their hypnotists, I come to an embarrassing revelation; I've had orgasms from half the guys up on that stage. I'm officially a groupie. When Jamie told me I wasn't one, I didn't pay any attention to it. At the time, I thought it was just more hurtful words from him, but now I know why he said that. In my mind, it was just an expression, but he compared me to the chicks who are tossing their bras onstage and doing anything they can to get one of the guys' attention. That's what he thinks of me. "I can't believe this is happening."

"It's fate that they're here."

"God, it all makes sense now."

A sensual beat fills the auditorium, and the lights dim. I close my eyes and sway to the rhythm; the shock of what's taken place since yesterday still gives me the nervous butterflies.

After Jamie left my apartment last night, I didn't move from my couch. I was almost in a trance, and once I dragged my body to the cushions and fell on top of them, I couldn't move. Charity tried to get a hold of me, I knew it was her from the ringtone, and when I didn't answer, she came over, worried something happened since I always pick up when she calls.

I must not have locked the door after Jamie left because she walked right in; not that she didn't have a key, but she didn't need to use it. All she had to do was take one look at me, and she knew I needed her.

She simply said my name, and it all came out. I bawled my eyes out, and through hiccupped sobs, I finally told her everything. For three years, I'd hidden it from her because I was afraid of what she'd tell me. I thought she would tell me to move on, and I didn't want to hear it. I wanted a reason to justify why I was hanging on to him, but I knew she wouldn't give me that. She'd tell the truth, she'd tell me to forget about him, but there was no way I could.

And after all these years, I could no longer keep it all inside, so I told her everything from the beginning. How I first met him at the hospital and laughed at him, and then seeing him again at the bar and how I fell hard and fast. I told her I was with Chad for all the wrong reasons and how I was the most horrible person ever. She, of course, didn't agree with me, but I know I am. It was selfish to do what I did to him. I finished my sob story by telling her everything up until yesterday when Jamie successfully tore me apart.

Once I was finally finished, she asked, "You said his name is Jamie, and his friend is Kolby?"

"Yes." I tossed another tissue on the huge pile on my end table. "Why?"

Instead of answering right away, she grabbed her phone and was looking at something on the screen, scrolling with one hand and holding her finger up in the air with the other. Her knees hit the carpet and she held her phone out. "Is this them?"

I looked at the screen and covered my mouth when I saw them in a photo. "Oh my God."

"Holy shit, Merc. Do you have any idea who they are?"

"I told you I didn't even know his name! They're in a band?"

She fell to her butt and stared at me like a deer in headlights. "They're not in *a* band. They're in *the* band. They were only a class or two younger than me, all of them except Kolby. He's new because the drummer quit the band to be with his girlfriend. I think they're married or something now. You would have just missed them in high school, but I'm sure you've heard of them."

I couldn't believe it. "I think I remember hearing something about them, I didn't pay much attention. Let me see that." She handed me her phone, and I avoided looking at their faces because it was too hard, and found the about me section.

Front man, Mike Baker, was born in Dallas, Texas, but

moved to south eastern Wisconsin when he was in second grade. Born with a microphone in his hand, it was a natural progression that he found Reason to Ruin founders and stepbrothers Liam Anders and Jamie Cooper in eighth grade. Which is when they also asked guitarist Gabriel Hunter to join.

The band supported Liam's decision to leave to pursue other avenues and welcomed Kolby Rappaport, who has proven to be an asset to this award-winning band.

I scrolled to the bottom.

Double Platinum. World Tour. Number One Album. Multiple Grammy Wins.

"Oh my God." My hands were shaking, and I dropped her phone when another truth bomb exploded in my head. "Liam is Meara's husband. Meara who owns Kelly's Pub. The one Jamie said that night he knew the owners so he couldn't hook up with me inside the bar."

My sister gave her head a little shake. "If you knew he knew the owners, why didn't you ask her about him? My God, Mercy, you went three years pining for a guy you very well could have found if you had just asked."

Could I have? What would I have done? I don't know what I would have said…

I was trying to process it all because on top of being a slut, I'm also an idiot. How did I not figure it out before? How could I not have known they were related? Liam and Jamie look nothing like each other. I replayed conversations with Meara in my head, and I didn't think a band ever got brought up. I knew Liam owned a music center, but not that he used to play in a band.

And I think I remembered her saying Liam's brother Jamie randomly, but I didn't know *his* name to put it together. And because my mind was just so messed up, I didn't even think about the fact that Jamie said he knew the owner. I tried to block out that night, and some parts I was successful at keeping away.

Dammit.

Charity ran her fingers through her hair, almost angrily, her movements short and rough. "You spent those years with a man you weren't in love with but didn't even ask... How did you not know Meara and Liam were related to him? You were at their house; did you not see pictures?"

"The only time I was at their house, it was dark out, and I went straight to the baby's room because she called me in the middle of the night worried Melody was sick. Maybe she assumed I knew... how could I not know? Why would I know anyway? What difference does it make who her brother-in-law is?"

"Weren't you there for a birthday party or something?"

I nodded. "Yes. But I never went inside. Chad talked to Liam for a little while, too, but God... how did I not figure this out? How could I not know?"

"Well, now you do."

"Yeah." I fell back into the couch and crossed my arms. "Now I know."

Only a minute of silence passed before she sat up straight. "So what are you gonna do about it?"

My eyebrows drew together, making my headache worse. "What do you mean?"

"I mean... they're playing in Chicago tomorrow night."

"So?" I saw that when I was looking at their site.

She pushed up on her knees and grabbed mine, squeezing gently. "Don't be that girl, Merc. I've watched you walk around a shell of yourself for the last three years, and I didn't know why. But now I do, and there is no way I'm not going to tell you to at least try. You feel something for him, after all these years and—"

"Well, he doesn't feel the same."

"That's crap."

"It is not. He was so pissed, Charity. His face was so… so angry. I almost didn't recognize him he was so disgusted with me and whatever the reason he had not to call me before… he has an even bigger one now. At least I know why this time."

Her fingers tightened. "Think about it. If he didn't feel something, he wouldn't be mad. Why would he care if some chick he banged screwed his roommate if you meant nothing? You left him your number, right?"

"Yes, and he never called."

"How do you know he got it?"

I tilted my head, the possibility not a possibility at all. "Because I left it for him."

"What if he didn't see it? What if housekeeping came in and took it?"

"There's no way he didn't see it. I left it on the nightstand."

"Men are stupid, Mercy. Do you have any idea how many times Mark asks me to help him find his wallet, and it's right in front of his face? Or his keys or phone. I swear, for a damn doctor, he can be an idiot sometimes. Maybe Jamie didn't see it. Did you ever let that thought penetrate?"

I shook my head. "No, because there is no way he didn't."

"Don't be that girl." Her voice softened. "The one

who sits back and doesn't say anything. I know you're not her. Or at least, you never used to be. Ever since the night Mom got attacked and you started dating Chad, I saw my vibrant, fun, optimistic sister change. You don't laugh like you used to, Mercy.

"You've been living with a broken heart. And maybe, maybe you were trying to fix it with Chad. You're not selfish for trying to move on. You tried to be happy, but it didn't work, and that's okay."

My throat was dry when I swallowed. "It's not. I was with him for three years, I took three years of his life. I agreed to marry him, Charity, knowing I was totally in love with someone else. I honestly don't think I ever gave him a fair shot. He was unknowingly competing with a man whose existence he wasn't aware of. Who does that?"

Sweet sister was gone, and she laid into me. "Fine. If you can't say it, I will. You were with him to make Mom happy. After she was attacked... she was never the same. The issues that guy caused when he squeezed her hand gave her permanent nerve damage. She had to quit her job. She was depressed. You being with Chad made her happy, and you wanted to see her happy. But she's better now, she loves her new job as a professor, and she's happy. Frankly, I think she'd be pissed if she found out you were going to marry someone you didn't love." I disagreed but didn't verbalize it because that's not anywhere near accurate. "I get why you did it, I do, but it's time for you to find your happy now, little sister."

"Whatever, even if I decided to go see him to ask him why he never called, what am I supposed to do? Show up and jump on the stage. He's a fucking rock star, Charity. I'll never be—"

"How about this? Go to his house first and see if he's there to talk. If not, then we'll go to the concert. Deal?"

I didn't answer right away, and she shook me.

"Don't be that girl. Stop it. Where's the fighter? Where's the girl who does whatever she wants and doesn't care what other people think? I know she's in there. And now I know why she went away, but you can bring her back."

Even though every word my sister said was right, I couldn't do it. "I can't. It's stupid."

"It's only stupid if you don't try. You know why me and Mark have lasted this long?" She continued without waiting for my response. "It's because we talk about everything. All of it. The good stuff, the bad stuff, insecurities, hopes, dreams; we talk about how we feel. How will Jamie know if you never tell him?"

"Yeah, okay. I'll just walk up to him, tap him on the shoulder, and say, 'Hi. I've been in love with you for years. Why didn't you call me? Oh and by the way, I was engaged to a guy who I went on a blind date with the same night I met you. He broke it off, though, because he knew I didn't love him the way he loved me. And yesterday was the day we were supposed to get married and to make myself feel something other than despair and heartache, I fucked your friend."

"Yep, say exactly that. Except I maybe wouldn't remind him about the friend, and I'm not sure he'd want to hear that you were engaged. Not yet. So come on. Let's go." She stood and yanked the blanket off my legs. "Up. You never know if you don't ask, right? Ask him why he didn't call you. Ask him why he's so mad at you if he doesn't care."

She was right. I would have in the past. In fact, before him, I wouldn't have taken his shit when he first saw me in the kitchen. I'd never let a man talk to me that way. But after everything with my mom and Chad... Charity's right. I lost myself somewhere along the way, and the catalyst for it was feeling so much for Jamie and letting myself believe he reciprocated, then never hearing from him again. That broken heart shit sucks.

And it'd been killing me not knowing why he didn't call. If I at least knew that, I thought I'd have some type of closure. "Okay."

She smiled and pulled me toward my bedroom. "Get dressed. Hurry. I'll go buy tickets online if there are any left, just to be on the safe side. If not, we'll have to find a scalper."

I pressed my hand to my queasy stomach. "I feel sick. Like I'm going to puke. This is so stupid. I won't even get to see him."

"You will. We'll find a way. I promise."

So after I was dressed, she drove me to Jamie... and well, Kolby's house. It was pretty late, but come on, they're rock stars. I knocked on the door, and Kolby answered a minute later.

"What's up?"

Seeing him again under the porch light with a clearish head made me dizzy. He was really attractive, and I remembered why I fell for his shit, too. "Is, uh, Jamie here?"

Kolby shook his head. "Nah, got shitfaced and crashed somewhere else."

"Oh. Okay. Thanks." Yeah, that wasn't awkward. I turned around and walked down a couple of steps partly relieved he wasn't home but mostly disappointed for the same reason.

"Hold up."

I paused but didn't look at him. I didn't hear footsteps, so I assumed he was waiting for my attention, so I twisted my neck slightly, just enough that my eyes caught his. "I'll leave you some VIPs for tomorrow's show in Chicago. He'll be backstage after. You can come find him and say whatever it is you have to say then, but not before. Don't need his head getting all fucked up more than it already is over you."

That made my entire body swivel. "What?"

He shook his head. "Nothing. Pick up the tickets. Talk to him. Get your shit figured out."

"Oh… okay, thanks." I was still confused by what he just said.

"No prob. You were a seriously good lay. I can see how he wants more."

I cringed at his words, wondering how women do the one-night stand thing on a regular basis and still have self-respect. Then I went back to my apartment where I cried myself to sleep while my sister ran her fingers through my hair.

And now here we are, standing in the nosebleeds. Swaying to some of the best music I've ever heard. Listening to hauntingly beautiful lyrics.

The VIP tickets Kolby left for me were front row, but there was no way we were sitting that close and risking that Jamie would see me. So we used the tickets Charity bought. I open my eyes and watch in the big monitor, and my heart skips a beat every time Jamie comes on the screen. Jeans that hang dangerously low on his hips, shirt with some kind of logo on it with what looks like the sleeves ripped off so you can see his sides all the way down to his belt. I feel my face heating as I watch Jamie saunter up to the end of the stage. His cocky smile and smooth gait do nothing but scream confidence.

He looks good up there. Like he was meant to be a performer.

I feel the nerves fluttering in my chest, actually feel them. They're going up my throat and making my belly empty, then back down, making me swallow the bile they stir up. But I owe it to myself to do this. I'll probably end up regretting it, but I have to at least try to see him.

After the concert is over, and I'm just on the right side of tipsy, we rush to the stage where Charity looks around for a door to get us into the back. "He gave you the tickets, so you belong back here. Just follow me and just act natural."

"I can't act natural." I stumble a bit, but right myself by pushing on a chair.

A couple of deep voices raise, and we look over to see two guys fighting. A group gathers around them, and she grabs my hand and pulls me in the opposite direction. The rent-a-cop at the door glances at our passes, nods, then takes off toward the fight. "See."

After pushing through the door, she pulls me aside into a darkened corner, probably sensing I need a second. We need a plan. The closer I get to him, the more nervous I feel. This isn't me. I don't chase after guys, but he's not just a guy. It scares the shit out of me to know I'm just going to face his rejection again, but it scares me even more to walk away from him again. I need to know; I have to at least talk to him so he knows how I feel. So I know why he didn't call. "Now listen to me. This isn't you coming here to grovel and beg for his forgiveness or whatever. It's you wanting to talk and figure things out... whatever way that goes. I do not want to see you shed a tear over this guy. He's not worth it. You hear me?"

I nod at my sister even though I disagree. He is worth it. I thought about him so much after that night, always wondering where he was and what he was doing. If he is thinking about me or ever thought about me.

"Why are we hiding? Let's go," Charity whispers as we stand behind a black velvet curtain. There are wires taped all over the floor, and it is relatively dark over there, but we have a good view of the hustle and bustle of what happens behind the scenes.

Doubt begins to strangle me. "This isn't smart. He's going to be so mad. I've already come between him and Kolby, and he made it clear he didn't want to see me again, so what am I doing? We should just go... this was a bad idea."

Charity offers a sympathetic smile. "You're talking and making sure he listens to what you have to say. That's bullshit that he laid that all out on you, then just vanished and didn't give you the courtesy to say anything back."

"But... I slept with his bandmate."

"So."

"I don't think he can just get over it. That'd be like you sleeping with him. I don't... I don't think I'd ever be able to look at either of you the sa—" I grab her arm and squeeze it. Tight. My nails dig into her skin, and I give myself whiplash I turn my head so fast. Because there he is. Walking down the hallway. *I love him.* I swear it looks like he's coming right for us. *He's gorgeous.* Charity smiles, but when we see a woman with bright red high heels and a pair of black leather pants following him, her face falls, and my heart stops beating because I'm dead.

We duck back, huddling in the corner in the dark, and both of us stop breathing as he stops with his back on the wall on the opposite side of the curtain, right next to us. I see her as she drops to her knees just on the edge of the thick material, her lipstick the same color as her shoes. I can't watch. Hearing his belt buckle is bad enough. Then his zipper. I'm pretty sure I could die again right now.

I thought my heart was broken before, but now it's demolished. Normally, when I cry, my throat gets all tingly, but I feel that all the way down to my toes. I have to fight to keep my knees locked and squeeze my eyes to block out the scene before me, but when I close them, I still see it.

I can fucking hear it.

We shouldn't be here. Not only is it tearing me up, but it's wrong to sit here and be witness to this when they don't know. Plus, I want to be a catty bitch and rip the fake, bleached hair out of her stupid head. This is such a bad idea. Totally what I get for daring to be adventurous for once in my life.

Charity's fingers bite into my arm now, so I open my eyes. She's looking at me like the time she almost got caught after she had a house party when she was seventeen. My parents went out of town for the weekend and trusted us to behave. It was the first time they left us alone, and it was just for one night as a test that we failed.

Charity was always the wild one, so of course she didn't listen. And because I'm a good sister, I helped her clean up until the moment my parents walked in the door that Sunday night. They were suspicious and when my dad turned his back to my sister and asked me point blank if there was a party, Charity's eyes practically bugged out of her head as she shook it, pleading with me not to tell.

That was pretty much the only time I ever lied to my parents, and I felt awful. But it also is the thing that drew Charity and I close. Not that we weren't before, but that show of solidarity was the catalyst that made us as tight as we are now. She realized I wasn't just the annoying little sister who always begged to borrow her clothes.

I shake my head at her, telling her without words to stay still and be quiet. The rush of excitement is long gone, and I hate how powerful my feelings are being shredded right now. I shouldn't be surprised. Why am I surprised? I'm not. He's a rock star. This is what they do. This is what both he and Kolby did with me. Meaningless.

My ears are ringing, and I swallow hard enough for them to pop, just in time to hear him say, "Leave your shirt on. I don't care about your tits. Just suck it, okay?"

"Whatever you want, Jamie," she purrs... fucking purrs.

"I want my dick in your mouth," he commands. "That's all I want from you."

I feel a tear roll down my cheek, and if I wasn't afraid I'd make noise, I'd wipe it away because it's so irrational. I don't have the right to be upset. Charity bites the bottom of her lip as she peeks between the curtains.

"What?" I mouth.

She makes her cheeks puff out and holds her hands like two feet apart, indicating his length, and I lose it. I choke, trying not to laugh, and she does the same.

"The fuck?" I hear Jamie grumble, and Charity grabs my hand, yanking me away. We tear off running as fast as we can down the hall. Faintly, I hear him yelling

something, but we keep going, her laughing and me trying not to cry, but also laughing. It's very odd.

We pass by a flurry of people, and I'm so glad they
help block his view of us. If he finds out it is me, I'll be
totally mortified.

"Hurry up."

"I'm trying." I gasp as I round a corner and scream
when I run into a guy, or more like get flung into him.

Kolby's arms wrap around me to prevent me from
falling, and Charity's grip on my hand is so tight I cry out
in pain when the force of my stopping yanks at my shoulder. "Whoa."

"Let me go," I screech, trying to pull away. I need to
get away.

"Chill, babe. Jesus. Why are you running?"

His arms fall, and I scramble away, but not before my
back slams into another body. I already know it's Jamie because it feels like home, and if I didn't recognize his smell
and… and *him*, the panicked look on Charity's face would
give it away.

"This is ironic," Jamie rumbles, his chest vibrating
against me sends a chill down my spine.

"You're such a dick." Kolby grunts at Jamie as he
walks away, back to the hustle and bustle of the afterparty
backstage. I hear hushed voices behind me, but have no
clue how close the people who we just ran past are.

My entire body trembles, and Charity clears her
throat. She widens her eyes at me, silently telling me to
say something. But I can't. I can't move again. She finally
speaks up. "I'm Charity. Mercy's sister."

"Figured as much." He glides his fingertips along my
arms, all the way up to my bicep, tingles poking my flesh,

then he grips them and turns me around. No doubt he sees the tears in my eyes because the sharp angle of his jaw softens for a millisecond, but when I blink, it's hard again. Everything about him is stone right now. "What are you doing here?"

Oh God. We have an audience. There are probably about twenty people standing behind Jamie. Including Mrs. BJ. "Nothing... I, uh, got tickets, and we were, um, just leaving, so..."

I try to pull away, but he won't have it. "You enjoy the show?"

"Yeah. You guys were great."

"Not that show." His lips tilt up into a sarcastic smile. "Did you enjoy watchin' me gettin' head?"

That hollow feeling in my stomach turns as people snicker, and again, I try to back away. "Let me go."

"You interrupted, though."

"Let me go."

He tilts his head. "You wanna continue where she left off?"

Charity gasps, and I narrow my eyes at him, avoiding the crowd of people who just witnessed me getting humiliated. "You're an asshole."

"You're still beautiful." His head tilts to the other side, and he drops his arms. "But you're a beautiful bitch. Not me who left a bogus fucking number after what we shared, Mercy. I didn't screw one of your best friends." I'm about to tell him he's nuts because I left my number, but then he looks at Charity, and I know what he's going to say. "Although, maybe if I fucked your sister—"

"Oh my God. I can't believe you," I snap. "You really are a dick."

"No. I have a dick that needs to be sucked. So either drop down or get the fuck out of my sight."

He reaches for his zipper, and I don't know how it happens, but I slap him across the face. Hard. The smack echoes throughout the hallway and the sting buzzes down my arm to my shoulder. He snickers as the crowd gives a collective gasp, and I feel my bottom lip quiver, knowing I lost him. I lost the best thing that ever happened to me. He rubs his reddened cheek and watches as I fight back tears but doesn't make a move to even give me a chance. I thought I deserved at least that. After what we shared, yeah, I deserved that.

"Come on, Merc. Let's go." Charity tugs my arm, and I close my eyes, knowing when I open them again, he'll be gone.

And I'm right. But the crowd is still there. Everyone drops their heads or looks away, trying to pretend they didn't just witness that. She pulls me down the hallway, and I want to turn around. I want him to come after me. I want him. So stupid. God, I'm so stupid, but I still want him.

My vision is blurry, but I see it all clearly now. "He's nothing like what I remember."

"He's nothing like what you told me he is, so the way I look at it, you did the right thing. It just took you three years to realize it. Now you can move on."

"Yeah." I wipe beneath my eyes. "Now I can move on."

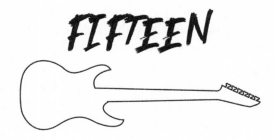

FIFTEEN

Jamie

"**H**OW THE FUCK DID SHE GET BACK HERE?" I SLAM the door to our dressing room, then yank it back open when I see more than just the guys are in here. "Get out."

The girl sitting on Gabe's lap crawls off and scurries away.

Kolby tosses back a shot of whiskey, dropping the plastic cup into the trash. "I gave her a pass."

"You gave her a pass?" I mock.

"Yup."

"What the fuck is wrong with you?"

He shrugs like what he did was no big deal. "She came to the house lookin' for you, told her to come back after the show to find you." I don't even have words, so he keeps running his mouth. "Her face was all puffy and shit, looked like she was crying."

"So the fuck what?"

He crosses his arms. "You've sure got lots of anger for a chick you don't give a shit about."

My palms dampen, and I feel sweat dripping down

my back. My damn jaw is still throbbing from her slapping me… deservedly. God, she fucks me up.

"Who is this chick?" Gabe asks.

"Not mine anymore, is she, Kolby?"

"God, not this shit again. What do you want me to say? I fucked her. So what? Didn't mean shit. You want her, go get her. I don't give a fuck."

"You wouldn't."

"What's that supposed to mean?"

I shake my head, curling my lip in distaste. "I'm outta here." I can't stand to be near him. I could barely last night and I don't know how I managed to perform with him at my back, but there's no way I can look at him right now. Mike follows me but doesn't say anything until I'm in the parking lot. I don't want to hear what he has to say, either. "Leave me alone."

"No way." He grabs my arm but I yank it out of his grip. "What the hell is going on with you and this chick?"

"Nothing. She showed up because Kolby's a fucking moron."

"Why aren't you with her if she's here?"

I shake my head, the truth forcing its way to the surface, hitting me with the knowledge that it's so much easier to be pissed at her than admit how I feel. How she makes me feel all the things I never knew I needed. "I don't know," I admit. Should I go after her? Maybe. Probably. Yeah… I should. I should just ask her, grow a damn set of balls and ask her why the hell she played me like she did. It'd have been less insulting if she didn't leave a number at all, but to leave the wrong one?

"Well, you've gotta figure this shit out 'cause the last thing we need is you and Kolby at each other's throats."

Just then, Kolby comes out, and before he can open his mouth, I cut him off. I don't give a shit what he has to say. "You're going the wrong way. She went out the front."

"I don't want her."

"Yes, you do."

He waves me off and turns to go back inside. "I'm over this shit."

"Bet you like it when you're under her."

"Fuck off, Jamie."

Mike moves to stand in front of me. "I don't know what happened with you and this girl, but you've gotta get your shit straight. We can't lose him, Jamie. You need to fix it. We've come too far to get knocked down again."

"Whatever." I turn and head toward the bus, ignoring him calling my name and trying to forget about her.

And for the next few months, that's pretty much status quo. I seek Kolby's ass out just to fuck with him, to play games and get in his head so maybe he feels a little of the torment I feel. We manage to keep our hatred for each other off the stage, but that's the only place. He tells me to fuck off before I even open my mouth because he knows the only thing I have to say to him is shit to piss him off. One of us eventually gets in the other's face, but someone's always around to separate us.

I can't stand the sight of him, and it's gotten so bad that when we're done with this leg in a few months, he's moving out, which is something he should have done earlier, but we've barely been back. It's not like he lived with me permanently or anything, but he's got all of his shit in that room.

My muscles tighten thinking about his room and her in it.

I'm buttoning my jeans as I step off the bus, just as Kolby gets back from the gym. Beth, Bell, I forgot her name trails behind me. "You want a go at this chick?" I angle my head. "I know you like my seconds."

He drops the wallet he was holding and charges me. Bring it, asshole. I've been waiting for this shit for months now.

I let him get the first punch in, because I know I deserve it, my teeth crash together from the force of his fist. I get a left jab to his jaw, then hit him with a right cross before he can protect that side of his face. His skin splitting beneath my knuckles feels fuckin' awesome. The chick who I just fucked screams, and after a couple of minutes of Kolby and me beating the shit out of each other, we're ripped apart.

"Goddammit," Mike chastises us as Lincoln yanks me off him. "Not cool, you guys. Not fucking cool."

"You've gotta get your shit straight, bro." Gabe looks at me as he helps Kolby up. "We can't lose him and do that to this goddamned band again." Yeah, it's always the damn band. That's the only thing anyone gives a shit about. The stupid fucking band.

Fuck this. Fuck them. Fuck her.

I storm away from everyone with no destination in mind, using the bottom of my shirt to dab some of the blood from my face. I have no clue where I am, somewhere in Colorado is all I know. That's about all I know lately… don't think my head has ever been this fucked up in my damn life.

I find a bench to sit on and plop my ass down and don't move. I just think. Torment myself with jealousy and rage. I should be able to get over it, but I can't. She was it. She was the game changer. She was mine. For a night, she was all mine.

I drop my elbows to my knees and stare at the concrete, mindlessly watching ants march back and forth. I stay there until the sun goes down. I ignore my phone going off like crazy in my pocket. When the moon fully rises, I lean my head back. The silence is welcomed although I shouldn't be alone with my thoughts.

My neck is stiff, and I've gotta take a piss, so I think about getting up to go back. But I don't want to. I don't want anything but her and because I'm a colossal dick, I'll never have her again.

An incessant buzzing irritates me enough to finally answer my phone. "What?"

"Where the fuck are you?" Liam yells.

"No clue."

"Are you insane? What the fuck's the matter with you, Jamie. Jesus Christ. Everyone's worried sick."

No, they're not. They're just pissed because I missed the show. First time ever. Through sickness and everything else under the sun, I've played every show. I've happily given my life to Ruin, but I just couldn't tonight. Not with the way things are. There was no way I could stand on that stage and not want to fight Kolby again. "I don't know if I can do this anymore," I confess to my brother.

He expels a breath. "You've gotta figure out how, Jamie."

"I love her, man. It's crazy and it doesn't make sense, but it's true. Even knowing she slept with him." It's not like everyone doesn't know what happened, but it still is almost embarrassing to me when I say it out loud. "I can't look at him and not want to kill him. I swear, I imagine my hands around his throat every time I see him. It's jacked, I know that, but it's like he… I don't even know. I just hate him."

"I get it. I had a moment when I was worried about Nik and Meara, and it made me insane. But you're not even with her, Jamie. You've gotta get over it." If I wasn't such a pitiful excuse for a man, I'd ask him more about what he's talking about. Nik is like part of the family; I had no clue Liam ever had issues with him.

But then again, Lee is notorious for hiding shit from everyone.

"I know, and I think that's the problem."

"What is?"

I squeeze my eyes closed to alleviate some of the tension in my head and rub the back of my neck. "That we're not together."

SIXTEEN

Mercy
three months later

THE CHATTER OF VOICES SURROUNDS ME, BUT MY MIND IS nowhere near the baked ziti on my plate right now. "Mercy!" I jump at my mother's sharp tone and sit up.

"Yeah?"

"I asked how work was. Where is your mind at lately? I know that you've had it rough lately, but you can't even give us twenty minutes of your attention over dinner?"

Charity squeezes my leg beneath the table. "Give her a break, Mom."

"I have been giving her a break since she let the best thing that's ever happened to her walk away."

"Let's not do this, please. Once a month, I have all my girls together, and I don't want it spoiled over nonsense."

My mom huffs. "Her being disrespectful isn't nonsense. I didn't raise her to be a snot."

"We raised her, Faith. You and me. And she's not being disrespectful. She's going through some things... Charity is right, give her a break." I love my dad.

148

I fiddle with the handle of the butter knife, wondering if I could cut the tension with it, or if I'd need to go to the kitchen and grab a steak knife. "I don't want to talk about me." I take a drink of water.

"Fine. We'll talk about your brother. Has anybody talked to him recently?"

And just like that, I've managed to disappoint my mother again. Seems par for the course. I've always been such a failure to her. During my relationship with Chad was the only time I didn't feel like I was a failure to my mother. I wish I knew what I did to make her feel that way about me, but I honestly have no clue.

After we finish dinner, instead of staying around to talk like I normally do, I leave. I'm too depressed right now to deal with my mother's shit, and pretty soon, I'm going to go off on her. All the things I've been saving up to tell her will probably ruin our relationship for good. The years of feeling unloved by her and the way it's caused me anxiety because I'm always so afraid of what people will think would explode in a way I'd never be able to get back.

She made me that way. I question everything because of her and I'm so sick of living my life that way.

My dad walks me to my car, his penny loafers clicking against the concrete. "She means well."

"Sure."

"She does."

He's such a good husband, always defending her even when she's wrong... which is a lot. The comments she made a while ago about not having a spark have never left my memory, and it kills me to look at my dad, how loyal he is, and know how his wife truly feels.

"Talked to Chad this morning."

His name makes my stomach drop. "Oh, yeah."

"Yeah. I know you don't want to talk about it, but—"

"I don't. Please, Dad. Just don't."

He presses his lips together and puts his hands in his khaki pockets, rocking back on his heels. "Okay. But I have to say something, so just let me all right?" I press my lips together and he grabs my shoulders. "Only you know what makes your heart happy. I don't want you to care what anybody else thinks about your choices. I want you to be happy. You hear me?"

I nod. "Yeah, I hear you."

"Good. Now have a good night, sweetheart. Drive safe home."

I wrap my arms around his neck and absorb the familiar smell of home and wish I could take that feeling with me all day every day. "Night, Dad."

He stands on the porch until I'm out of sight, and as I drive home, I think about what he said and try to tell myself he's right. But it's hard to think like that when you've never even been good enough for your mother. And after the colossal mess I've made of my life, I know I'll never be.

After I get home, I collapse onto the couch and groan when there's a knock on the door. I knew she'd come, and as much as I appreciate her, I don't want to fucking talk about it right now. "Dammit, Charity," I grumble to myself as I drag my feet through the kitchen to let her in.

"You still haven't talked to him?" She falls into the chair at my kitchen table, and I cringe at the squeak the legs make against the floor.

"Why would you say that?"

She motions to my wrinkled scrubs, disheveled hair,

and dark circles beneath my eyes. "You look like shit, and you haven't taken your nasty scrubs off."

Leave it to my sister to tell me like it is. "Gee, thanks."

"Don't be sensitive. You know what I mean."

No, I haven't talked to him. It's too much, and I'm a huge chicken shit. But I've been following their tour schedule, and they're home for a few weeks, so if I was ever going to have the guts to do it, it was going to have to be now. "No, I haven't, Charity. And I don't know if I even want to."

She's been so great since the night of the concert about five and half, almost six months ago, doing nothing but supporting me and being there for me in every way possible. I tried to move on, and I think I did a pretty good job of pretending to be okay. She knew I needed to confront him but didn't push because there was no way I was going to show up at another concert. Nope, that's never happening again.

But when I made the mistake of telling her he was back in town, she's been hounding me ever since. I don't want to go to his house, but I know I have to.

So with very hesitant hands, I grab my keys. "Fine, you're right. Might as well get it over with, right?"

She nods. "Want me to come with?"

"No. Go home, I need to do this on my own." Except I'm not alone anymore. I never will be again.

We walk out together, and she hugs me before she gets in her car. It takes no time to reach their house, a house I drove by a thousand times and looked up at, praying to catch a glance of Jamie, despite how much I hate him. My palms are damp, and I wipe them on my jeans before I push the doorbell. I don't want him to be here, but I also want to just rip the Band-Aid off.

The lock clicks, and Jamie answers. My teeth clench, and I have to hold my breath to rein in the tears. I've cried more in the last six months than I have my entire life combined.

He stands there and just stares at me. And if I could, I'd look at his handsome face for the rest of my life. Even though he looks like I feel. Confused. Hurt. Torn. Even after all this time, he's still the hottest man I've ever seen. "What are you doing here?" He has a bite to his words that tells me he hasn't changed the way he feels about me.

Well, screw him. He's hot, and he's the love of my life, but I'm done pining over an asshole. He thinks I left a bogus number when I didn't. I wrote down my number. But he didn't even give me a chance to explain. Instead, he treated me like a whore and humiliated me in front of my sister and an audience, including the groupie who had her mouth wrapped around his dick not even two minutes prior. I'm so done with him. Done with men. Done. I'm not here for him anyway.

My throat is swollen, and I can barely swallow. "Is Kolby here?"

"Yeah. Why. Wanna fuck him again?" I still don't know how somebody who looked at me like I was the only person in the world can treat me like I'm dirt. I don't get it. But it doesn't matter anymore.

I keep my head high even though the weight of the world is on my shoulders holding me down. "Can you let him know I'm here, please."

The door swings open, and Jamie makes an exaggerated sweeping motion with his arm. "You know the way to his bedroom." Such an asshole. His back is to me before I can blink, and I wait until he's out of eyesight to step inside. It hurts too much to look at him, no matter what I tell myself. Every fiber of my being is drawn to him, no matter how hard I try to fight it. Damn him.

Kolby is just coming around the corner and freezes when he sees me. I notice some boxes stacked outside his room and briefly wonder if he's moving or something. "Mercy. What are you doing here?"

I close the door and take a breath. A big one. The deepest I'd ever taken before in my life. My body shakes, and my palms go from damp to wet. Tears sting the back of my eyes, but I push them back. Then I open my mouth. "I'm pregnant."

SEVENTEEN

Jamie

I TRY NOT TO THINK ABOUT WHY SHE'S HERE. WHY SHE CAME for him and not me. When I opened the door and saw her, beautiful but terrified, I wanted to pull her to me. The need to drop to my knees and beg for her forgiveness was so strong I had to grip the edge of the door so I didn't fall.

I feel like that's all I've been doing lately, simply holding on for the sake of not falling.

One look at the beauty of her gorgeous face, and I wanted to tell her how sorry I am for what I said to her. How every day since then, I barely sleep because I worry that she thinks I hate her when that's so far from the truth. I almost did, but then she asked for him.

The motherfucker who's moving his shit out of my place because we can't stand the sight of each other anymore. We've only got a few more days on this tour before we get a break, but I don't want him back. I don't want to give an ultimatum, but I know I won't be able to work with him again. We're supposed to be like brothers, but he's more like my enemy, and it's not conducive for the band at all.

We're closing out this tour with a show in Minneapolis, and after I get home for our hiatus, I'm going to put the house on the market. I can't look at the room she fucked him in anymore. I squeeze the bridge of my nose in frustration.

"No fuckin' way. Do not come at me with this shit." I hear Kolby yell, and for whatever the fuck reason, I feel the need to make sure she's okay. Despite how much I want to hate her for ripping my heart out, I still love her. It's been months, and nothing's changed about the way I feel; if anything, it's only intensified. "No fuckin' way. I don't know what fuckin' game you're playin', but straight up, bitch, I'm not playing."

The fuck? She doesn't know how to play a game if the pieces were handed to her, or maybe she does. But I know he didn't just call her a bitch. I don't have the right to get pissed at him for it when I said the same damn thing. God... worst day of my life, and something that I'll never forgive myself for. I wish I could take it back; I wish things could have been different, but they're not.

I round the corner and see her with her hands resting on her stomach over her oversized coat. "I'm not playing a game," she whispers and wipes at her face, but it's pointless. Tears are pouring out of her eyes so fast she can't keep up. "I don't expect anything from you. I just wanted you to know."

If I thought my chest was crushed before, that was nothing compared to right now. No. *No.* Fuck no. "Know what?" I demand. Please, Jesus fuck, please don't let it be that. Anything but that.

Kolby clenches his jaw, and Mercy licks her lip nervously.

"Know fucking what?"

"I'm pregnant." The words are whispered, but they're rattling around in my head so loud I can hear nothing else.

Pregnant.

With another man's child.

The woman I love, the woman who's supposed to be mine is having someone else's baby. The woman who, after Kolby was gone, I was going to try to fix what I broke. I wanted to give her time, and I needed the separation from her to pull my shit together enough to even think about being with her again… because despite how much it hurts, I need her.

I barely sleep, and when I do manage to get into a REM cycle, I dream of her. Food all tastes the same; bland. Anytime I laugh, it's fake because I only smile thinking of her.

But now… Christ Jesus, now I'm back at square one. Square negative twelve.

The knife that was in my heart twists, and I actually have to clutch my chest to alleviate the pain.

"Until I get a paternity test, stay the fuck away from me," Kolby's punk ass yells at her.

"It's yours."

"You expect me to believe that? You had no problem spreading your legs for either one of us, so how—"

I have my hands in Kolby's shirt, and I shove him against the wall before he finishes that sentence. "Do not fuckin' talk to her like that."

"Why not? Clearly she's a slu—"

I pull him back and slam him against the wall and if I wasn't blinded by rage I'd think it ironic that we were back in this same position. "Don't. Fucking. Talk about her like that ever again, Kolby. I won't warn you again." There's something ingrained in me that wants to protect her. At least from everyone else. I'm the one she needed protecting from, and if anyone treated her the way I did, I'd have laid their ass out.

He pushes me away, but I don't let go of him. He needs to really hear what I'm saying. "Get your hands off me 'cause this time I won't stop until I knock your ass out."

I ignore the goading. "You gonna chill? She's fuckin' pregnant and doesn't need to deal with you scaring the shit outta her because you're a dick."

He glares at me. "I've gotta get the fuck outta here." I drop my hands, and he looks over my shoulder at Mercy, then shakes his head.

He shoulder checks me as he passes, but I ignore it, and I wait for the door to slam. My breath comes out in harsh pants, and I can hear my pulse in my neck, thundering around and trying to force blood through my veins.

Mercy sniffling makes me turn around, and when I see the absolute turmoil tightening her entire body, I forget that she left me. I forget she fucked one of my friends, and I forget that I'm supposed to hate her. Because I don't. I never did.

You can't hate the only person you were meant to fall in love with. No God can be that cruel.

I take an abrupt step towards her, grabbing her hand and pulling her with me. She follows easily, and with her fingers intertwined with mine, I know I'd gladly go anywhere she took me. When I sit on the couch, she collapses and burrows into me. I wrap my arms around her and put my lips to the top of her head. Completely loving her in my arms again, where she belongs. "It'll be okay." God, she smells good. So clean and sweet. "Everything will be all right." So fucking right.

Her small body shakes with the effort of her sobbing, and I hold her tighter, kissing her forehead, letting my lips linger since she's allowing it. I don't know how long we sit here for, and I don't want her crying, but for all the times I wished to have her in my arms again, I don't want to let her go.

I never wanted her to go.

And it's time I tell her that. Time to see if she'll ever forgive me.

"There's a thin line between love and hate, gorgeous, and I ruined us because I blurred that line. My ego got pummeled, and I didn't handle it well. You didn't deserve me to treat you like that. I was a fuckin' dick, and I don't know what any of this means, but whatever you need, whenever you need me, I'm here." I'll always be here. I never should have left. I'm never leaving you again. I want to tell her all of those things, but I don't think she'd believe me.

I was hoping that might give her a little comfort, but she just cries even harder. I don't expect her to forgive me, but at least, she knows where I'm at. It's been eating away at me, the shit I said to her. The words that never should have come out of my mouth. I didn't mean that, but I mean what I said just now. If she needs me, I'll be here.

"I don't need… need your symp… sympathy." She hiccups, and I hold her tighter. Too tight? I don't know because she doesn't try to push me away or anything. I can only hope that she lets me do this again.

"Believe it or not, I want you to be happy. I wanted to be the one to make you happy… I thought I was the one who would be." I laugh humorlessly. I still want to be.

EIGHTEEN

Mercy

HIS ARMS AROUND ME ARE WARM, STRONG. HIS SCENT calms me. His heartbeat steadies me. His body cushions me. But his words cut. They slice through my skin like a knife through butter; fast and sharp, hit my veins, and drain the life out of me... whatever life I had left in me after the way he destroyed me.

God, he's a jerk. I still wake up some nights thinking those horrible things he said to me were just a dream because it's almost impossible to believe the same guy who promised me heaven so ruthlessly put me through hell.

But I have a reason to fix it now... to fix me. And it has nothing to do with him, not anymore. Never again. No way. I'm no longer the only person whose well-being I have to look after.

What am I doing? I push off him, and his arms tighten before he lets up.

I stumble backward, and he jumps up, reaching for me. "Stop." I put my hand out, and slam against the wall. "Stay away from me."

"Mercy, I—"

"Fuck you," I whisper even though I want to scream. "Fuck you. Do you really think I'm gonna let you... let you *comfort* me? You? After the way you treated me the last time I saw you, you motherfucking asshole."

His body strains while his hands ball into fists. "I just apologized for that. It was fucked up, I know. I didn't mean it. But you—"

"You treated me like a whore, and from the looks of what I saw that night, that's not even a step up from groupie. You humiliated me. You told me to get on my knees to finish off a fucking blow job that some other woman started." He opens his mouth, but I talk over him. "With an audience!"

"I fucked up."

"Yeah, you did."

"I know, please just let me—"

I cut him off and start to blindly walk backward toward the door. "I don't care what excuse you're gonna come up with. I will never forgive you for that. That was humiliating."

"I know, *I know*. I feel horrible about it. It was degrading and insulting and uncalled for. I know that, and I'm sorry, Mercy. Seriously, genuinely sorry that I hurt you. You have to believe me. You have to know how hurting you is the last thing I want to do." He swallows, and the look that crosses his face tells me he really is ashamed.

"You're so sorry you came running to me to apologize? No, you waited until I came here, not even to you, to tell me you're sorry? And you expect me to believe you?"

He shoves his hands in his pockets. "I should have come to you. I was going to, I swear. God, I want you to believe me, to look at me with all the trust in the world

160

like you did that night. Shit... that night, I was so fucked up over you."

So he's gonna try the sweet guy act now. "And I was over you. That was what I went to the concert for because I thought that what we shared was worth a conversation. I wanted to talk, wanted to explain..."

"Good. Tell me now. Tell me why you left the wrong number."

My head shakes, and I can feel the tears on my cheeks sliding to my ears with the aggressive movement. "I didn't, and it's too late now. You wouldn't let me explain before, and I'm not letting you explain now."

His jaw clenches, clearly not believing me. "Whatever. That doesn't even matter anymore. Neither of us can change the past; the good and the bad. What matters is now. You. The... the baby." His lip curls in distaste as though it was actually hard to say it.

"No, that's where you're wrong. Now you get nothing. You're nothing to me. And since it seems your friend wants nothing to do with the child he helped create, he'll be nothing to me either. You and him, your whole fucking band... all of you guys are nothing to me. Not anymore." I release a rueful laugh. "Just like I was nothing to you."

Then I yank the door open and run. Well, I run as fast as my pregnant belly will let me. As soon as I reach my car, with my hand on the handle, I hear him. "Stop."

That night crashes into me along with him, his chest flush against my back. His scent surrounding me. His strength holding me up. Memories become palpable, and the hitches in my breath become uncontrollable.

I'm not drunk, but I am intoxicated by you.

Smile if you wanna have sex with me.

I want you.

Watch me.

Nothing will ruin this night, Daisy-girl. I won't let it. It's been the best night of my life.

See how far inside you I go?

You'll feel me forever. I promise you that. Fuckin' forever.

God! Why did he have to be such a liar? Why is he such a jerk?

"Shh," he whispers against my ear and lifts me into his arms. "I got you."

"No, I—"

"Just relax, Mercy." I squeeze his shirt and hold on, hating that I love being in his arms. Using the excuse that I'm too emotional to fight with him, when really, I need him for just another minute. I could have used him like this a lot over the past few years. Especially right after my mom's attack. "Please. Let me just help you right now. Please at least let me be a friend and make sure you get home okay."

I don't agree to it, but I don't disagree, either, so he takes that as an okay to proceed. I thought he was carrying me to his house, but he bends down and deposits me in the passenger seat of my car. More memories hit me, and I can't breathe when he shuts my door. It's like sucking air through a straw. I panic when he digs in my purse, but he ignores me trying to grab his arm and successfully gets my keys. He doesn't say a word and pulls away from the curb. I can't help but remember the last time I was in my car with him.

How he made me touch myself and watch him. God, I could watch him all day. All night. He's the most handsome man I've ever seen, and in the three years since I saw him last, he's only gotten better.

He's grown some hair on his face and put on muscle. His piercing green eyes see through me, and in a moment of weakness, I want to tell him how much I missed him. How I don't even care that he didn't call. I just want him now. I want him forever.

But when he stops the car in front of my apartment, my door is ripped open by my sister. "What did he do to you? Why is he here?" She pulls me out and slams the door closed. "Why the hell are you here?"

"I thought you went home?"

"I drove around the block. I was afraid of something exactly like this happening. Why are you here?"

She's not talking to me, and even if she was, I don't have the energy to argue with her right now, too. "I'm going to take care of her tonight." Jamie states.

"No, you're not," Charity snaps. "She doesn't need you."

"Well, I need her." My head snaps up at his admission, and I find him almost shocked. He recovers quickly. "I need to make sure she gets inside okay, and I need her to give me some information so I can figure out how to deal with this problem."

I can't believe he just said that. "The baby is a problem, now?"

"No." He runs his hands through his hair, and I remember doing that same thing and how smooth and soft it was compared to the rest of him. "I'm totally fucking this up again." He mumbles it to himself and is about to say something else when a couple jogging slows and points at him. "Hey, you're from Reason to Ruin."

Jamie's irritated; I can tell that without a doubt. "Yeah, but I'm in the middle of—"

"Cool, dude. So awesome to meet you, I'm a huge fan."

Charity tugs on my arm, and I turn my back on Jamie taking a selfie with the couple. "Hurry. Get inside so we can lock him out."

"You're not locking me out."

We both scream at how close he is, and Charity flails her arms and hits me in the face. I scream again, and Charity and I grab onto each other in a fit of laughter and practically fall to the ground. Jamie is reaching for me. "Jesus, are you okay?"

I wave him off and can't catch my breath as my sister and I laugh harder than I have in months... maybe even years. We're both really jumpy people, and every time we get scared, we can't stop laughing.

"Mercy, gorgeous. Are you okay?"

The concern in Jamie's voice makes my laughter die down. It reminds me of the Jamie I used to know as Donny. The one I miss.

I wipe beneath my eyes, and Charity and I stand to our full height. "I'm fine."

"Christ." He wipes his palms on his holey jeans and breathes a huge sigh of relief. "Let's get you upstairs so you can rest."

"You can leave." Charity speaks for me, but I put a hand on her arm and gently shake my head. "You can't be serious, Merc. Him? After what he did?"

"Trust me."

She glares at Jamie. "I do. It's him who I don't trust." Her finger jabs Jamie in the chest. "If you hurt her again, I will personally find you, rip your balls off, and then sell them on fucking eBay to one of your stupid rock

164

star whore groupies and then you can sleep at night knowing—"

Oh God. "I'm gonna be sick." I put my hand on my belly and rush inside. I can't even make it to the bathroom, so I grab the can from the kitchen and heave into that, but nothing comes up. The door closes behind me with a soft click, and a heavy hand rests on my back.

"Are you okay?"

"Fine." I wipe my mouth and put the garbage back, then turn around.

And there he is.

The flutters from my belly manage to tickle my throat, and I look away from him to avoid letting him see into my damn soul.

"I called."

"Called what?" I whip my head up.

He pulls his black leather wallet out of his pocket and takes a crumpled-up piece of paper out. He runs his fingers along the crease and presses it open, then hands it to me. My shaky fingers take it, recognition making my throat scratchy.

"That. I called that. You. Or at least I thought I did."

I look down at my writing on a piece of paper with the logo of the hotel on it and can't help but feel all the tingles when I reread my note, remembering exactly how I felt writing those words. I was so full of hope and so much love. But when I see the number, I gasp, dropping the paper to the ground. "Oh my God."

"Why'd you do it? I... I thought you felt it, too."

"That's not my number." I rasp, my heart crumbling and the past three years pummeling my brain. "That's my mom's... I... " I can't breathe. Oh my God. It was me. I messed us up. I ruined it. I lost three years of my life pining after a guy who I could have been married to already, whose baby I could be having... not a one-night stand's. It's all my fault. Everything. All of it. It's all my fault. "I'm really gonna be sick this time."

I jump up from the couch and rush to the bathroom, yanking off my coat as I go and processing how big of a mistake I've made. By the time I'm on my knees and hugging the bowl, Jamie is holding my hair. "Leave." I hurl and reach up to flush, embarrassed and mortified beyond belief. Not just for puking in front of him, but for everything. How could I be such a moron?

"I'm not leaving." He stands firm, and once I'm done, he drops my hair and hands me a cool, wet washcloth.

"Thanks," I mumble and then wipe my mouth. As I go to stand, he helps me up, and I lean over the sink to brush my teeth. "You should go."

"I'm not leaving."

I'm too weak to argue, so I simply nod. He wraps his arm around my waist and leads me to the living room, but I shake my head. "I want my bed."

"Whatever you want." I press my lips together at the words Chad would always say.

He turns the light on, and when I practically fall onto my comforter, I'm surprised that he sits next to me. He rearranges us so he's sitting up, legs straight in front of him, and my head is resting on his lap. He absentmindedly runs his fingers through my hair, then my back, applying pressure toward the lower part where I'm sore from carrying a baby.

"I'm sorry," I apologize. But those two words aren't enough, are they?

"I already forgave you, but there really isn't anything to forgive, is there?"

I cuddle closer, practically crawling onto his lap and allowing myself this. I'll take his comfort even though I don't deserve it. I'm so tired. Everything is pushed past the point of exhaustion, and my eyes begin to close. But when I shut them, I remember seeing another woman on her knees for him, and that reminds me of the cruel and haunting words he said to me.

He said he forgives me, but I don't know if I can forgive him enough to move on.

But then again, maybe he wouldn't have been with another woman... and I know she wasn't the only one. There were probably hundreds. Maybe he wouldn't have been with them if it wasn't for my careless mistake. I messed up, then he did.

Mine wasn't intentional, though. I would never say something just to hurt him. And he did. I made a mistake, but he humiliated me.

His hand molds around my butt, and he squeezes slightly. A tingle between my thighs that's been absent for years returns, and I know I'll forgive him. I'll learn to understand that he didn't mean it, that he thought I fooled him and played a player. I get it, but it still hurts. "Where'd you go?"

He doesn't need to ask more because I know what he's referring to. "My mom was attacked by a patient and was in the ER. I rushed out, and I guess in the chaos and with my mind all messed up, I wrote down hers instead of mine. My number is just the last two of hers switched."

"Why didn't you wake me up?"

"You looked peaceful... and... and I was afraid that if I told you I was leaving, you'd just tell me goodbye."

His chest rumbles. "You know I'd never have just said goodbye."

"I thought that, too... but then I realized that I couldn't say goodbye regardless. You told me you had to leave, and I didn't know when I'd see you again, and I just... I don't know." Tears leak out of my eyes, but I cry silently.

He wraps both arms around me and holds me tight. "Get some rest. You've been through a lot."

"You don't have to stay. I know you're mad at me and—"

"I'm not mad, Mercy." I don't have it in me to argue about anything or to think about anything. All I know is right now, he's here. And for the moment, that's good enough for me.

NINETEEN

Jamie

MY ASS IS NUMB, BUT DAMN IS MY HEART FULL. I WANT to ask her so much more, want to know if she stopped loving me... if she ever did, or if it never ended for her, either. I want to know if she can ever forgive me for being such a colossal asshole to her. I need to explain to her that it was the only way I could cope... that I thought she'd played me, and my only defensive play was to hurt her before she hurt me worse than I already was.

I want to know if there's a future even though I don't deserve one.

She turns on her back and snuggles her head into my leg, her face pinching in pain. Her eyes stay closed, and once she settles, I realize she was probably uncomfortable. Her stomach is swollen so beautifully, and I itch to touch her skin, but it's not my place. Not yet.

When I thought about if I could forgive her for leaving me a bogus number, I lied to myself by saying I couldn't because it was easier to admit I'd take this girl however she came. I'd let her destroy me if only to beg her to put me back together again. I'd let her scar me and revel in the fact that a part of her would be with me forever. Liar, cheat, thief—she belongs to me. But the baby growing in her belly doesn't.

And as much as I want her and with how fast things have progressed, I haven't actually thought about what being with her with another man's baby would do to me. If I could look past it and love a kid as if it was my own.

If I could forget it was Kolby whose blood ran through their veins. If I'd be able to look into eyes that were neither hers nor mine and see beyond the irises and into the soul. I give into the curiosity and gently press my palm to her stomach and softly caress her, bringing my hand down and sliding it back up so I can feel her taut skin and a few bumpy lines from where the marks are stretching.

Will I ever be able to see those battle scars and know it wasn't my baby who put them there and simply appreciate them for what they are, which is a testament to how strong she really is.

Smiling when I feel a little movement, I splay my fingers across her abdomen, and the baby kicks again. Her baby, not mine... and not Kolby's... it's just hers. Just Mercy's. I can live with that. I can pretend the father is nameless and faceless and be happy with her. I just might be able to live with that.

I think. Because if I know Kolby like I think I do, he's gonna want not one thing to do with her or this baby. If he wants to be involved... I'd have to figure out how to swallow my pride and accept it. It would gut me, but I'd do it for her.

I settle in, keeping my hand where it is, wanting to get as close to her as I can right now. Her thighs rub together, and she writhes, scooting closer. I continue caressing her and sense her eyes on me. Caramel swirls and needy whispers of a whimper, she begs me for it.

She needs me to touch her almost as much as I do. I lick my lips, and she closes her eyes, fighting the desperation she feels and wanting her anger to outweigh her desires. But when she bites down on her lower lip and her lids pop open to reveal dilated pupils, I know exactly what she needs.

I know how she needs it.

And I'm gonna give it to her.

"Are you wet for me already?"

She nods feverishly as I experiment and graze my knuckle over the crotch of her leggings to find her just how I like her. Soaked.

"Jamie."

"Yeah. Right here."

"You're really here, right?"

I'm never leaving you again. I turn on my side and run my thumb just below the waistband of her pants. "I'm really here."

Her eyes well with desperate tears as I continue my journey south. My fingers graze her swollen clit, and her mouth parts. "Please."

"I've got you." I shove my hand in the tight confines of her bottoms and don't waste any time. I can feel how much she needs this. Two fingers find her clenching hole, and with her juices lubricating my fingers, I push them in easily, growling at how amazing she feels. Her back arches, and with just a press of my thumb to her sweet spot, she detonates for me. And it's breathtaking. "There you go, gorgeous. Come all over my fingers." My words spur her on, and she spasms around me even harder, her breath coming out in jagged pants and her thighs fuckin' shaking.

Beautiful.

I wait for her to relax, her pussy to stop spasming, and slowly remove my hand. I bring my fingers to my mouth and suck her essence off, moaning at the taste of sweet redemption. "Just like I remember."

She throws her arm over her face, and her shoulders shake. I can't tell if she's laughing or crying, but when I hear the hiccup, I know it's the latter. "Hey now, none of that."

"I can't believe I just let you do that... I'm such a whore, and the biggest crybaby known to man."

I yank her arm down, holding it roughly at her side, and grab her face with my other hand. "You are not a whore. You needed me to make you feel good, and that's what I did. I'll always want that privilege. We've got the most insane chemistry, Mercy. From the moment I saw you in the coffee shop to even now, I get hard. Always."

She glances down at my lap, but I lift her head. This isn't about me. "Ignore it."

"It's kind of hard to do that." Her lips quirk, and I swoop in and kiss them while they're smiling.

"Nice pun."

She shrugs. "I try."

"And one more thing. You're not a crybaby. I did and said some really shitty things to you, and you're allowed to be upset about that. And you're pregnant. Your emotions are all over the place, so I don't want you to think you need to hide how you're feeling from me, okay?"

"When did you become so rational?"

I laugh. "Baby, nothing I feel about you is rational." I brush the pad of my thumb over the apple of her cheek. "Why don't you go take a shower, and we'll order some food. Now that you've got a nap in, we need to talk."

Her lids flutter, and I bring both hands up to hold her scared face. "We'll figure it out. Trust me." The heat that was in her eyes vanishes and punches me in the gut. "I'll make it up to you. I swear. I'll make you trust me again."

After a few long minutes of her deciding whether she believes me or thinks I'm a piece of shit, she whispers, "Okay."

I breathe a sigh of relief that I don't deserve, and kiss her forehead. Then her nose. And finally her soft, warm lips. God, I missed her, missed this. It doesn't matter that we only shared one night because all it took was one glance to know she was my forever. I knew it then, and I know it now.

We just have some bumps to get over. Speaking of. I bring my hand to her belly. "You're beautiful pregnant." She opens her mouth to speak, but I shush her. "Just that. Just know that you always were and will always be the most beautiful woman I've ever seen."

Just then, her stomach growls, and she giggles. God, I love that sound. "And apparently hungry, too."

"I am. I haven't eaten a lot today. My nerves were all messed up."

"What sounds good? I'll order it while you take a shower." I see a flash of disappointment, and I wonder if it's because she wanted me to join her. Of course I want to, but for lack of a better term and admittedly sounding like a bitch, I'm not ready. I don't know that I can make love to her with another man's baby in her stomach. I can forgive the mistake with the number—it's already forgotten—and I know I'll get to the point where the fact that she slept with Kolby isn't a factor as long as I don't have to look at him on a daily basis. But the baby... it'll take some time.

"I normally don't like it, but since I've been pregnant... I've craved Chinese."

I help her out of bed and bend down to kiss the top of her head. "Whatever you want."

Her face falls for a millisecond. "I have menus and stuff in the kitchen. Let's go order, then I'll take a shower."

We head to the kitchen where she grabs a bottle of water out of the fridge. She takes a long drink, then hands it to me before retrieving the menu. After a few minutes, she decides on the sweet and sour chicken and beef and broccoli. And she wants egg rolls and cream cheese wantons. And egg drop soup. I place the order and have to raise my arm in the air while I read off my credit card info since she tried ripping it from my hand so she could pay. As soon as I hang up, she puts her hand on her hips. "Why do you have to be so tall?"

"Why do you have to be so short?"

"I'm not short, I'm petite."

I smile, widening my stance and fitting her body between my legs. I place my hands on her hips and pull her as close as I can. "You're both of those things, but you're also insane if you think I'd ever let you pay for anything, let alone a meal while I'm around." I pat her backside that's only gotten juicier since I last saw her. "Go shower."

She scrunches her nose at me but goes down the hall without protest. The water echoes in the quiet little apartment, and I dig through her fridge for a beer. Instead of sitting on the couch waiting, I check out her place, sipping a Miller Lite and looking at her DVD collection. She has the movies alphabetized, and I quirk my lips at how cute she is. I'm also surprised she has a huge flat screen, fucker's almost bigger than mine.

There's a wall with photos on it, and I start to head in that direction when there's a knock on the door. I set the beer down on the kitchen table and open the door for the Chinese delivery. A man, but not one delivering food, stands in front of me, appearing confused and nearly frantic. "Can I help you?" I ask, crossing my arms.

"Where's Mercy?"

"Who the fuck are you?" I find myself already in total protective mode defending my territory and guarding my mate. Refusing to let anything touch her.

He pulls his head back. "I'm her fiancé."

I have to lift my chin off the floor and have him repeat it because I know I didn't hear him right. "Excuse me? Her motherfuckin' *what*?"

"Where is she? Are you the asshole who got her pregnant?"

"No, I'm a different asshole." He tries to step in, but I put my hands on his chest and shove him back. "Not happening, bud." I don't know the story, but I will after I get rid of this guy. I do know he's not getting in here, not getting close to her, he's not fucking up what I just got back with her. Nobody is.

"Let me through. Where is she? Mercy!" He bellows her name, and I'm about to slam the door in his face when she steps up behind me, wet hair and a pink towel around her curvy body.

"Chad." Her voice is laced with surprise as she stands

next to me, leaning her weight into me. Picking me. Choosing me over him. I wrap an arm around her waist, palming her hip and holding her close.

His angry eyes go from my hand to the bump in her stomach. "Who is this guy?" he asks her.

"Who I am isn't any of your business."

He steps up to me, and I gently push her away because if things keep going, we're gonna have some blood shed, which is fine with me. I could use something to get all of the aggression out.

This guy leans closer to me. "It is when she's going to be my wife."

I hear her gasp without looking away from him, I ask her, "You gonna marry this guy?"

"I was," she confesses, and I grind my teeth together so hard I feel my filling crack. Of course. What, did I think a woman like her wouldn't get snatched up? I knew it was a possibility, but since I never moved on, I was hoping it'd have been the same for her, but nope. She had no fucking problem starting over without me while I was a loser who hung on to the broken promise of a one-night stand for years.

"Are. You. Still?" I grit.

Her head shakes, water droplets falling down to her clavicle. "No." And as much as her word means shit to me, I hear the truth in her voice. She doesn't want him, not anymore.

"I wanna know if that's my baby," he yells, and I go on alert as she freezes.

"How dare you?" she whispers.

"It's not too farfetched to think it could be mine, Merc. How do you know it's not?"

I straighten to my full height, fists clenching and nostrils flaring. "Shut your fuckin' mouth."

"It's not yours, Chad. We hadn't had sex for months. There's no way it's yours."

I let the knowledge that he had her in his bed and didn't take care of her flow through me. What an idiot. How can you have her... her with all her beauty and grace and humor and killer body next to you and not pleasure it?

He doesn't like that answer, probably because he knows what an idiot he is, and starts to charge inside. "We need to talk," he demands, and I've finally had enough and shove him back into the hallway, then slam the door instead of following him out and pounding his face in because what I really want to do would upset her right now, and she doesn't need any more stress. Chest heaving, I lean against the door and ignore his pounding and screaming her name. She stares at me, lips parted, cheeks pink, pulse thrumming in her neck.

The steam from her shower followed her into the kitchen, because the air is thick and hot, and until he stops, and I hear his footsteps fading away, I can hardly catch my breath. "Explain."

"I... he was there for me when everything happened with my mom, and it was... I never loved him, not in that way, and I agreed to marry him, but he called it off three weeks before the wedding about six months ago because he knew that I... he wasn't the one for me."

My nostrils flare. "If he wouldn't have called it off, would you have married him?" When she doesn't answer, I know the answer. I pace as the knowledge fucks with my head. "You're good," I whisper cynically. "Really good."

"No!" she screams and reaches for me when I turn the doorknob. "No, I thought you didn't want me. You didn't call, I was... I wasn't with him because I loved him the way I loved you, I-"

"But you loved him?"

Her hand trembles over mine. "Do you want the truth, or do you want me to sugarcoat it?" she asks, throwing my own words back at me.

"Truth," I grunt.

"I didn't love him. Not really... but in a way."

"What way is that?"

"Like a friend."

Jealousy, that irrational green doesn't tint my vision, it blinds me, and I step into the little space she left between us, my pelvis rubbing against her belly. "A friend who makes you drip? A friend who can touch your pretty little pussy and have you screaming in a matter of minutes? That kind of friend?"

A pained sound comes out of her mouth as she shakes her head and backs up, walking until her thighs hit her couch and she falls back onto the cushions. I let her have her space. "He wasn't you. That's why he left me; he knew I wasn't in love with him."

"But you would have married him."

"Yes."

"Would you have divorced him if you saw me again?"

Her brows draw together. "Why are you doing this? You're the one who asked me to finish off a blowjob some skank was giving you. And since we're on the subject, how many more of them were there, Jamie? Huh? How long did it take before you replaced me with one of your groupies?"

"You left me the wrong fucking number."

"On accident, it was an accident. You insulting me like that was degrading and embarrassing and intentional. I might have pretended with someone else, but it was just one guy. Just one."

I shake my head and then point at her belly. "You forgot someone."

TWENTY

Mercy

"**B**UT I NEVER FORGOT YOU." I BEG HIM WITH MY eyes, pleading for him to see the truth. To see me. "Even when I should have, I didn't. I don't get why... I didn't understand it, and he was simply there, Jamie. He wasn't the person I thought about when I closed my eyes at night. He wasn't the one I thought about when I climaxed," I admit embarrassingly. "All this time, I thought I was hung up on the what-ifs with you, and that's why I could never forget, but God... when you touch me, when you look at me, I feel it in my bones."

The sharp lines of his face soften, and he steps closer. "I do too."

"I don't want to fight with you anymore."

He nods and continues toward me. "What do you want?"

"To focus on this baby. To get to know you. To try to come through this season of my life with some type of dignity and not hate what I see when I look into the mirror."

His hands seize my face, calloused fingers grazing the

180

apple of my cheek. "How can you hate all of this beauty?"

I reach up, the towel cascading off my body, but his eyes don't leave mine.

"I hurt a good man and have to live with that for the rest of my life."

"No." He grunts. "You'll be with me the rest of your life; he will not factor."

I want to believe him… so badly I want to. But it's too much. Too soon. "Don't," I plead. "Don't make promises you can't keep."

His grip tightens, and he tilts my head back. The angle elongates my neck, and I watch his eyes turn to fire as they trail down to my collarbone and back up. "I'd have kept the promises I made three years ago, gorgeous."

He would have. I believe that down in the bottom of my soul. "I know."

"Good."

"I would have, too."

"I know."

I'm naked, in front of him, and he's doing nothing but talking. Listening. And I want to show him how much it means to me. I reach for his belt buckle.

"Mercy, baby." He grabs my hair and yanks my head back. "You don't have to do that."

I pant, desperate to taste him again, hot desire courses through me. "I want to."

My fingers fumble with his zipper, and once it's open, I tug on his jeans. They fall to his thighs, and I reach inside his black boxer briefs and attack his hard cock. "Fuck." He hisses when my lips pull, suction drawing pre-cum out of the tip. "Jesus." I grip the base and stroke, my desire to start gentle vanishes, and I squeeze. He groans, and when

I tilt my eyes up to see his face, all that's in my view is the underside of his scruffy jaw.

I moan at the flavor of him when it hits my tongue. Salty and sweet at the same time. I cup his balls, and his hands in my hair tighten. "Mercy," he warns already. "You've gotta slow the fuck down unless you want me comin' down your throat."

I want that. I so want that. I want to make him lose control, but not yet. So I pull back. His grip just barely loosens, and I lick the mushroom tip like a popsicle. My tongue swirls and flicks at the notch, and he pushes his hips up, forcing his shaft into my mouth. If he wanted to, he could fuck my mouth and take what he wanted, but he's letting me give him what I need to. His thighs are straining and the muscles in his neck are corded.

My fist tightens, and I look up this time to find his eyes blazing on me. "I thought you wanted me to slow down."

"I did." He pushes my head down. "But I lied. Use that pretty little mouth and wring me dry."

I bring my lips to the tip and begin to spread them around the crown, when I have a moment of doubt. When I feel like the words he's saying to me aren't anything special. He must sense the shift in my mood because he cups my jaw and lifts my head, his dick falling out of my mouth with a soft pop.

"You know it's only you, and if you can't feel it, if you don't believe it deep down, then *listen to me*. Trust me. It was always you. You were who I thought about, you were the only one who I ever gave myself to in the ways that count, and you are the only one who has ever mattered. I promise you that, Mercy. Swear. Cross my heart and hope to die, I swear it's only been you in any and every way that means anything." I swallow, fighting the declaration from him and what my brain is telling me. "You don't have to do this. We don't have to go there yet. I'm happy just being with you. Knowing your name. Seeing your eyes. It's all I need."

"I need you, Jamie. All of you."

He rubs his thumbs across my cheekbones and he bends down to lift me off the couch when the doorbell rings. I giggle when he drops me back down, pulls up his pants, and waddles to the door. After he gets our food, he drops it on the table. "We'll eat later." Then he rushes to me and lifts me up again, and then carries me to my bed. Then gives me what I need. I finish what I started. And then... then he gives me what I didn't know I needed. His fingers and his mouth give me everything.

An hour later, he lies on his back and looks at my ceiling, his shoulders shake and he turns his head towards me. "Why do you have glow in the dark stars stuck to your ceiling?"

My breath expels, and I don't want to tell him, but I don't want to lie either. "Chad put them there."

The humor that was in his voice disappears. "Why?"

I shrug.

"Why?"

"I was complaining one night that being in the city ruined the stars at night, so he wanted me to have stars to wish upon."

I hear him swallow and he rolls all the way to his side. "Did you ever make any wishes?"

"Yes." I roll to him, too.

"What do you wish for?"

"One of them already came true."

He traces my jaw with his finger and wraps me up, pulling me to him as best we can fit in this position. My face is tucked into his throat and his chin rests on the top of my head. "What wishes haven't come true yet, gorgeous?"

I smile against him. "If I tell you, they'll never come true."

"I'll make 'em," he vows, the certainty in the deep vibrations of his voice is almost my undoing.

God, he's so damn sweet. "Some wishes are out of your hands, honey."

"Nah." He squeezes me gently, his calloused fingers digging into my skin, taking ownership of my body and claiming my heart. "All of mine are in my arms right now."

I should melt at that. My heart should soar, but instead, I feel a tingling in my throat, and I sit up. He follows me with confused eyes. "You need to leave."

He bends at the waist. "Excuse me?"

"Just for a couple days. I... I need to get my head sorted, Jamie. I can't get caught up in you again. I need to think. I need to plan my future. I want you in it, but you're not the only one." He watches as I rub my stomach. "I can't tell you how much I want you or how desperately I want things to just fall into place, but—"

"I get it."

My lips snap closed. "You do?"

"Yeah. I don't like it, but I get it." He sifts his fingers through my hair and wraps them around the back of my head. "Kiss me then walk me out so you can lock up after me."

I lean into him, but I don't kiss him. I hold his eyes

and rest my forehead on his. "I'm sorry I left you the wrong number."

"I'm sorry I was such a dick I didn't let you explain."

"That's also something I need to come to terms with, Jamie. That the reason for us not being together was my fault. After that night…" He tries to talk over me, but I don't let him. "It was my fault. It wasn't intentional, but nevertheless, it was a mistake I made, and I blamed you for far too long."

"Blame me."

I lick my lips and we're so close, the tip of my tongue touches the corner of his mouth. "What?"

His eyes shift in hues from emerald to hunter. "Be pissed at me. Let me shoulder it."

"But—"

"No. Blame me. Hate me right now if it'll make you feel better, just as long as you promise to love me when I get back."

"Do you promise to come back?" I ask cautiously.

"Did I ever really leave?"

He waits for an answer, but I don't take long. "No. You were always here."

"And I always will be. I promised you that three years ago, and I'll say it again. I'll be with you. Forever."

He watches as a single tear falls down my cheek. "I want that."

"I want you."

"You have me."

He smirks. "I know."

"Don't be cocky."

His tongue parts my lips, and I close my eyes, enjoying the moment. Living in the now, loving having him back.

He groans into my mouth and pulls back, looking deep into my eyes, then slams his mouth to mine once again. I hold on for the ride, letting him do what he needs. There's no way I could take control if I tried; he's dominating me and saying without words how he feels. When his fingers flex against my scalp, he pulls back, panting.

There's a lot happening right now, so much emotion between the two of us and too much for me to deal with in front of him, so I have to get him out of here. "I hate to see you go, but I wanna watch you leave."

He grins. "Before I go, can I borrow something?"

"What do you need?"

"Your heart. I promise I'll give it back."

"You already have it."

His eyelashes brush the top of his cheekbones when his lids lower. "You're giving me a toothache, Mercy. Stop being so sweet." He kisses me again, fast and hard. "Come on. Lock up behind me and eat."

He helps me up and I walk unhurriedly to the kitchen with him where he opens the door. "I'll give you space. But not much. I'll be back in a few days. You need me before that, call me."

"Okay." I should have told him to stay, especially since he ordered all that food and paid for it, but if I do that then I'm afraid I'll never ask him to leave again and I need a couple of days to myself.

"Okay, baby." He kisses my forehead. "Lock up."

I nod, and once he's through the door, I close it and slide the chain, then engage the deadbolt. I head to my window and watch him drive away. Standing there, I rest my head against the glass, and it takes about twelve seconds to know that I can put the past behind me and move forward with him because if I can forgive him, I can for-give myself.

After I come to that conclusion, I go and eat a little food and am putting the leftovers in the fridge when I hear my phone ring, not recognizing the number I still answer it. If it was Jamie, his name would pop up since he pro-grammed it in. "Hello?"

"Please don't hang up."

"Chad."

He sighs. "Look, I'm sorry. I didn't mean to just show up like that, but your mom called me and told me everything—"

"My mother called you?" I ignore the fact that Chad disconnected his old number, so somehow my mom got his new one.

"Yes. I was worried, I… I still care about you."

"I'll always care about you, Chad, but right now I need to focus on this baby."

He snorts. "And that guy, too, right?"

I don't want to hurt him, but it needs to be said. "I've been in love with him for over three years, Chad."

The line goes silent, and I pull it back, thinking he hung up, when I see I'm right. I bring the phone to my forehead and give myself a moment to come to terms that I've found yet another way to hurt him when it wasn't my intention. But maybe now he'll understand. Maybe now he can have his closure and move on.

It's not worth the energy to bring it up to my mother, because I don't want to listen to her lecture me. I'm done. Jamie makes me happy. And I refuse to let my mother try to control my love life anymore.

My phone rings right by my head and I jump,

answering it before I see who it is but assuming it's Chad again. "Hello?"

"Hey, it's Kolby."

He's not who I expected to call. "Oh. Hi."

"Listen. I'll do whatever, pay for you to do whatever, but I don't want anything to do with the kid. If you wanna still have it, that's up to you. Far as I'm concerned, it doesn't exist."

Every protective instinct I have as a mother heightens, and I wrap my arm around my belly. "I'm six months pregnant, Kolby. Even if I wanted to, which I never would, but even if I wanted to have an abortion, it's too late. God, what's the matter with you?"

"Nothing. I just don't want to deal with a kid."

"Did you use a condom?" I blurt.

He doesn't answer.

"You didn't."

"I did."

"You're such a liar. Jesus, how many other women have you screwed without protection, you pig?" I hated being humiliated when Jamie said that Kolby gave his wife an STD, but at the same time I was thankful for it because I went and got a test to make sure I was clean. Which I was, thankfully.

He laughs. "Most women if they go whoring around are at least on birth control. Unless they're trying to hook a man with a baby."

"I'm not trying to do shit to you."

"Whatever. Listen, I don't need this to get out, so just keep it between us right now, and when I'm done with this show and Ruin, I'll get some shit drawn up."

I see red at the way he so carelessly talks about our

fucking child. "No, you won't, motherfucker." I point at my chest as if he can see me. "I'll get it drawn up. I'll take care of it because if you're seriously telling me you will never want to have anything to do with this baby, then there is no way I'm letting you leave some kind of loophole to come at us later."

"I won't do that." He actually sounds regretful now.

"I know you won't because I won't let you." I drop my phone from between my ear and neck, then jab the button to end the call.

And when I move to sit on the couch, I fall into it instead, because the cramp in my stomach makes my knees weak.

TWENTY-ONE

Jamie

MY FINGERS TWITCH AS I SIT HERE ON A FOLD-OUT chair outside the bus. It's been two days since I left her, and I haven't slept since then. Worrying about her, feeling her still, smelling her. We performed our final show of this year last night, and are chillin' by our bus at the outdoor venue until we take off to go home tomorrow. It was also the final show with Kolby. I'll make sure of it.

Nobody else knows what's happening right now… at least not the details. Obviously, they know that Kolby fucked my woman, but anything more than that isn't theirs to know yet. Mercy didn't want me to, and plus, it's not my place to tell them, but if Kolby doesn't man the fuck up, and soon, we're gonna have major fucking problems. Huge. Bigger than we ever have before.

I can't even fathom how much of a pussy you have to be to get a woman pregnant and not give a shit. But especially with someone as amazing and beautiful and funny as Mercy. How can you not want all that good shit in your life? I mean, she's perfect.

No words can express how deep the connection I feel to her is and I hope to God I spend the rest of my life trying to figure out how I can show her what she means to me. I don't know what's going to happen between us, but I know what I want to happen. What I need my future to be. And it's all her. She's what I look forward to, and if she can forgive me enough for what I did in the past, I know I can give her everything she'll ever want.

I'll work my ass off to give her whatever she needs. I've been working my ass off, and now that I have her, I know why. It's for her. Everything I have, everything that I'll ever be is for her.

Mercy insisted on having a couple of days alone to clear her head and come to terms with what's happened between us so quickly. It was terrifying when we spent that first night together, and it's even more scary now.

That first night started out as an insane attraction, but as the night went on it became more. Greater. Everything. But now... after what we've been through and what she's actually going through, it shouldn't still feel that way. But it does. *It's just right* and I don't want to waste any more time not being with her, but I have to respect her wishes.

And truthfully, it's probably for the best for both of us to have a minute to process everything that's happening.

When she said she thought the reason she never got over me was because of the what-ifs, I felt that statement in my gut. But it wasn't just that. It was just her. *Mercy.* She's the reason. She's why I was so messed up without her because I can't survive unless it's with her. We were meant to be together, it's just that simple.

And knowing that I know where she lives, that I have her number and could call her and hear her voice, that I know her name and can't communicate with her are killing me. But I fucked up enough; I messed up so badly that I'm willing to do anything and everything she needs to trust me again.

So if she needs space, even though I feel like that's all we've had, I'll give it to her.

We've got some brats grilling and a cooler filled with beer and water, a table with all sorts of junk food on it, and the background music comes from the other bands playing. I hold a beer in my hand but can't even take a swallow. My stomach is in knots, and my head just isn't here. It's with her. I managed to get through the performance last night only because I knew when it was over I could really begin with her. It was motivation to go balls to the wall. I don't know exactly what the future holds aside from her, so I gave it my all and know that if this ends, which I hope to God it doesn't, but if it comes to the end I know I went out with a bang.

I think Kolby was in the same boat as me on stage yesterday, but unlike me who is unsure, he's *gotta* know this isn't going to end well for him. I shouldn't do it, but I have to confront him about this. I stride over to Kolby and turn my back to everyone else. "What are you gonna do?"

"About what?"

"Don't play dumb, asshole. That baby might be yours, but Mercy is mine and I won't let you fuck with her more than you already have."

He smirks. "Finally got your head outta your ass, did you?"

"Shut the fuck up." I narrow my eyes. "I swear to God, if you hurt her…" I don't finish the sentence because the threat is implied.

He crosses his arms. "Pretty sure you were the one who not only hurt her but also humiliated her."

I stab myself in the chest. "I know what I did. And I'll spend the rest of my life making up for it, but that's not what I'm talking about, and you know it. Because make no mistake, I will marry her, so that kid will be in my life, and she already loves it, so that means I will, too." Eventually.

"It's harder than you think," he whispers cynically. "You think you'll be cool with only one woman, think her pussy's lined in gold enough to hold out for, but it's not." He tilts his head. "I see you, Jamie. I see how many bitches you've fucked at once, seen the damn look on your face when—"

"You don't know shit, so shut the fuck up. I had fun, no doubt, and I don't regret it. But I'm not you. I'm not looking for more than what I've got. And I've got her." Which was easy to prove when bitches were lining up, practically panting after the show and I didn't even see them. All I saw was her. She's all I need. "So again, you think to do something to hurt her, prepare. I'll make yours a living hell if you even think about doing something that will make her do anything but smile."

With that, I turn and walk away, needing to get gone from him. It's pointless trying to talk to him rationally. In his defense, I didn't make it easy on him when he tried to talk to me after *the night that shall not be remembered.*

I'm heading to the keg when I see Lincoln take his phone out of his pocket, and his brows scrunch together when he looks at the screen. "Excuse me guys, I need a second."

They nod at him, and everyone else goes back to doing their thing, but for some reason I watch him. He looks tweaked. He holds the phone to his ear, and his big ass body freezes. His jaw tightens, and he barks some words into the phone. Slowly, like something you'd see in a movie, his head turns, and his eyes drill into Kolby.

He's oblivious to the sudden tension in the air, but I'm not. I stand still and watch what's about to play out.

With a roar, Lincoln drops his phone and charges at Kolby. His fist high in the air, Lincoln brings it down and slams it into his face.

Blood spurts from Kolby, maybe his nose, a gash, I don't even know. And then Linc does it again. And again. I should probably try to stop him, but because I'm a god-damned asshole, I just watch. By the time Gabe and Mike make it over to him, Kolby is groaning and rolled onto his side. Lincoln kicks him, and as much as I hate the bastard, I can't help but wince when he whimpers at the contact.

"Jesus fuck, Linc. What the hell?" Ian barks as he runs toward the commotion.

Lincoln ignores anything else but Kolby's bruised face. "You knocked up my sister? Got her pregnant and left her alone? Told her to have an abortion?"

What. The. Fuck?

He struggles against the holds of the guys, and rips free, his anger giving him the strength of four men. I think he's going to hit him again when he reaches for him, but instead, he grabs his T-shirt and yanks him so their heads are practically touching. "If Mercy dies because of you, I will kill you, do you hear me?" Lincoln whispers cynically with promise.

My heart falls to the ground, splattering all over the hot blacktop. My chest tightens, and I grab my throat. "What." I choke for air. If she dies? "What the fuck?"

Linc throws Kolby down and marches back to his phone where he picks it up. "I'm on my way."

He doesn't look back as he shoves it in his pocket, and I get with the program and run after him. I need to see her. "What happened?"

"Stupid motherfucker got her pregnant... told her to kill it. Fuck! He's dead. I'm still gonna kill him even if he makes it."

"Who's she?"

"My sister! My niece who is too little to come yet are both fighting for their lives in a goddamned hospital right now."

"It's a girl? She's having a daughter?"

"Yeah."

I can't move... it's a girl. God, I bet she'll look just like her mom. I hope she does. She'll be beautiful. "Mercy." I mouth the word, then run to catch up again. "Mercy!" I scream her name and that makes him stop.

He glares at me. "What?"

"Mercy... she's... long hair, works at the hospital. Lightest brown eyes you've ever seen. That's your sister?"

He unlocks the keys to a shiny black Escalade, and I don't ask as I jump in the passenger seat. "What the fuck are you doing? I don't have time for your shit."

I ignore the guys yelling my name and slam the door. I need to get to her. I need to see her. I need her.

"Your sister. She's Mercy?" I don't know how many other Mercys are out there who Kolby knocked up, but I feel the need to be sure because I don't want it to be her. I want him to say no. I don't want it to be her who's in a hospital. I wish he'd tell me his sister had blond hair.

"Yes!" he snaps and continues to breathe heavier

than I've ever seen someone breathe. More forceful than I thought possible. "She's my sister. My baby sister." His voice cracks, and I see through the anger to the straight-up fear. Fear that I'm feeling thinking she's hurt, that she could die. That I couldn't have more time with her.

"I'm coming with."

He shoves the key in the ignition, and if I wasn't afraid that he'd beat my ass if I questioned, I'd ask if he was okay to drive. We've had him as security on and off for years, and though we shot the shit every once in a while, we never talked about anything personal. He'd been gone on some type of special assignment, a personal protection thing or something for the past year or so, and we just got him back.

"Why do you want to come with? I'm straight. I'm cool to drive." He's impatient as he asks me, but so am I. I need to get to her, and I needed it yesterday. I needed to never leave her.

"I've known her for years, Linc. I didn't know she was your sister, but she means something to me. Swear." I'll beg him if I have to. I'll do whatever to go with him.

He studies me for a second, his pained eyes assess me, the years of training he has come to a decision, because he nods tersely. "What the fuck ever. How do you know her?"

"She's mine."

As he's driving, he pulls up the GPS and the large screen on the dash illuminates the directions. Six and a half hours.

"She's not yours."

Now is not the time to argue about this shit. "She will be," I mumble, nerves making my knees bounce.

"If you think you, or any one of you fuckers who go through women in one week like most people do their entire life, are gonna claim my sister, you're sorely mistaken."

I lean my head against the window. "She'll never see Kolby again."

"She'll have to see him every time she looks at her daughter and know some stupid piece of shit knocked her up and disposed of her like she was trash." His hands tighten on the steering wheel. "But you're right. He's never getting near her again."

I am, though. I'm practically obsessed with looking into her eyes again and getting my arms around her. Holding her tight and keeping her safe and loving her. Forever.

Just like I promised.

TWENTY-TWO

Mercy

I WAKE UP IN A HOSPITAL BED AND THE FIRST THING I SEE IS two men hunched over, sleeping. One of them I'm not surprised is here even though it's been a while since I've physically seen him. My brother Lincoln works a lot, and it's hard enough to get in touch with him on the phone, let alone get him to come home. We usually only see him in July for a long weekend, which sucks. But if someone in his family, particularly his baby sister, ends up in the hospital, he'll drop everything to be here.

Case in point, his wrestler's body slouched in the pastel green chair with his normally slick-backed dark hair disheveled, and wide, broad shoulders moving heavily as he breathes. Knowing he's here gives me comfort.

The other man who's in much the same position gives me anxiety. His brown hair is also disheveled, but it always appears that way. His jeans have the usual tears in them, and his black T-shirt looks like it's been washed one too many times.

I wince as I sit up, a cramp in my stomach making

my entire body ache. Jamie lifts his head, in tune to me, which isn't a surprise since I'm convinced he's my other half. "You okay? Do you need anything?"

I swallow and glance over at a bottle of water on the window ledge. He follows my gaze. "Thirsty?" He's already reaching for it and looks around for something else. "I can't find a straw, but here." He brings it closer to me and cups my chin as though he belongs here. As if he has every right to touch me and look at me like he loves me. "Open, baby."

The softness of his voice and the way he so tenderly strokes my skin brings tears to my eyes. When I bring them up to his, wetness is behind his lids, too and the strangled sound that comes from my throat has nothing to do with being parched. "Open for me," he mouths the words.

I nod, parting my lips, and let him pour some of the cool liquid in my mouth. A little bit dribbles out, and he catches it with his finger, then runs it across my lip. I forgot what that felt like, his attention on me that night was so sweet, his caress all consuming. That's the man I thought I knew. This is the man I know. The only man I've ever loved.

I squeeze my eyes shut when I swallow and nod, telling him that's enough.

I don't know how he knew I was here, and I want to ask him why he even bothered showing up, but my brother wakes up, and when he stands, I see his raw knuckles. I quickly look over at Jamie, and when I double check that his handsome face is unscarred, I look back at Lincoln. "What happened to your hand?"

He shakes his head and bends down, hugging me

as gently as a six foot two, two-hundred-and-fifty pound man can. "What do you need?"

"What happened to your hand?"

Linc shrugs.

"What happened to your hand?" I ask more firmly, but because of what my brother does for a living, I have a feeling my guess would be accurate. "And why is Jamie with you? Why are you with him?"

"He says you're his or some shit, but I don't give a crap enough to care about him right now."

Jamie stands on the opposite side, sensing my agitation at not knowing what's going on and takes my hand in his, comforting me with a simple touch. "He was our security on tour. Got the phone call wh—"

"Oh God, did you kill Kolby?" I grasp his hand tighter and squeeze his fingers. And how did I not know my brother was security for them? He never told us before who he was working for because of NDAs and stuff, so I shouldn't be surprised. But the way things have happened between Jamie and me, I shouldn't be surprised that we're connected in another way. The town we're from is the smallest large town in the world, I swear. Everyone knows everyone, and unless you're a moron like me and don't put it together right away, you'll find some connection with the person in line behind you at the grocery store. "Please tell me he's okay."

"Why do you care? He's a piece of shit who told you to kill your baby, and you ended up in the hospital because of the stress of it."

"You're overreacting, I don't know what Charity told you, but I'm fine. It was just Braxton Hicks."

My big brother shakes his head. "You don't have to lie to cover for him."

"I'm not. Charity's imagination is all over the place." Her and I have gotten into it over the past couple of days. Bad. She doesn't agree with my decisions. I don't know what she told Linc or why, but he clearly misunderstood the severity of the situation. "Yes, he doesn't want to have anything to do with the baby, but he's not why I'm here. I mean, obviously he's the reason I'm pregnant, but the reason I'm in this bed is just some false contractions."

"Why are you hooked up to an IV then?"

Before I can answer, we're interrupted by Meara running into the room. She's frantic as she searches the bed. She briefly glances at the two men, her confused eyes stopping on Jamie for a moment, then darting back to me. "Oh God... are you okay?"

"I'm better now." She pushes my brother out of the way, and he actually allows it. When she bends down and hugs me, I hear murmurs between the two men but can't decipher what they're actually saying because Meara is crying into my ear. "I'm sorry. I shouldn't be crying, but I was freaking out, and I'm so glad you're okay."

She stands and wipes her eyes and then turns to Lincoln, sticking out her hand. "I know him, but not you. I'm Meara. Her friend."

"Lincoln." He checks her out while he shakes her hand, and Jamie growls. "She's married to my brother, asshole."

"That's a shame."

"Lincoln," I snap. "Don't be a pig."

Meara sits next to me. "Are you okay?"

"Yeah. I don't know what you all heard, but they were just Braxton-Hicks. I had one a couple days ago, but they got super bad this morning. My blood pressure was really high, so they're monitoring that, but we're fine now." I hold my belly, and thank the lord, she's healthy.

Lincoln rubs his hands down his face. "Charity said you were having contractions and under so much stress. She spit out the whole story in like two minutes, and after she explained, she said you were in the hospital... I thought all the shit you were dealing with is what put you and the baby in here."

Meara sighs of relief. "Thank God you guys are okay."

"Not that I'm not happy to see you, how did you know I was here?"

"Apparently after Lincoln beat the shit out of him, Kolby filled everyone in on what a douchebag he is, and Mike called Lee. I had no idea you two, you and Kolby were ever a thing."

"Kolby is nothing to her," Jamie grinds out.

"Whatever, we'll have to talk later about how we didn't figure out that you were... connected to the band the way you are." Meara says to me with a smile, but then turns her head and looks at Jamie. "Why are you here?"

He holds my hand, kisses my knuckles. "Because she's here."

"I'm so confused."

"We met years ago. Fell in love." Meara gasps, and Lincoln grunts. "I made a mistake that made it so—"

"It wasn't your fault," Jamie interrupts.

I shake my head. "It was. But regardless, it was pretty, um... intense, and when I ran into him again, we've been, sort of, reconnected."

"And we're gonna stay that way," he adds. "So get used to it."

"But she's pregnant with Kolby's kid."

"So." Jamie shrugs. "If it wasn't for her going home with him, she never would have walked out of his room and back into my life."

I drop my head, never looking at it that way. Loving that that's how he chose to see it. Loving him. And never wanting to let him go.

Throughout the evening, several nurses I know come and go, most of whom freak out when they see Jamie. They all assume he's the father, and I don't tell them any different. He will be; this baby will grow up to have him as her daddy, and that's all that matters.

Especially since my oh-so-lovely phone call with Kolby. What an ass.

Meara left almost right away, after seeing for herself that I was okay, and Lincoln left when she did, saying he'd follow her out to make sure she got to her car okay. Now I'm just sitting here, watching Jamie sleep. I roll to my side, and my face pinches in pain, but after I settle my hand on my stomach, the pain subsides, and I relax and breathe deep again.

I run my fingers through Jamie's hair and he snuggles into me. I love him being here, love that he came, that he fought to be with me. "Why don't you go home?" I whisper. He sits up with a kink in his neck and lifts his head from the bed to find me smiling sleepily at him. "It's late."

"I don't care." He winces as he straightens out. "You're here. I want to be with you. I know you said you needed space, but I'm sorry, I don't want to give it to you anymore."

"I don't want it, either. The past couple of days..." I trail off.

He finishes my sentence. "Have been miserable."

"Do you think… do you really think we can do this?"

"I know we can."

"This is asking a lot, Jamie. I'm pregnant. I'll have a kid now. That doesn't just go away."

He swallows and I stop breathing. "I love you." He's implied the words but never flat-out said them. Hearing them is even better than I ever could have imagined. "And I'll grow to love that baby."

"She's a girl." I found out as soon as I could, there's no way I would be able to wait.

"She's gonna be beautiful."

"It's happening so fast."

"It started three and a half years ago. It's not fast."

I stare into his determined orbs, getting lost in the assurance. "I love you, too."

"I know." I yawn, and he kisses the top of my head. "I don't want to leave you, but I'm going to because when you come home, I'm gonna be there, and in order for that to happen, I've gotta go clear out my house. You good with that?"

Simply nodding, I give him my answer. Sharing my space with Jamie. Yes, please. "You want to live with me. Us?"

"Yeah. I do. I don't want to miss a second with you if I can help it. But if it's too quick I'll wait. I understand it's moving fast for you."

"No, I want you with me."

"Unless you want to move in with me, but I wanna get rid of that house. We'll get something bigger soon, but I want you comfortable and safe in your own space until the baby is born."

"Okay."

He rubs my cheek with his thumb, then pushes my hair behind my ears. "I'll be back in the morning, but you need to promise if you need something, you'll call before that."

"I promise."

He kisses me before he leaves, and I hug my arms around my body. It's not but a few minutes after he's gone that Charity walks in. She was here earlier but had to get some work done, so I knew she was coming back, just not when. "I saw him leave."

"So."

"Is he coming back?"

My defenses rise, and I push myself up to sitting. "Yes. He's going to get his stuff and bring it to my apartment."

"Are you sure this is what you want?" She sits on the end of my bed. "After what he did to you time and time again."

"Yes."

"What makes you think he's going to be able to handle having a baby. I mean, God, Merc... you've known him like a day. And you suddenly—"

I interrupt her. "It's been over three years. It's not sudden."

"You spent a night together. One. Singular."

"I love him. From the moment his lips touched mine for the first time, Charity, I knew. I've never felt that before, and I never felt anywhere near that connection after. He makes me happy... he makes me feel whole and before him I didn't even know I was incomplete."

"He asked you to finish a blow job with his dick still wet from a groupie's mouth."

Sighing, I nod. "I know. But he was hurt, Charity."

"So he treats you like shit because his *little feelings* were hurt? I don't know who's worse, him or Kolby."

"Don't you dare, Charity. Don't you ever compare them."

"Whatever."

I move on from that because I legitimately don't need the stress. "Look at what happened with Lincoln and Scarlett. He was the biggest jerk, but it wasn't because he's an ass. It was because he's a guy, and men don't know how to accept that their feelings got hurt, so they lash out in anger."

She rolls her eyes. "Whatever. There is no excuse for what Jamie did, and I'm sorry, but I'm not feeling the Jamie love right now. I wasn't really before all this, but I knew you needed to get closure with him, but nope... not feeling it."

"You don't have to. I do. And that's all that counts."

She shakes her head and stands, clearly pissed with my decision, and I've gotta say, it sucks. She was always on my side, but right now, she's nowhere near. "No, it's not. Not anymore. You have a baby now, Merc. A child. For the rest of your life, you're going to be a mother, and she's what counts."

"I know that," I snap at her. "But if you want to be pissed at somebody, be pissed at Kolby." Reaching for my phone, I pull up my email and hand it to her.

She reads through the document and shakes her head. "What an asshole."

"I know. He called to give me a head's up, but couldn't believe it when I opened it up. He doesn't even want to have visitation. He wants to pay me a hundred grand to sign an NDA, and in turn for keeping his identity as the father secret, he'll sign over all rights."

"What a prick."

Since she's a lawyer, I know her brain is working over-time right now. "I don't want his money, but I'll sign it."

"Don't you dare without me and Dad, Mercy."

"Well, of course. I told him I'd have my own papers drawn up, but if you think these are good, then I'll sign these." I take my phone back and rub my sore temples. "Kolby wants nothing to do with me or his child. I have a guy who I've been in love with for years wants to be there for me, so why would I push him away?"

"History."

I shrug. "People change."

Her eyes narrow at me. "Not true, because I know I can't change your mind. Don't agree to be with him just because the real dad bailed."

"That was low."

"Sorry, but it's the truth. You go and let him tear you apart over and over again. I'm sorry, but I won't sit around and watch it. Not again." She wipes away tears that ha-ven't fallen yet. "I love you, but I think you're making a huge mistake. You'd be better off without him."

True to his word, Jamie showed up first thing in the morn-ing. He helped me to his car and took me back to my place. Which was filled with flowers. Dozens of roses in all colors filled each room, and I hugged him, burrowing my face in his shirt to hide the plethora of emotions over-whelming me.

He let me have my moment, then started the shower

for me. I wanted him to join me, but he didn't. Maybe he was trying to give me privacy, thinking I needed it, but in all honesty, I didn't.

The entire day he was attentive and loving and being with him around him, just being in the same space as him was amazing. It's been so amazing that I feel like I need to tell him.

Before I fall asleep for the night, I rest my palm on his freshly shaven face, "It was never him," I whisper, needing him to feel it in his guts that nobody compares to him.

Jamie's head snaps up, and he grabs my hand. "Stop it."

"It was always you."

His jaw tightens beneath my hand. "It's the same for me. You know that, right? Nobody replaced you; nobody came close. They were nothing. You're everything."

I want to believe it, and I know that in my situation, I'm forgiving him a lot faster than I should… if I should at all. But he's a part of me, and I need him right now. I don't want to do this alone. I want someone at my back other than family. I want a man who believes in me. Charity's words keep bouncing around in my head, and I can't help but let some self-doubt creep in.

Am I making a mistake? Jumping in too fast with him? Is what I'm going through with Kolby right now clouding my judgment, and in a desperate desire to not be alone, I'm settling for whoever will take me… take us?

"I want to believe you." I bite the inside of my cheek.

"I'll prove it to you. Promise. I know I don't deserve it, and I know it'll take time, but I'll prove it."

I lick my lips nervously. "Charity thinks I'm making a mistake."

"It's not her decision to make."

"I know, but she has a point. I mean, look back at the past six months, Jamie. I'm an idiot if I don't question that. If I just pretend it didn't happen."

"She doesn't understand what we have. What we feel. I can't make her change her mind, but I can make you trust me again. Because I know you love me still. I knew it the first time I sank inside you. Knew it when you looked at me after you walked out of Kolby's bedroom, but the thing is, gorgeous, it's mutual. It never stopped for me no matter how hard I tried to move on." I wince at the statement, and he shakes his head, fingers scraping against my collarbone. "It might not make sense to anyone else, and that's okay. We're the ones who have to be good with what happens next, not anybody else."

I don't give him the answer he's looking for, and he drops his head.

"I want to make this work, Jamie. I can forgive you, but I don't know if I'll ever be able to forget what you said to me and how much that destroyed me."

"And I don't know if I'll ever be able to get the sound of you through the walls outta my mind, but it's not stopping me from moving forward with what we both want. You have to decide if you can forgive me enough to forget it because I won't have it be something that's thrown in my face forever. I'll work my skin to the bone to prove how serious I am, but you have to give me the chance. You have to trust in us enough to try."

I get it. And I want to… I know I will. I am already, really.

"Let me ask you this. If you had given me the right number, and you had picked up when I called you that morning, what would have happened?"

"You called me right away in the morning?"

He bows his head and then nods in earnest. "Yes, Mercy. I woke up without you and I freaked out. At first I was worried that something happened to you, then I saw the note and it was like I could breathe again. When I dove to my phone to call you my hands were shaking. Then when I figured out the number you left wasn't yours, I'd never been so infuriated in my life. But that's not the point. I'm asking about if you had answered when I initially called."

He thinks it's not the point, but he's wrong. It matters. It matters a lot. "I don't know what you're asking, Jamie."

"What do you think would have happened between us if you gave me the right number and when I called, you answered?"

I swallow, hoping my reply is what he's looking for. "I would have wanted us to be exclusive. To get to know each other more, to continue what we started."

"Same, Mercy. That's exactly what I would have wanted. So a mistake tore us apart and we both fucked up in one way or another. Me worse than you. That shit's gonna happen in any relationship. But you're the only woman I've wanted any relationship with in the first place."

"Why didn't you tell me who you were that night?"

He bites his lip. "I liked who you were with me and who I was with you, and I was afraid that if you knew who I was, that would change."

I shake my head. "It wouldn't have changed."

"I know that now."

"You know you were in the same graduating class as my sister, right?"

He shrugs. "Not surprised."

"I can't believe that I was friends with Meara, and I didn't figure out you were Liam's brother."

"You didn't know my name. Why would you have? We traveled so much over the past few years, needing to show our fans that without Lee we were still the band they loved. It's hard to lose an original member, and a lot of times, the band falls apart when that happens. But somehow we didn't."

I pull away from him, guilty. "But now you will. Because of me, right? Lincoln told me that you and Kolby got into it with each other."

"We did. But it's not just about you. When Kolby leaves it won't be your fault."

"He's leaving?"

"Either him or me, so, yeah."

"It is."

"It's not. We'll figure it out. Ruin is due for a break, a well-deserved one, and we're taking it. During that time, we'll figure shit out. Bottom line, Mercy, we're all good guys. The fact that Kolby can knock up a woman and do what he's doing to you doesn't sit right with any of us. We don't want that shit associated with our name."

I want to say some remark about all the groupies the guys sleep with, but he shakes his head, almost stopping my thoughts in their track.

"Fuckin' some groupies and having a good time living the life isn't the same as what he's doing. Liam was faithful to Meara for years on the road. None of us have ever done anything even close to what Kolby is doing to you."

"I can't believe he doesn't care."

"Me either." I'm sure he doesn't want to sit here and

talk about another guy. He wants answers. Reassurances. "I want to make us work, Jamie. I do. I'm just scared."

He smiles, but I notice through his teeth that the bar is missing. I noticed it when he was kissing me, too, but never asked him why he took it out. "I'm scared, too, baby. But everything I've ever wanted is on the other side of that fear, and I'll never make it through unless you're holding my hand while we trample that shit together."

TWENTY-THREE

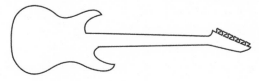

Jamie

RESTING MY HEAD ON HER BELLY, I HAVE MY ARMS wrapped around her waist, and I hold her tight as I apologize over and over and over again. I feel like it's all I can do right now, just give her words. It's me sticking around that will ultimately be the true test, that I fully intend to pass, to show her that I'm committed to this relationship. It's my fault she's hesitant, and maybe I'm pushing too fast. I shouldn't have put my clothes in her drawers until she asked me, but dammit, I want to be with her. I need to. She needs me, too.

"I'm such an asshole. I don't deserve your forgiveness."

Her fingers tighten. "It's not your fault."

It is. And there is another way I can show her how sorry I am. "I have to make it up to you. Have to prove you wrong about me."

"Jamie."

I sit up and grab her hips, yanking her down. Her back hits the mattress, and before she can utter a word, my mouth is on hers. I silence her protest, and as I pull back and she sucks in air, I rip her stretchy pants off her legs. I don't even give her time to kick them off her ankles before I have her clit beneath my tongue.

"God." She presses into my face, and I lift her by her ass, kneading the globes as I apologize as best as I can without words. I slide my hands around and press my longest finger against her pussy and feel her getting wetter as the seconds pass. "God, Jamie."

My tongue shows her what I struggle to say, and I growl against her when I feel her clenching around me already. I give her what she needs, again and again, until her body becomes limp. Until I'm sure she understands. She throws her arm over her face, and I kiss the inside of her thigh as her breathing evens out.

"You okay?"

She peeks at me through her fingers. "More than okay."

"Good. Be right back." I disappear to grab a washcloth, my stride constricted by my stiff cock. After taking a second to calm down, I head back to find her smiling lazily.

"Well, that's one way to apologize." She suppressed a giggle as I wipe between her legs with a warm, wet cloth.

I chuckle and kiss her stomach for the first time, reveling in the fact there's a baby in there. That her little body is protecting and growing a human being. The thought of something happening to either of them makes my gut tighten and bottom out, and I know... I know they're both mine.

"He can't have her," I vow.

"What?"

"Kolby. He can't have her."

She presses her lips together and then licks them as

her gaze ping-pongs around the room. "If he wants to, though, I—"

"He won't."

"He might."

"No, he won't." I sit up and hold her hands. After I left yesterday, the band had a conference call and I've been waiting to tell her this because I know it's going to hurt her. "Kolby's wife wants him back. And if she finds out that he got someone pregnant, it'd be a deal breaker. He wants her, not you and not the baby."

Her eyes bug out of her head. "I thought he cheated on her left and right. Why would she suddenly want him back?"

I knead my shoulder. "I don't know. Love? She must have missed him or something to call him out of the blue and tell him she wants to reconcile."

"I never wanted him. God, no. But... how can he not want to be a part of his daughter's life? To watch her grow and... and live. I don't understand. How can he not?"

"I don't know. But I do know that she's not mine, and I already love her like she was."

"She's yours, Jamie. We both are. I want us to be, and I want to try. I really, really do."

"I want that, too. More than you'll ever know."

She giggles. "Well, you did move your stuff in after being kind of together for a day."

"Again, gorgeous, it was more than a day."

"Yeah, yeah."

She burrows into me and sighs in contentment and I love every second. It doesn't take long for her to doze off, and I really should get up and make some calls, but I refuse to let her go. Not now and, if I had it my way, not ever.

A sudden knock on the door forces me to get up and answer it before it wakes her. When I look through the peephole and see that it's Liam, I almost keep it shut because I don't know why he's here. The past twenty-four hours with her have been the best of my life. So clear, so precise. She's what I need, all I ever needed, and from here on out, I'll always pick her... even over my brother if it came down to it. I open the door and am surprised at what I see from him.

Normally, my brother is calm and confident. He always knew what his end goal was, and even though the road to get there was a little bumpy, he didn't falter in his decision. From what I can tell, he's happy with it. I mean, he's got an adorable daughter and a wife who stood by him during what most women would run from.

But right now, his hair that's normally styled in some way lies flat on his head, and his shoulders are slumped over. I'm assuming it was Meara who gave him Mercy's address, so instead of asking him how he knew where she lived, I say, "You look like shit."

"Feel it, man. Can I come in?"

I open the door all the way. "She's in bed sleeping." He just steps inside and leans against the wall. "So what's up?"

"What's up with you? You know I talked to the guys. Ian. Everyone's saying you were gonna be done, but the one person I haven't heard shit from is you."

"Never said I wouldn't go back, but I'm not doing anything until this baby is born and I know Mercy's going to be okay. I was prepared to walk if Kolby stayed." Even though I know that there's no way the label or Ian or any of the guys would allow me to leave over Kolby. "We're on hiatus anyway, so it doesn't really matter."

He rubs his chest as if he's in pain. "I get it. You know

out of everyone just how much I get it, wanting to be with your girl. Having to choose. Feeling like you can never satisfy every demand."

"I understand that things were kind of rough with you, but if I ever have to pick, it'll be her. Every time."

He draws in a breath and laughs humorlessly. "Yeah. Just... don't make any permanent decisions right now."

"Uh, a baby is pretty final, and I promised her I'd be here for both of them. I don't know yet what that entails, but I'm gonna find out, and whatever it is, I'll do. She deserves it, Lee. After what I did to her, she deserves it more than whatever I can give her. I promised her, and I won't break her trust ever again."

"But will she?"

I cross my arms, irritated as shit at my brother for questioning her. "Get at what you're really here to say."

"Listen. Once you leave..." He watches his Vans as he crosses his legs. "You lose a part of yourself that you'll never get back without Ruin. This girl could be it, and I've only met her a couple times and she seemed cool. From what Meara says, she's an awesome person—"

"She is."

"Yeah, well if she's it, and you're happy, dude, that's great. But if you've already walked away from Ruin, and this goes south..." He shakes his head. "Just really weigh your options, bro. Really, truly think about what leaving means. Not just what you're leaving behind, but what leaves *you* in the process."

I tilt my head and look behind me real quick to make sure Mercy isn't awake. "You're mistaken, Liam. I never said I was leaving. I said I would, but chances of that happening are slim. But man, are you okay?"

"I'm fine."

"Don't give me shit."

He scrubs a hand over his face. "I fuckin' miss it, Jamie, like you wouldn't believe, and there's nothing I can do about it."

Shit. As happy as he seemed, I was afraid this would happen. Ruin was just as big a part of him as much as Meara was, and when he gave up the band for her I knew the high of being with her wouldn't satisfy his addiction to the music forever. "Ah, damn, man."

"When I was with the band, I always knew Meara would be the end game. Christ, I've known since I was a kid that I'd marry her. I love her, still do, now more than ever. I never have and never will want anyone else. I love our family, I love our life... but I, *me*, I'm missing a part of me that I'll never get back."

"You ever tell Meara?"

His eyes widen. "Fuck no. If I do, she'll just tell me to go back on tour. Record again. Go back to it all."

"So if you know that, why don't you just do it?"

"Because she'll be miserable again. She'll pretend to be okay just like she did for almost a decade. She waited for me... through everything, through my shit, my mistakes, she stood by me, and I can't put her through it again. I won't. It sucks to know that I can't have both, but what I have with her is worth the fuckin' gaping part of my soul missing from what I lost with Ruin. It's worth it because I have her."

I nod in agreement. "That's how I feel about Mercy."

"But if you leave and then something happens and you don't have her... I just want you to really make sure it's what you want before you decide. I talked to Mike and

I know it's crossed your mind, but I just really want you to think about it, man."

I stand tall and reaffirm my decision to him. "I fell in love with her over three years ago when she laughed at me. I spent the best and most memorable and meaningful night of my life with the woman I was meant to be with, and then I lost her. And then... I almost ruined her... *us*. I was such a motherfucking dick. I don't deserve her, Lee, but if she'll have me, I'm gonna take her and never let her go. And I'll do whatever I have to for that to happen. As of right now, I don't have plans to step away from Ruin, but if that's what she needs, I'd do it."

"I know you would, but you have to make sure she can give you what you'd be missing."

We stand in silence for a moment as I let what he's saying sink in. I know it'd be hard. It's not just my job but it's who I am. Without it I know it would be a struggle. But being without her is something I can't even pretend to think about. It's just then that I hear the door open and feel an extra beat in my heart knowing I get to touch her again. Her tiny feet barely make any noise on the wood floor, and I turn around when she walks into the kitchen. "Hey, sleepyhead."

She rolls her eyes, but then does something I'll remember for the rest of my life. Coming right to me, she grabs my shirt and nuzzles her face against my chest, leaning all of her weight into me like she trusts that I won't let her fall. That I'll be here to hold her, my arms will protect her. That I'm the only one who she wants, who can give her whatever it is she needs right now.

I wrap her up and bend down to kiss the top of her head and then suck in a lungful of her flowery, powdery smell as if I'm afraid I'll forget it. Which I won't. I never forgot, and I'd even get a small whiff of it sometimes if I was at a store or something, and I'd look around frantically for her.

"I'm hungry."

I chuckle. "Okay. Let's get you some food then."

I make a move to separate from her, but she squeezes me tighter. "In a minute."

When I adjust my stance, I catch Liam's regard and I know what he sees. He sees himself. Him with Meara. How she needs him in all the little ways that mean the most. "I get it," he mouths, and I close my eyes, feeling like finally somebody is on my side since it's been nothing but a losing battle on my end.

"Hi, Liam," Mercy mumbles against my chest.

"Hey, Merc."

"Where's Meara? She should come over, and we can order some food."

Lee looks at me to see if it's okay, and I shrug. If that's what she wants. "Let me call her. She's at home with Melody."

While he grabs his cell, I rub Mercy's back and absorb the warmth of her. Liam is here, but it feels like we're alone.

"She's on her way."

Mercy tilts her head back and I bend mine down to brush my lips against hers. "Do you want a beer?"

"Sure, gorgeous."

"Liam? Beer?"

"I'm good with water if you've got it."

She gives my hips a squeeze before she grabs us drinks, and we stand around talking about nothing until

Meara and Melody arrive. As soon as my niece sees me, she runs over and squeals. "Uncle Jamie!"

I scoop her up and kiss her nose. She pushes my cheeks together and gives me a sloppy kiss before her little arms wrap around my neck and don't let go. If there was ever any doubt I had about loving a kid who wasn't mine, Melody just made them all disappear.

TWENTY-FOUR

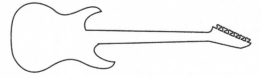

Mercy

"**A**RE YOU OKAY?" I ASK MEARA AS WE TRAIL BEHIND the guys who are swinging Melody.

She shrugs and kicks at a rock. It's a beautiful night, and it's been a lot of fun hanging out. Dinner was great and so was the impromptu sundae bar we had, but through all of that, she seemed off to me. Now we aren't the bestest friends in the world, but we've hung out quite a bit and I've come to understand her better. "Kolby leaving is bringing up all sorts of memories for me with Liam."

"I'm sorry."

"It's okay. It's just... I know he regrets it. He misses the band, the life. I'm not a moron. I knew it would happen eventually. I want to tell him to go back on tour, especially now that Kolby's gone... sorry, by the way. I know when I saw you at the hospital, I wasn't very sympathetic."

I wave it off. I'd rather not have anybody's sympathy, especially since my own carelessness is what put me in the position I'm in now. "It's fine." I haven't processed the fact that my baby's father wants literally nothing to do with her. That me wanting to forget about my life for one night

222

turned into the destruction of their band. That Jamie is back.

Melody screams when she's swung high, and a melancholy smile tugs at Meara's lips. "He won't go."

"Jamie?" I ask in confusion.

"No. Liam. He won't go on the road again."

"Do you want him to?"

Tears glisten on her eyes, but she looks away from me. "I want him to be happy. And I know him… Mercy, I know that man better than I know myself, and I know he's not happy. He can't pretend with me, and I'm scared shitless that Kolby leaving is opening up the door for him to walk right back in."

Great, that makes me feel even worse. "But you said he won't go."

"He won't, unless I push him to. Unless I lie and tell him that I want him to tour again. That I fully support his dream and I don't want to be the reason he doesn't fulfill it. The same bullshit I've fed him since he left for the first time at eighteen."

"I guess I don't understand it enough to know what you mean."

She laughs and runs her fingers through her hair. "They're gone all the time. Weeks, sometimes months at a time. You have to see pictures of them online with other women, and no matter how much you trust them, it's still nauseating. You have to make them think everything is okay back home because if they think something is wrong, it throws off their game and messes up their performances. You have to sacrifice your happiness for theirs." She stops walking, so I do too. "You have to share them with the world."

Melody runs to her, and in the blink of an eye, she's supermom. The guys wait for us to catch up to them, and when Jamie links his fingers between mine, I lean against him on the walk back. He and Lee talk music, and I can hear the passion in his voice. I saw him on stage and witnessed it firsthand.

And yeah… over the past six months, I spent almost every night looking at videos of him and the band online. I read all the interviews. Scrolled through all the pictures. And Jamie wasn't mine, so I didn't even have a right to, but whenever I saw a photo of him with another woman, it did make me sick.

But none of those women are me. None of them share what we do. And I know that none of them love him like I do. They see him as a rock star first, but I saw him as a man. My man. I honestly never believed in love at first sight, and I definitely didn't have it with Jamie. It was still fast, what I felt for him, but it was right.

It is right.

He brings his arm around my shoulder, and I fall into him even more, my finger hooking into his belt loop and my other hand grasping his shirt.

I like to think that everything happens for a reason, and the past three and a half years didn't really make sense, but everything is coming into place now. There is no other choice but for things to work out.

Meara, Liam, and Melody come back to the apartment, and as they're getting their stuff, there's a knock on my door. I look through the peephole and see my brother's ginormous frame filling the hallway. "It's Linc," I tell whoever is listening.

"Hey." He greets as he opens the door. He looks

around, nods at the guys, and smiles at Meara. "Hi, Meara."

"Hi." She stands up straight and swallows. "How are you?"

"You know each other?" Liam steps in front of his wife protectively and directs his question at Lincoln.

Oh shit.

"We met at the hospital." Meara moves around next to Liam, but he pulls her back, wrapping his arm around her waist and claiming her without words.

"Hi." Melody looks up at my brother. "You're tall."

"I am." He crouches down and pokes her nose. "And you're little."

She giggles. "Daddy says I'm a princess, just like my mom."

"I'm sure you are, you're pretty"—his gaze flickers to Meara—"just like her, too."

Tension fills the room, and I gasp at the nerve of my brother. "Lincoln."

He stands slowly, his eyes never leaving Meara, who shifts on her feet, and finally replies to me. "Mercy."

"What are you doing here?"

"Get your eyes off my wife," Liam thunders and Meara jerks in his hold.

She rests a hand on Liam's stomach.

Lincoln smirks, then turns his attention to me, putting his back to Liam, telling everyone in this room that he's not afraid in the least of him.

"Linc. Jesus." I grab his hand and drag him out into the hallway, then shut the door to my place. "What the hell was that?"

He shrugs. "I'm leaving. Just wanted to say bye."

"So soon?"

"Got another job. Let me know when you're having the baby, so I can come back. And take care of yourself." He hugs me, and I hold onto him tight. I love my brother, and he's never home, ever since he and his girlfriend Scarlett broke up out of nowhere in college. It sucks.

"Don't stay away too long."

He pulls away and ruffles my hair. "Send Jamie out here."

"No."

"Merc, do it."

"No. I'm not going to let you threaten him."

He shakes his head. "I don't threaten, little sister. Now go get him or I'll do it in front of everyone else."

"I'm not a child, I don't need—"

"It's fine." Jamie comes out of my apartment, sexy swagger and confident in himself, and rests his hand on my lower back. "Go back in. I'll be there in a minute."

"No way, this is ridiculous. You know him, Linc."

He nods. "Exactly why we need a word."

"Go." Jamie pats my ass. "I'll be right there."

I point to my brother and narrow my eyes at him. "Don't be a dick." Not that I want to, but I listen and go back into the apartment, only to find Meara with her arms crossed, and I swear it looks like she's got tears in her eyes again. In the few years I've known her I've never even seen her upset, she's always happy and super outgoing.

Liam leans on the counter with his jaw clenched across the kitchen from her, which is also really unusual. Every time I've seen them together, he's close, but if he happens to be further than arm's length, he's watching her lovingly, not with disdain. Melody is happily oblivious and playing with my collection of gel pens at the kitchen table.

"I'm sorry about that." I shouldn't have to apologize for my brother, but I feel the need to. I also need to break the tension. I hate small talk.

"Not your fault," Meara tells me.

I swallow nervously and avoid looking at Liam, I don't want him mad at me for my brother being a jerk. He probably already doesn't like me and thinks I'm a whore, but he at least has the decency to not show it. Awkward silence fills my small space, and I expel a sigh of relief when Jamie comes back in a minute later. He looks unscathed, and Lincoln sticks his head in and finds me. "Later."

"Bye, Lincoln. Stay safe."

His eyes catch Meara as he starts to close the door, then they go to Liam, then back to her. He stands up straight as he squints a bit. "You okay, babe?"

"Oh, hell no." Liam pushes off the counter with his fists clenched like he's ready to go to battle, and Jamie steps in front of him. "Melody," is all he says. I see the strain in Jamie as he holds him back and go to my brother.

"Lincoln, you need to go. That's not cool." I reach for the door, and he nods, observing Melody as she watches him. "Call me when you get to wherever you're going."

He shakes his head, then his eyes do a head-to-toe sweep of Meara before he says, "Change of plans. I'm staying." He disappears behind the closed door, and I turn to Meara.

Her face is pale, and her hands are shaking. "Mama. Look." Melody holds a pen up. "It's pink sparkles."

"Pretty." She answers her daughter without looking. "We need to go. Melody, let's go."

Jamie moves aside, and Liam walks to his wife aggressively. "You got something you need to tell me?"

"Are you serious right now?" Meara stutters.

"Oh, I'm dead serious, princess. Get your stuff. We need to go home and talk about some shit," he snaps, razors sharpening his voice.

"Gladly." She grabs her purse, and he lifts Melody. "Bye, you guys."

Liam storms out the door, his footsteps thundering down the hall, and Meara follows close behind.

I enjoyed having them up until my brother acted like a douche. Now I'm worried for her and what's going to happen when they get home. "What the fuck was that?" Jamie asks as he locks the door.

"I have no clue."

"He was straight up hitting on her in front of her husband. Your brother is a scary mofo and if he and Lee started going at it, that would not end well for Liam."

"I know. I swear... I have no clue what he was thinking. He's always been kind of cocky, but that was a new low."

"I've known Meara forever, and I've never seen the two of them fight like that, and it wasn't just about Lincoln, but there's something else going on. Damn. Whatever it is, I do not like. Did she say anything to you?"

I want to tell him about Meara's and my conversation, but I can't. She confided in me, and I need to honor that. Because if this thing between us lasts like I want it to, I'll need her someday, I'm sure. "I hope everything is okay." I avoid lying by not answering.

"It will be. Those two can make it through anything... after what they've been through, I know they can."

"I hope so. Hey, what did Lincoln say to you?"

He waves me off. "Don't worry about it."

"Um, no. I will. What'd he say?"

"Just gave me a warning about what he'd do to me if I hurt you, and before you get mad, I respect it. He's your big brother, and I hate to bring up shit, but babe, he's seen me without you, and I'm not proud of some of the shit I've done. So I get it. He's just someone else I need to prove myself to."

"You don't need to prove yourself to anyone."

He shakes his head. "That's where you're incorrect. But let me worry about it. The last thing I want to do is continue this back-and-forth about who was wrong, what mistakes were made, and how we're going to move on. We're just gonna do it, and we'll come out on the other side stronger than Liam and Meara, all right?"

"All right." I'm with him. I want to move on.

"Let's get to bed."

"I've gotta clean up real quick."

He shuts all the lights off while I put away the leftover food and load the dishwasher.

He waits for me, and while I'm changing into pajamas, he takes his turn in the bathroom.

He kisses me before I go brush my teeth. After I rinse, I look into the mirror as I take my makeup off and realize I didn't even put any on today. The pink flush to my cheek isn't manufactured; it's because of him. He makes me glow and shine, and I like it. I like him with me. I like the fact he'll be the one raising the baby with me.

By the time I'm back in my room—or is it our room now?—he's sitting on the covers in nothing but his boxer briefs. I stop in the doorway and bite my lip. That attraction I feel for him only intensifies every time I look at him.

He looks up from his phone, and his eyes drop from my breasts, that are larger than ever, down to the barely there hem of the pink nightie I'm wearing. I can see his breathing get heavier along with feeling the same for the air, but I need to get this off my chest now. "So if we're going to really give this a go, we need to be honest with each other, right?"

His brows draw together, and he drops his phone to the nightstand, giving me his undivided attention. "Uh, yeah."

I pad to the bed and sit on my knees next to him, my butt resting on my heels. His arm comes around me, and I immediately find comfort from his touch. I love that he always touches me gently. Always says things without words. "I will never, ever forgive you or give you another chance if you cheat on me."

He leans into me. "I wouldn't ev—"

"Let me finish." His mouth twitches and he nods, his hands trailing up and down my back. "I'm serious; that's a deal breaker. I need you home for her birthday and Christmas and the Fourth of July because my family always goes up to the cabin, and it's important to me." He swallows and looks even more confused than he was a second ago. "I want you to change your status to *in a relationship* so all those stupid bitches know you're taken. And I need you to never let me go." My words fade as my throat dries up.

He sits up and grabs my face. "What are you talking about?"

"I love my job, and I would resent you if you asked

me to give it up for you. I know how much you love what you do, and I don't want you to give that up for me." His eyebrows draw together, so I explain further. "Meara told me that you were thinking about leaving the band."

His face relaxes, and he give me a lazy smile. "If I did, it'd be my decision. If you needed me here more, if you ever need me here, I'd drop everything to get to you, no matter where I am. I wasn't planning on quitting because it is actually my job. I just happen to fuckin' love my job. It's what pays the bills, and it's what's going to pay for her diapers and put her through college. I want you to work if you want, quit if you want, but always know I've got you no matter what. That I can provide for you and give you a home and a fuckin' fantastic life, but I need money to do that. And unfortunately, the way I make my money means I'm gone sometimes."

"And I don't want you to quit what you love because of me."

He contemplates my words. "This is new to me, Mercy. You may have been on my mind since that night, but actually being together is new. I don't want to risk doing anything... or anything more than what I already did to fuck that up. So I won't make promises about the future as far as the band is concerned."

I chew on the inside of my lip. "What's happening with the band... ya know, with Kolby."

Jamie's jaw spasms, and he grinds his teeth. "When you came by, he was actually packing. He and I haven't exactly seen eye to eye for the last six months." I drop my chin, but he lifts it back up. "It's not your fault."

"But it is."

"It's not."

"Kolby wants to pay me to sign an NDA." The muscle in Jamie's cheek clenches again. "He also doesn't want any parental rights. Jamie, if we… if this sticks, you need to be all in. One hundred percent. No more bailing or lashing out if things get tough and then thinking I'll take you back."

His forehead falls to my chest, and he rocks his head back and forth. "I know what I have with you," he mumbles into my breasts, then lifts his head. "I won't do anything to risk you, ever. I want you forever, Mercy. I always have. Let me prove it to you."

TWENTY-FIVE

Jamie

THE PAST COUPLE OF WEEKS HAVE BEEN SURPRISINGLY UN-eventful but yet the most fulfilling of my life. Mercy and I have fit perfectly together. We've gotten into a routine and it's been so easy and so fucking right. That calm I used to get when I'd step foot inside my mom's house after being on the road for months at a time and I'd feel about twenty pounds lighter just from one whiff of home? Yeah. Waking up with Mercy is like that... except multiplied by about a thousand... a million. It's indescribable.

And right now, holding her hands in both of mine as we watch a little monitor with the *actual baby that's in her belly* moving around on the screen... I've never experienced anything like this in my life. It's surreal. It's like magic. It's unimaginably beautiful.

"That's her?" I marvel and instantly fall in love. There is simply no question anymore of if I can love this baby. None.

"It is. And she looks perfect, Mercy. You're doin' good, mama."

"Thanks. It's been a really easy pregnancy, I've been lucky."

The technician pushes some buttons on the machine but I can't stop looking at the baby on the screen. "I know it's cliché, but I've gotta ask, do you have a name picked out yet?"

I tear my eyes away from the monitor to give her my attention. I don't know why but I never thought to ask her that and now I'm really curious.

"I have, but I'm keeping it a secret." She looks at me with glistening eyes.

"I'll get it out of you before she's born." I promise.

"You won't. Do you have any idea how good I am at keeping a secret?"

I wink and look back to the screen. As we were walking up to her appointment, Mercy decided that she wanted to keep it a secret that I'm not the biological father. She stopped before we reached the door, turned to me and said, "As far as anyone is concerned, you are this baby's father, got me?"

And true to my word, whatever she wants I'll give her. So if her desire is to have people think I'm the baby's father, then that's what she'll get. Not only because it's what she wants, but for all intents and purposes, I am and will be this child's father.

I feel the vibration of my phone in my pocket, but ignore it as I continue staring at the baby… our baby. It's probably just Ian or Mike calling about our schedule. We've all enjoyed our break and have a little longer before we hit the studio again so we've made some arrangements with a few guys for tryouts for a new drummer since Kolby is officially out. Just like I assumed he would, as soon as we were officially on hiatus, he bounced.

It really was sheer luck that his wife wanted him back, and I've never been one to look a gift horse in the mouth, so I didn't ask questions.

But none of that is my priority right now. What is a priority is the human life that Mercy is carrying right now. I... I can't honestly believe it. I mean, everybody knows where babies come from, but to actually see it like this is insane.

I listen to them talk about measurements and dilation and all sorts of stuff I have no clue about. The only thing that matters is that both my girls are healthy, and they are. I forget about everything else going on and focus on the screen.

It's as if my life has had no purpose up until this point. I knew I had a place in the band, knew my family needed me, but never felt like my sole intent for breathing had a reason. Until now. Now I know my reason. I understand why Mercy and I went through what we did. I get why the climb was so rough because the view from the top is the absolute most beautiful and ethereal thing I've ever seen.

When the appointment is over, we walk to my car where I help her in and take her hand again after I get to the driver's side. I can't be close to her and not touch her. She grounds me, levels me in the best way possible.

"That was..."

She smiles and rubs her stomach. "It's pretty neat, huh?"

"Neat doesn't begin to describe it."

"I can't wait to meet her."

"Me, too." I agree. "Me too, gorgeous."

She made her appointment late so we could go to her monthly family dinner right after, which sucks because the buzz I've got from seeing the baby for the first time is going to be ruined. This is the first time I'm meeting her parents, and even though I couldn't care less about what they think of me, I know they'll disapprove of the way I've treated their daughter, which I fully expect. What I'm looking forward to the least? Charity.

Mercy told me how they had a falling out at the hospital and I couldn't believe her sister would be such a bitch. But also, she told me that her parents don't know who the father is... meaning she never told them it was Kolby, which ultimately means she wants them to think I am. Charity and Lincoln know, of course, but not her parents.

On top of me being a new man in her life which her mom and dad won't like just because, I'm also the man who knocked her up and then left her alone. But I'll take whatever they have to dish out and walk away with her, so it really doesn't matter.

We arrive and Mercy takes my hand as I help her out of my car. When I pull her up, I realize this vehicle isn't going to last forever, and I need to get something safer, bigger. If I'm going to be driving them around, they need to be more protected. They need the best. Mercy deserves it.

Her little coupe needs to go as well, but I'm not sure how that conversation will end, especially since things have been so good between us. We haven't disagreed on anything or even gotten angry; it's been perfect. It was like she came home from the hospital and everything fell into place.

Kolby got his shit out, and I sold my house. I've found the lot I want to build on and have been working with my dad on the plans for our house. I want to build something new, not only because my dad owns a construction company and I want him to do it, but because I want Mercy to have everything she ever dreamed of.

I need a fresh start and to make sure she wants for nothing. There are going to be so many times when I'll be gone, so I want her to feel safe and comfortable in her home. *Our home.* Her life may not have begun with me, but I'll be damned sure to do everything humanly possible so that it ends with me.

I'm going to marry her. And soon.

But putting any extra stress on her right now isn't a goal of mine, so I'm just waiting until the time is right.

We're having dinner at her parents' house tonight, and she seems really nervous. I actually haven't met them yet, but I'm sure they've heard all about me from Charity, who still isn't talking to her sister. I know how upset Mercy is about that, but she won't talk to me at all about it, so I don't push.

"You okay?" I bleep the locks and tuck my keys into my pocket.

"Fine."

"You're a shit liar."

She giggles. "I'm not my mom's favorite person, and she doesn't approve of my choices, so it's not like it's going to be a fun dinner or anything."

"Well, don't worry, gorgeous. I've got your back."

"I know."

When we get to the front door, she takes a deep breath, pushes it open and walks in before me. "Hey. We're here."

Her father emerges out of a room from the left

immediately. "Hi, pumpkin." He folds her into his arms, and she relaxes. I close the door behind me as they embrace and glance around her childhood home. It's huge. Looks way bigger inside than it does from the outside.

All of the decorations and furniture are obviously expensive, and it almost doesn't seem fitting of who she is. She's down to earth and funny and so sweet.

"You must be Jamie." Her dad holds his hand out, and I shake it. "Franklin Hall, but please call me Frank."

"I am. Nice to meet you, Frank."

Mercy grabs my hand and pulls me down the hall. "I'm gonna grab him a beer."

"Okay." He chuckles. "I'll meet you at the dinner table. Just have a few things to finish up first."

As soon as I step foot into the kitchen, I'm met with her mother, who I've had yet to see face-to-face. I've answered the phone to her calling but never actually seen her. I've heard enough stories about her to know that Mercy has taken enough shit from her to last a lifetime.

"Hey, Mom."

Shannon straightens from the pot she's stirring. "Hi. Hello, James."

"It's Jamie, Mother."

"Oh, I apologize. Jamie. Welcome to my home."

"Thank you." Merc grabs a beer from the fridge, and I take it and twist the top. "Thanks, babe."

Her mom clears her throat. "Have you been drinking enough water, Mercy?"

"Yes, Mom. Is dinner almost ready?"

She nods. "Yes. You can have a seat and I'll be right in. Charity will be here shortly."

"Okay."

Mercy grabs my hand and I lift my beer at her mom, who turns her nose at me. Great. "She's nice."

"Yeah, sure." Merc rolls her eyes at me.

As soon as we sit down at the dining room table, Charity announces her presence. Mercy's leg shakes, but I put my hand on it and squeeze. "Relax, gorgeous. It'll all be good."

"Hey." Charity sits across from us and throws her purse on the ground.

"Hey. Where's Mark?" Mercy asks.

"Work, where the fuck else?"

Mercy raises a brow at me and before she can says anything else, her parents walk in and we all dig in. Dinner is fine. Nothing special about the meal of ham or the stilted conversation. Frank clears the plates and excuses himself to his office, and I excuse myself to go to the bathroom.

I don't really have to piss, but I need to get out of that stuffy ass room. I splash some water on my face and by the time I get back in the room, I hear Mercy sniffling. And when I get close enough to get eyes on her, I see why. Her and Charity are having some sort of heart-to-heart. I hate that she's crying, but happy they seemed to have made up.

"I just want you to be happy. My little sister was miserable for so long, and I didn't want to see you go through that again."

Mercy reaches over and hugs Charity. "I am. He makes me happy. And I love you."

"I love you too."

I'm glad that's behind us now, and hope that Charity will be there to support Mercy through everything, because it's obvious that their mother won't be.

"I think they could use a minute." Shannon stands from the table and leaves me no choice but to follow.

When we get to the kitchen, she points at a barstool. "Have a seat. Can I get you something else to drink? You're driving, so it won't be another beer."

I raise a brow and shake my head. "I'm good."

"So what are you going to do to support my daughter and her child when your little band goes on the road again?"

Okay. I see how it's gonna be. I've never had to impress the parents because I've never met any, but I'll be damned if I'm gonna let my woman's mother treat me like shit. After witnessing the tension between them at dinner, I already don't like her. I might deserve Mercy's anger, and I'd happily take it, but not anybody else's. "Well, when our little band goes back to performing in sold-out arenas, I'll probably hold my bass, strum some strings, and sing into a microphone."

She narrows her eyes at me. "And how do you plan on taking care of my daughter. Her daughter?"

I push up, no longer able to sit still. "She's my daughter, too, so get that shit straight. And how I take care of *my family* is none of your concern. All you need to know is I'd do anything, anything to make them happy, and I'll stop at nothing to give them what they need. And absolutely *nobody* is going to get in my way of that." The underlying threat isn't subtle, nor do I want it to be.

Her hand goes to her throat, and she huffs. "I don't know who you think you are, talking to me like that." Yeah. Not gonna deal with this shit. I turn around to head back to my girl when Shannon starts talking again. "You're not good enough for her."

Pausing, I look over my shoulder. "No shit."

"Your language is foul, your attitude is abhorrent, and the way you dress is completely innaprop—"

"Don't say another word." Mercy walks right to me while glaring at her mother. "Don't you dare talk to him like that."

I pull her to me and rub my hand up and down her arm. "It's fine."

"It is not. How dare you?" She brushes me off and leans over the island, pointing at her mother. "How dare you think you can have a say in who I spend my life with?"

"You can't be serious. I did have a say because you were going to marry Chad."

My fists clench automatically. I hate hearing that shit.

"And I would have been unhappy. Is that what you want? Chad didn't make me happy. He was a friend at best." She points over her shoulder to me. "He makes me happy. Him, I love. But you don't care about that, do you?" She shakes her head, and turns her back on her mom, who is standing there with her mouth agape. "Come on, Jamie. Let's go."

She waves to her father who already went into his study and hollers to Charity that we're out. Neither her dad or her sister try to follow her or see what's wrong, which leads me to believe this isn't the first time something like this has happened. And that sucks. I hate that she's had to deal with that shit her whole life. It takes a good twenty minutes to get to her place, and by the time we get inside, she hasn't spoken a word. But when the door shuts, she tells me what she needs with just a look.

Her back arches, and I straighten my arm, watching her climax and loving how beautiful she comes for me. Her eyes pop open, and she reaches for me desperately. I lower my body as much as I can, and she pushes up, her big belly impeding her movement but her tits smashing against my chest. "God. Fuck me, Jamie."

"I wanna taste you, gorgeous."

"You already did."

"I wanna do it again."

She sits up and rolls me to my back. Of course I could fight her, but there is no way I'd risk hurting her. "Get na-ked." She dives for my jeans, but I put my hands on hers. "What? Why are you stopping me?"

"Slow down, ba—"

"I don't want to slow down. I want to fuck you, Jamie."

I clench my jaw; my cock is so painfully hard right now. "Climb up here. Come sit on my face so you can wrap your lips around my cock."

She stares down, and Christ, is she beautiful. Her face is rounder with the baby weight, and her tits are huge. "Why won't you have sex with me?" She pants and pushes some hair off of her damp face.

"What are you talking about?"

Her weight lands on my thighs, and she crosses her arms protectively over her breasts. "Is it because I'm fat?"

My head rears back. "You are not fucking fat, Jesus. What the hell are you talking about?"

"Is it because I'm pregnant? Are you afraid you're going to hurt me?"

I don't answer her because she's not looking for one. No, she's been waiting to lay this out, and I'm not prepared to deal with it.

"Do you think I'm stupid, Jamie?"

"Come, on Mercy. Of course not."

"Then answer me. Why won't you make love to me?" Her voice is breathy, and she grinds her pussy against my leg. "Why won't you fuck me?"

I sit up and grab her hair, which has gotten so thick during her pregnancy. "Why are you bitchin'? You just came three times, Mercy. You want more, I'll give it to you how I want, and you'll love it."

"I want your cock. Now. I want it inside me." I can't hide the uncertainty, and she stills. "Why won't you give it to me? We've lived together for two months, and we haven't made love once."

I fall to my back and close my eyes. I knew this would happen, as much as I was hoping it wouldn't and we could get through it. I knew she'd bring it up, she's not a moron. It's my hang-up, and I feel like shit that she's upset about it.

"Why?"

"I love you, Mercy. Everything about you. And I'm going to be by your side as long as you'll have me. But please, let it go. I'm asking you to just let it go."

"But... I don't understand. You don't find me sexy?"

I shake my head against the pillow. "You're the most beautiful and sexiest woman I have ever seen. Being pregnant only makes you more so."

"I love you."

My eyes pop open and land on her heartbroken face immediately, and it kills me… completely tears me up that she's questioning her beauty.

"I know you do, gorgeous. I love you, too."

"It's because it's his kid, isn't it?" The way her voice becomes heavy tells me she knows. Maybe she was in denial before or just hadn't figured it out until now.

I scrub my face roughly. "What do you want me to say?"

"I want the truth."

"Merc—"

"Tell me!"

"Let it go."

"Tell me!"

"Mercy."

"Just fucking say it!"

"I can't fuck you with his kid inside you, okay? There. You happy now?" I grab her under her arms and set her off me, then storm out of the room and go to the couch before I end up saying something I'll regret.

She follows me, naked and pissed off, which makes her even hotter. "If you're so disgusted by me, why are you even here, Jamie? Why not just go crash at one of your groupie whore's houses and come back once my pussy's clean enough for you."

"It's not about that." I keep my voice even, knowing she's goading me. "Don't insult yourself by playing dirty to get a reaction from me."

"Why not? It's the only thing I can think of since I've been nice and patient and understanding but you still won't give me what I really want."

"That's not fair, Mercy. I've given you everything you've asked for."

She straddles me and reaches for my waistband. "No, you haven't."

"I can't," I confess. "Please, baby."

Her fingers make quick work of freeing my erection, and I drop my head back when she strokes me. "It's okay, Jamie."

"Mercy." I whisper her name because it's all I can do. I've wanted inside her desperately but haven't been able to bring myself to do it because I'm as what Gabe would call a baby back bitch. It fuckin' freaks me out to think of my dick inside her while another man's baby is growing where my cock could touch. It's been killing me even more than I thought possible, especially because I know I'm clean and I could sink inside her without protection.

"Do you think I'm a whore, Jamie?" She rubs her thumb over the tip of my cock.

I right my head. "Fuck no."

"Do you think I'm dirty?" Another stroke.

"Dammit, you know I don't."

"Am I yours?" She tugs hard enough to make my hips buck.

I grab her thighs. "You know you are."

"That's right. So that means my pussy is yours, too."

She straightens, and I dig my fingers into her legs. "Mercy."

"It's all yours, Jamie. You can have it whenever you want. I don't care if you're on stage and you want me to bend over in front of the crowd so you can sink inside me. I'd do it."

I groan when she rubs back and forth, letting her wetness coat me. "Dammit." I curse her name but feel the opposite, loving her determination to get what she wants.

"Take it, Jamie."

I have never fucked without a condom before, but just the centimeter that's inside her feels like ecstasy. "Baby, fuck."

"It's yours, honey. Take it. Claim it. Mark it. Own that pussy, Ja—"

I have her flipped over to face the couch and mounted before she can finish my name. I slam inside her bareback and bottom out in one stroke. She cries out in what I think is pain. "Fuck. Shit, I'm sorry."

"Don't stop."

"No?"

"God Jamie, don't stop."

"Okay, gorgeous. I won't."

She arches her spine, and I grab her hips and do exactly what she asked. I own her pussy. I fuck her so hard she's gonna be sore tomorrow. I make sure I pound into her so desperately that she'll forget anyone who came before me. My hips slap against her ass, and the sound of our flesh meeting is savage. My grunts are stifled by her keening moans that fill the room.

"You wanted this."

"Yes."

"Needed my cock."

She grips the cushions and sinks her teeth into them.

"Needed me."

"Yes. Your cock. You. I need everything you... have..." Her body jolts when she climaxes, and it takes an ungodly amount of willpower to slide out of her while she's clenching around me.

Her hips are still undulating when I turn her around, and when I lift her into my arms, she claws at me, desperate for more. Sweaty, flushed, out of breath. I carry her to the bed and lie down. She straddles me, and we both take hold of my length. "Take your cock, Mercy."

She slides down slow and rotates her hips in circles. "God."

"That's right," I encourage when she lifts up and starts riding me. "Take what you need."

"Yes."

"Good girl, gettin' you some."

Her pace picks up, and she falls forward, her hair curtaining our faces.

Lips a breath apart, she pants into my mouth. "Jamie."

"Get it, baby. Fuck that cock, show me how much you wanted it."

"I wanted it so bad."

My balls were already tight, but I hold on. I clench my teeth together and squeeze my eyes closed and grunt every time she sinks down.

"I know you did."

Her nails dig into my chest, and she pushes up. I can't miss her like this, so I open my eyes. "I've got it now."

"You always did."

"I want you to come inside me, Jamie." She stills, and I fight to push my hips up and fuck her from below. "I want you to want to come inside me."

She rises, stopping with me at her entrance. "Christ." I moan. "Jesus Christ."

"Tell me."

"Baby, what? What do you need?"

"Tell me you want that, too."

I roll us over and bend at the elbows to brace myself above her. Her face is flushed, her chest is flushed, and her pussy is dripping. "I need to be inside you." With a shift of my hips, I slide in. "I missed this." I pull back and then push in again. Slow.

"Me too."

"I love you."

"Jamie." Her limbs convulse around me, and I drop my head.

"Gonna come now." I pound into her hard. God so hard but she's begging for more.

She screams, actually screams when she comes, and I can't hold off anymore. I explode and empty myself into the snug warmth of her and black out in the process.

I've never come that hard in my life and I don't know if I'll ever be able to again. Her legs unhook from my thighs, and when I slide out, her mouth falls open. "Yeah," I whisper. I roll off her and lie on my side, hauling her closer. My fingers trail down her stomach, and I graze her sensitive clit, then push two fingers inside her, feeling the aftereffects of her orgasm. "You wanted my cum, you keep it."

"Okay."

"Sleep inside of you however I can tonight, okay?"

She nods quickly, and I kiss her cheek, then drop my head and close my eyes. "Thank you."

"Don't thank me for giving you what I should have months ago. I'm weak for letting it stop me and pathetic for denying you."

"You're neither of those things."

"I am. A man's woman wants his cock, he should give it to her. And you were begging for it, not just tonight. I shouldn't have held back what I was feeling, I'm sorry."

"I get it."

I rest my head on her chest, and she runs her fingers through my hair. "And for the record, I'd never fuck you in front of a single person, let alone a stadium of people." I grind my palm against her flesh and she gasps. The fingers that are still inside her rub against her inner walls. "You're mine, your pussy's mine, and I don't share."

TWENTY-SIX

Mercy

JAMIE OPENS THE DOOR ON HIS NEW PIMPED-OUT, FANCY AS hell Land Rover. I almost had a heart attack at the price tag, but he said he'd go bankrupt to keep us safe. I twist in the black leather seat, and he clutches my trembling hands in his. "It's gonna be okay."

"I can't believe I'm doing this."

"I know, but it's for the best."

I bite the inside of my cheek, partly because I'm afraid, but also because I'm having another contraction and it's the strongest one yet. I just need to get through this meeting and then we can go to the hospital… they're not close enough together that I really need to be worried, but I also know that things can change in an instant. I've worked myself up for this day so much that I'm afraid if I don't follow through I'll never do it. "Is it? Shouldn't I fight more? Or at least work out something a little less… final."

"It's ultimately your decision, but in my opinion, if he doesn't want to have anything to do with the baby, he doesn't deserve to work out a compromise. You won't change his mind, and in an effort to do so, you'll just drive yourself crazy. Now that's not to say in five years he won't have a change of heart and you'll have to make decisions then, but for now? Yeah, it's the right thing to do."

Even though I know that, it doesn't make this any easier on me. And I also know that if Kolby wanted to be in our child's life, Jamie wouldn't make me feel guilt for agreeing to it. I truly do believe that he wants what's best for us. He's put aside his own jealousy and bitterness and stepped up more than I ever thought possible. "I guess."

"You have up until you sign those papers to change your mind, so let's get inside, and if you decide you're not ready, then we walk away."

God, I love him. So I tell him that. "I love you."

"I know. Love you too, gorgeous." He bends down to hug me and I wrap my arms around him, squeezing tight as a contraction pulses in my abdomen. I don't let him go right away, the pain too much to bear standing alone, but he doesn't release me. He just waits until I'm good. "Ready?" He finally asks, holding me at arm's length.

We're the last ones to arrive but aside from everyone who is in this room, nobody else is in the building since it's a Sunday. When I step into the conference room, my sister stands, blocking my view of Kolby. She smiles at Jamie, then looks back to me. "Are you sure you want to do this?"

"It's not my choice, but yes, I want him gone if he's going to leave."

Her jaw tightens and she gives me a curt nod. "Okay. Let's get this done."

"Yeah. Let's." We actually really need to hurry this along because if we don't, I'm going to find myself in a very uncomfortable predicament.

Jamie holds my chair out, and I sit down between my sister and him. The other guys from the band are here as well, along with their manager. Nobody's said anything to me. They've barely looked at me. Jamie told me they're on a hiatus right now, so everyone is just enjoying being home and nobody thinks anything bad about me at all, but I'm sure they all hate me and think I'm a horrible person.

I'm just at the point that I don't care what anyone thinks anymore. It's an extremely awkward situation for me to be in, but Jamie's hand on my thigh gives me the encouragement I need. "This should be quick. I trust you've all gone over the documents already?" Charity addresses the room as she thumbs through the papers. I didn't want my father involved in this, and even though I know he'd be supportive of me and whatever decision I made, I just couldn't do this in front of him. I hope he never finds out about Kolby, either.

I went over it with her last night when she came over, but we thought it was best to do it here with everyone present so any issues could be addressed. Basically, these documents state that Kolby relinquishes all claim to his child forever. And the band, knowing what they do, has to sign an NDA saying they won't share in that knowledge.

This really should have been done when he called me to tell me he didn't want to be a part of the baby's life at all. But the reason it took so long was because Kolby demanded a clause that if anyone from the band or myself leaked the fact that he was the father, there would be a ten million dollar fine.

After some negotiating, Charity got it down to five. It's not like anybody would ever tell, so the point is moot.

As far as the world knows, Jamie is the father. If it's wrong, I'll have to deal with the repercussions later, but for now it is what it is.

"Okay, then. You all have pens, if you could turn to page two…" I can't even look at Kolby as he signs all of his papers in record time. Every scratch of his pen is like a knife to my gut, a wound that won't leave physical scars, but the emotional ramifications I'm going to have to face for the rest of my life will be permanent.

When she grows up and is old enough to understand, do I tell her? Should I never mention it even when she's an adult. Would she hate me for keeping it from her or never talk to me again if I told her? And Jamie? What if he got upset at me for telling her? What if she got sick and I had to find Kolby to see if he was a match, and if he was then have to break the news… that the man who raised her really isn't her father?

I'm not trying to worry about things that haven't happened yet, but it's hard not to. When I get another contraction, I look down and squeeze my eyes shut, breathing through it as best I can.

It happens fast, but before the ink dries, Kolby pushes up and leaves the room without a word.

"What a dick." Gabe mutters.

The rest of the men and my sister all mumble an agreement.

And I finally can breathe. Even if my breaths are now coming out in short bursts. Even if my stomach is clenching. Even if my back feels like the bones are breaking. And even if my vagina feels like it's about to get torn in two… I can at least breathe free and clear.

It's also finally safe to tell Jamie. "Ugh, Jamie." I

squeeze his hand push my chair back, practically falling to the floor.

"Jesus, babe. What's wrong?"

He helps lower me, and I lean back on the carpet. "This baby is coming."

"What?"

"The baby. She's coming. Soon."

"Now?"

I nod frantically. "No, but soon. I've been having contractions all day."

"Holy fuck."

"Oh my God."

"Call 911!"

Everyone in the room panics, and as a contraction passes, I ignore them and suck air in through my nose and push it out through my mouth. I've witnessed so many deliveries and coached so many women through this, but it's nothing like what I expected. Holy shit it hurts.

"Let's get you to the hospital." Jamie frantically reaches for me.

"I'm not moving until the paramedics get here."

He grabs my face. "Tell me what to do."

"Take my pants off."

His hands have tremors as he reaches for my waistband, but then he looks over his shoulder. "Move, assholes." The fact that he didn't even joke about that command tells me just how damn worried he is.

The guys rush to get behind me so they don't see my crotch, but right now I couldn't care less, and Jamie pulls my leggings down along with my panties. "Oh my God. Oh Christ, Mercy."

I know exactly what he's looking at. I didn't have

nerves about giving birth until right now. No that's a lie. When my water broke this morning, I really started to think about it. I've witnessed so many that I thought I had an idea of what this would be like for me, but nope. It's nothing like what I expected. It's all happening so fast, though, and I know I don't have time to waste. "Is an ambulance on the way?"

"I called 911." Charity drops down at my head. "Ambulance is on the way."

"How long have you been having contractions?" Jamie is trying to hide the fear and anger but he's failing.

I swallow. "Hours."

"Christ, why didn't you say something?"

"I just wanted to get this over with before…"

He drops his head, jaw clenching. I know he wants to say more, but he's holding back. However, this little girl isn't. "Jamie." I look down to him, feeling fear for the first time since. "If she comes, you need to use my pants. She's gonna be slippery, but whatever you do, don't drop her." The contraction begins to build, and I fight my body's natural instincts to bear down. "Please, honey, when you get her, don't let go."

He leans over me so his eyes are the only thing in my line of vision. Through the intense pain, the fear, and the chaos, green is all I see. "I'll never let go."

"Is there something we can do?" I don't know which guy asks that, but I roll my forehead against Jamie's as an answer.

"Do you want them to leave?" He whispers.

"No, they're fi-" My sentence is cut off when I grit my teeth together from the pain and at the same time heavy footfalls sound down the hallway.

When Jamie sits back, I see a firefighter rushing in. "What's going on guys? Someone's ready to make their mark on the world a little early?"

"Travis, help her." Jamie addresses the firefighter who he apparently knows, but as he gets closer, I notice he looks familiar.

He crouches down and smiles at me with a freaking dimple. Of course some hottie is about to be all up in my space at the worst possible time. "I'm Travis. I think we've met before. My wife is Meara's cousin."

"Oh. Yeah." I pant.

"You're a nurse, right?"

I nod and feel sweat roll down my face.

"How are you feeling?"

"She's about to have a baby, how the fuck do you think she feels?" Jamie snaps at him.

Travis smirks but ignores Jamie. "She knows what I mean."

"There's no time to get to the hospital." I bite my lip and Travis nods, then moves into action. He pushes Jamie aside and preps the area as best as he can. "I've gotta push."

"Let's do it, mama."

"Holy shit." Jamie is at my left side, and he marvels as I bear down and push.

I vaguely hear Travis counting, but Jamie's encouraging words are loud and clear. "There you go. God, baby, look at you. Push, gorgeous. You got this, Mercy." And after only four pushes, my daughter is born. Her cry brings a sob of relief to me and I take her from Travis and hold her tight against my chest. No baby has ever been more beautiful. Jamie runs his finger down her cheek and then brings that hand to my face. "God, I fuckin' love you."

I don't have time to reply or absorb everything fully because I'm being loaded up onto a gurney and taken through the empty building to the ambulance.

We're quickly loaded on and I wince at the slight cramping still taking place inside of my body. The doors are slammed shut and Travis sits on the opposite side of Jamie.

"I can't believe that just happened." Jamie holds my hand and brings it to his lips. "Seriously, that was the most intense, most beautiful, scariest thing I've ever witnessed."

"Pretty cool, huh?" Travis agrees.

"Dude. It was badass."

Travis wraps a plastic band around my bicep, and I make a fist without him telling him to. "You know the drill." When he grabs an IV catheter, Jamie reaches across us and seizes his forearm.

"You can't do that in a moving vehicle. You'll hurt her."

He laughs and continues prepping my arm. "I could do this with my eyes closed."

"Don't fuck around, man."

"Jamie," I plead.

He turns to me and shakes his head, and I really want to laugh at how upset he is over it, but I know he's genuinely concerned. "It's not funny."

"Honey, he's already done."

"What?" Jamie gapes.

Travis tapes up the IV line. "Told you."

It's not long before we arrive at the hospital and everyone is rushing around to make sure the baby's okay. All of the nurses and everyone in the department come in to see me and give me shit for waiting to come in. It's exhausting and after a couple of hours, Jamie and I... and the baby finally have the room to ourselves.

I haven't called my parents yet, because I don't want my mom to ruin this moment of happy. I want to live in the bliss that I have right now, even though it's totally unconventional. It's mine. It's ours. My little family. *Our family.*

Jamie hasn't taken his eyes off her and I can't take mine off of his. They're so full of light and love that I can barely stand it. I could sit here forever and just watch them together.

"What are you going to name her?" he asks, his finger gently stroking her cheek, and I fight away the tingle at the back of my throat. Even though they'd be happy tears, I'm sick of crying. I had cried so much this past year that I don't know how I didn't become dehydrated.

I'm not sure how he's going to take this news and the meaning of it to me, so I take a breath before I tell him her name, her middle being the same as Jamie's.

"Kelly Taylor."

His eyes whip up to mine. "Baby."

"And if you'll be okay with it, I wanted her to take your last name, too."

He stares at me, jaw tight, the muscles clenching. But his eyes are soft. He licks his lip and tilts his head. "Kelly Taylor Cooper."

I laugh. "It's kind of a mouthful, but it's meaningful. I fell in love with you at that bar. And if nothing else ever happens between us, I want her to have a part of you with her always, because—"

He cuts me off with his lips to mine, and I feel wetness fall onto my cheek, but it's not from me. God, he's too much. "Shut up." His voice cracks, and he presses his lips to mine again. "It's perfect. But when we get married, I want you to take my last name, too. I want her to have it and I want to give that to you, too. I'll give you guys everything. I'll give you the world."

"If we have you, that's all we need."

He sits next to me, running his fingers through my hair, and we both admire the beautiful little bundle sleeping soundly. I manage to doze off for a little while as well. Of course the night is filled with nursing and diapers and pokes, but I've never been happier.

Jamie never leaves my side, and just as I put Kelly in the little hospital crib, he clears his throat. "Is that the sun coming up?"

I glance over to the window. "Not yet."

"You're right, that's just you, lighting up my world."

My lips purse as I fight back a smile and turn to him. "Are you a pulmonary embolism? Because you're making me breathless."

He chuckles. "Have you talked to the doctor yet today?"

"Ye…" He shakes his head, so I laugh and say, "No."

"You should. I think you're lacking vitamin *me*."

I roll my eyes. "If you were a pill, I'd overdose."

"Wouldn't we look good on a wedding cake?"

I laugh as quiet as I can. "You look a lot like my soul mate." Kelly fusses, and I lean over to watch and see if she's going to go back to sleep.

"There's only one thing I want to change about you." I turn to glare at him, but when I see he's on one knee, I immediately cover my mouth and feel my hands shaking against my lips. He holds out a huge ring, sparkly and beautiful and perfect. I just stare and he smiles. "Ask me what I want to change about you."

I shake my head, words unable to form.

"Ask me."

"Jamie."

"Mercy, ask me."

Through unshed tears, I manage to whisper, "What do you want to change about me?"

"Your last name."

NOTES AND STUFF

If you're reading this, then you've finished Jamie and Mercy's story! Yay! I hope it gave you the same feels (which was all of them) it gave me while writing it. I am so in love with this book and the entire series, and can't wait to ruin you some more.

Ever since I wrote Prove Me Right and we met the guys, I have been dying for their stories. I knew they'd be a little different than anything I'd ever written, but I have never been more excited for a series before. It took a while (obviously) to build up the courage to tell their stories as they needed to be told, no matter how raw they may be. Now that the first one is out there, there's no turning back!

I genuinely hope that you enjoyed the ride, and look forward to releasing the rest of the stories very soon. My books will always have happy endings, but in the case of the guys from Reason to Ruin, the road to getting there is going to be very, very rough. So thank you for reading and giving Justifying Jamie a chance. I am beyond excited to share the rest of the series with you all. Be sure to follow me on social media (I'm @annabrooksauth everywhere) to stay updated with teasers, release dates, and more!

Xo,
Anna

PLAYLIST

These are the songs that played over and over and over again while I was writing. You can check it out on Spotify, along with all my other playlists!

Addicted—Saving Abel

Heroine—Badflower

Let Down—The Palisades

Gone Forever—Three Days Grace

Not Meant to Be—Theory Of A Dead Man

Letting You Go—Bullet for my Valentine

What It Takes—Aerosmith

Breakeven—The Script

Even If It Hurts—Sam Tinnesz

ABOUT THE AUTHOR

The first time Anna tried to read a romance novel, her hair caught on fire when she leaned over a candle to sneak a peek at her mom's Harlequin. She thinks being hit on the head with a shirtless Fabio until the smoke cleared is what sparked the flame for her love of romance.

Anna was born in Wisconsin, but lives in Texas with her husband and two boys. She writes sexy romance that always has a happy ending and loves bringing characters back for cameos. Less than six degrees of separation connects any of her novels.

When she's not writing or reading, she's watching reruns of her favorite romcoms, talking to her dog and cat like they're human, eating carbs, or practicing hand lettering.

She loves to hear from readers and can be found on social media as @annabrooksauth everywhere, or you can contact her from her website annabrooksauthor.com/contact

Want to stay up to date with new releases, sales, and more?

Sign up for Anna's newsletter:
landing.mailerlite.com/webforms/landing/g2g3c3

Follow on Bookbub:
www.bookbub.com/profile/anna-brooks

She'd love to hear from you. Please visit her website for contact information

www.annabrooksauthor.com

Or send an email:
annabrookswrites@gmail.com

She can also be found on social media as @ annabrooksauth.

Please consider leaving a review for this,
and any other books you read.
They are appreciated more than you can possibly know. <3

OTHER BOOKS

IT'S KIND OF PERSONAL SERIES

Make Me Forget

Show Me How

Prove Me Right

Tell Me When

Remember Me Now

Give Me This

It's Kind of Personal Series Box Set

PLEASANT VALLEY SERIES

Fixing Fate

Love, Me

Steady

Pleasant Valley Box Set

STANDALONES

Not Your Hero

Easy Sacrifice

Bulletproof Butterfly

Heartbreaker